SPECIALTY PRESS AWARD RECIPIENT

NARAKA

BY ALESSANDRO MANZETTI

ISBN: 978-88-31959-00-1
COPYRIGHT (EDITION) ©2018 INDEPENDENT LEGIONS PUBLISHING
COPYRIGHT (WORK) ©2013 ALESSANDRO MANZETTI
TRANSLATION INTO ENGLISH: DANIELE BONFANTI
ENGLISH VERSION EDITING: DANIELE BONFANTI AND MICHAEL BAILEY
COVER ART BY WENDY SABER CORE
INTERNAL ILLUSTRATIONS: STEFANO CARDOSELLI
(EXCEPT PAGES 13, 19, 221)
INTERNAL ILLUSTRATION (PAG 221): ENRICO D'ELIA

नरक

PRAISE FOR NARAKA

"*I AM UNABLE TO THINK OF A MORE ORIGINAL NOVEL IN ANY GENRE. EACH PARAGRAPH IS A DELECTABLE NEW TREAT IN WHAT YOU SHOULD THINK OF AS A DIABOLICAL WHITMAN'S SAMPLER FROM HELL. I'VE NEVER TAKEN LSD AND NOW I DON'T HAVE TO; AFTER FINISHING NARAKA, ITS HIDEOUS, CHIMERAL IMAGERY RACED CEASELESS TARTAREAN CIRCLES IN MY BRAIN, LIKE A SPEW OF APPALLING LIVING THINGS, AND I WAS HELPLESS TO STOP IT. THIS BOOK IS A MUST-READ FOR FANS OF ANY TYPE OF HEAVY-WEIGHT NON-MAINSTREAM FICTION, AN UNPARALLELED LITERARY CARPET-BOMBING THAT WILL WARP YOUR MIND FOR SOME TIME TO COME.*"

—EDWARD LEE, AUTHOR OF THE BIGHEAD AND WHITE TRASH GOTHIC

"ALESSANDRO MANZETTI'S NARAKA IS A DARK, FRIGHTENING AND HEARTBREAKING NOVEL THAT TAKES AN UNFLINCHING LOOK AT EVIL AND COURAGE. HIGHLY RECOMMENDED!"
—JONATHAN MABERRY, NEW YORK TIMES BESTSELLING AUTHOR OF GLIMPSE AND V-WARS

"*ALESSANDRO MANZETTI'S NARAKA IS A WILDLY ORIGINAL TOUR DE FORCE, A FEVERISH AND FASCINATING NIGHTMARE OF A NOVEL THAT GETS UNDER YOUR SKIN AND NESTS THERE IN AN ALARMINGLY UNSETTLING WAY. MANY WORKS DEAL WITH THE DARKER SIDES OF EXISTENCE AND WHAT IT MEANS TO BE ALIVE, TO BE HUMAN, OR SOMETHING OTHER THAN HUMAN—ANYTHING BUT HUMAN—BUT I HAVE HONESTLY NEVER READ ANYTHING THAT DOES IT QUITE THE WAY MANZETTI DOES IT IN NARAKA. RAW AND DEEPLY DISTURBING, I CAN GUARANTEE YOU NARAKA IS UNLIKE ANYTHING YOU'VE EXPERIENCED BEFORE. NOT TO BE MISSED.*"
—GREG F. GIFUNE, AUTHOR OF SAVAGE AND A WINTER SLEEP

"*WELCOME TO NEW BELMARSH, NARAKA, A SPACE FARM OF HUMAN MEAT WHERE SLICERS DISPATCH FLEEING CAPTIVES, ORGANS ARE MECHANICALLY EXCISED FROM THE FLESH AND KEPT ALIVE, AND TORTURE AND DEATH IN A THOUSAND VARIATIONS AWAIT THE DYING AND DAMNED WHO RESIDE HERE. A GUT PUNCH OF A NOVEL THAT BRINGS TO MIND—AND THEN EXCEEDS—THE HELLSCAPES OF DANTE AND BOSCH, READ NARAKA AT YOUR OWN RISK: ITS IMAGES WILL INFILTRATE YOUR BEING AND TAKE ROOT IN YOUR MIND. YOU*

CANT UNVISIT *NARAKA* OR UNSEE ITS UNHOLY DELVING INTO WHAT AUTHOR ALESSANDRO MANZETTI SO APTLY CALLS "THE UNAWARE BESTIALITY OF THE HUMAN RACE."
–LUCY TAYLOR, AUTHOR OF THE SAFETY OF UNKNOWN CITIES

"A STARK, BRUTAL VISION OF A FUTURE SHROUDED IN DARKNESS AND STEEPED IN BLOOD. THIS IS SHARP-EDGED SCIENCE FICTION THAT CLAWS DEEPER INTO YOUR BRAIN WITH EVERY WORD YOU READ."
—TIM WAGGONER, AUTHOR OF THE MOUTH OF THE DARK

"NARAKA" IS A TERM IN HINDU AND BUDDHIST COSMOLOGY GENERALLY TRANSLATED AS "HELL." NARAKA, THE NOVEL, IS A BRUTAL, VIVID, HI-TECH PORTRAIT OF A FUTURE WORLD WHERE LIFE IS CHEAP, FOOD IS SCARCE, AND CANNIBALISM HAS BECOME THE ORDER OF THE DAY. ONE OF THE MAJOR STRENGTHS OF NARAKA LIES IN ITS LANGUAGE, WHICH WHIRLWINDS FORWARD WITH A KIND MANIC INTENSITY THAT SWEEPS THE READER ALONG WITH IT. MANZETTI IS A GIFTED POET, AND MANY OF THE PROSE PASSAGES HERE COULD STAND ALONE AS POETRY. HIGHLY RECOMMENDED FOR LITERARY AFICIONADOS OF DARK AND EXPLICIT HORROR."
—BRUCE BOSTON, SFPA GRANDMASTER, AUTHOR OF DARK ROADS

"THIS IS A WILD RIDE THROUGH A NEW KIND OF HELL. VISCERAL. REMINISCENT OF CLIVE BARKER. I DON'T KNOW HOW ELSE TO DESCRIBE IT."
—MICHAEL BAILEY, BRAM STOKER AWARD WINNING AUTHOR

NARAKA (SANSKRIT: नरक) IS A TERM IN HINDU AND BUDDHIST COSMOLOGY, USUALLY REFERRED TO IN ENGLISH AS "HELL" (OR "HELL REALM"). PHYSICALLY, NARAKAS ARE THOUGHT OF AS A SERIES OF CAVERNOUS LAYERS WHICH EXTEND BELOW JAMBUDVĪPA (THE ORDINARY HUMAN WORLD) INTO THE EARTH. THERE ARE SEVERAL SCHEMES FOR ENUMERATING THESE NARAKAS AND DESCRIBING THEIR TORMENTS. THE ABHIDHARMA-KOSA ("TREASURE HOUSE OF HIGHER KNOWLEDGE") IS THE ROOT TEXT THAT DESCRIBES THE MOST COMMON SCHEME, AS THE EIGHT COLD NARAKAS AND EIGHT HOT NARAKAS.

KĀLASŪTRA, THE "BLACK THREAD" NARAKA, INCLUDES THE TORMENTS OF SAÑJĪVA. IN ADDITION, BLACK LINES ARE DRAWN UPON THE BODY, WHICH HELL GUARDS USE AS PATTERNS TO CUT THE BEINGS WITH FIERY SAWS AND SHARP AXES.

SAMGHĀTA, THE "CRUSHING" NARAKA, IS SURROUNDED BY HUGE MASSES OF ROCK THAT SMASH TOGETHER AND CRUSH THE BEINGS TO A BLOODY JELLY. WHEN THE ROCKS MOVE APART AGAIN, LIFE IS RESTORED TO THE BEING AND THE PROCESS STARTS AGAIN.

FROM WIKIPEDIA.ORG

SUMMARY

A WEIRD INTRO

PART 1 – NARAKA

PART 2 - KALASUTRA

PART 3 - SAMGHATA

नरक

NARAKA

BY ALESSANDRO MANZETTI

For Caleb

A WEIRD INTRO
THE PERPETUAL COMMUNICATOR
नरक

I'm the last man on Earth, a fucking holographic recording, actually.

Don't be surprised. You're all dead by now, right? And yet, someone has turned me on ...

If you're those blue snouts from the BM-2 quadrant, go fuck yourselves. I only saw you through the Norman verticalizer, but that was enough. After the Hubble and its great-grandsons, they should have called it a day. The more you see, the more you fuck yourself up, like peeking at your sister in the crapper; there are other, less dangerous vaginas to explore. I'm talking as a scientist, but also as a first-row voyeur.

Anyhow, I hope whoever pressed the button – activating the apocalyptic ghost in front of you – is instead a human colonizer: two legs and two arms, no tentacles and see-through guts. Maybe you're wondering about this electric Moses. Yours truly, that is. What can I say? I understand bafflement about my messianic looks, but long beards were all the rage a hundred years ago, or two hundred, a thousand ... I mean, you know the century, *your* century now. Who gives a shit? I'm dead. The problem's yours.

Who are you? Who am I? To that, I can answer: not Jesus Christ, sorry to disappoint you; just one of the Perpetual Communicators on New Moon Corporation's paycheck – they planted us all around the planet. They wanted to have a say with posterity, and we popped out after the last red alert like many metaluminum artichokes. You just have to turn us on, with fingers and intellect.

One hundred credits for an hour's work. What do you think? And a billion possible repeat performances. We're all scientists, of course: credibility is important. Tallying it all up, if I were to receive royalty income for the image rights of my holy ass – available to eternity – by now I'd have earned like the Beatles of yore; or maybe, let me ride the horse of optimism – supported by several centuries of serial gigs as a frontman. Maybe this chunk of planet has now become mine, and you've landed on private property. Or perhaps I really am Jesus Christ, to you ... possibly someone is persuading you of that, to make a load of money. *Kneel before me!*

But beware: as the motherfucker I've always been, even and especially in my role of Perpetual Communicator, I modified the official version of the message, of my eternal self, to tell you how things *really* went down since the crash of Uxor-77, until the end of what they used to call "World." I'm sparing you the official version, which is all bullshit ... Cloud 7 did more harm than the damned, notorious meteorite.

Apocalypse, ladies and gentlemen, has on her ass the shining plate of New Moon Corporation and its shitty labs, where they cooked up their zombie super-drug. Apocalypse came from *this* World, blossoming out its own navel, not from outer space. Sure, Uxor-77 brought its good share of shit and new-generation poisons: it laid out the groundwork for human providence. That is, for the deathblow.

You may be thinking: *but what the fuck is this crazy old man saying?* I'll immediately explain, also because my battery life – with the permite cells of my age, probably antediluvian tech today – is about twenty-seven minutes, starting now.

Colonizers, open your ears well. Blue Snouts and other hypothetical alien races, go fuck yourselves once again. *Assholes, pieces of shit, faggots and cocksuckers.* You won't be understanding my words anyway. Don't bother spreading your gills or fiddling with your semantic scanners: you won't find dead languages in your hyper-updated databases.

If you're human, survivors of all the mess that went down here on Earth, that means you're descendants of those fuckers from the Impact Area, the lepers of AFRO4 Confederation, deportees sent to the hinge-colonies of Area 40. *It's cold in Vercingetörix, isn't it?* The dumping grounds for direct carriers of Uxor-77's venoms. They couldn't have shipped you to a worse place. Better to die right away. Goddamn ... now that I think about it, you could have tentacles and alien shit yourselves.

I've seen all sorts of things in the labs with some Contamination 1 subjects: phosphorescent lizard-sapiens with human eyes and a perfect understanding of the non-meaning of life; pseudo-snails with police badges fused into their milky bodies; women with five tits, spraying gushes of hydrochloric acid. Gross. Horror gardens of delight, farmed by psychedelic demiurges – maybe the same ones who sent to Earth their creative version of the A-bomb: Uxor-77.

So, if I'm right, best case scenario has its new Adam and new Eve as disgusting monsters and apocalyptic lepers. Hell, you'll be screwing like crazy and you'll multiply, you'll invade the planet and fuck it before us. *New dinosaurs or new humans?* Good question.

Therefore, I'm forced to address you, my dear sons of devastation, otherwise this recording would seem even crazier and more useless. What did you miss out, since they kicked you out of our orbits to put you into magnetic quarantine?

Thanks to New Moon's tech, now you'll see my belly turn into a display, showing you *Apocalypse pre-recorded*, after an opening recap, like in protohistoric *Star Wars*. As the digital guts are mine, and as I'm forced to give birth to a sort of ghost channel, I did some edits to the official video. No selection of authorized scenes, just raw reality.

I never cared for propaganda, let alone now that I am bottled up inside this neon artichoke. Maybe it would make more sense shooting into space the notes of a Mahler symphony, or an army of orbiting Marilyn Monroe promo-bodies.

Come on, look, and laugh out loud at human misery.

And you, Blue Snouts, listen to me: *Cocksuckers!*

They sighted it two years ago, that pregnant whore,
tumbling in space, pissing out its messianic yellow trail.
Boom! A meteorite, a trans-Neptunian bitch with its pocked skin
and the shape of a whale without ass or head; a Prussian blue,
ultimate torpedo.
We all saw it coming, approaching day after day. Giving birth to
poisoned meatballs.
We slaughtered each other over a piece of meat, over a slice of
cheap human being.
Uxor-77. The Apocalypse trigger. Look over your shoulder.
Beware of the day after tomorrow, sit in front of your door with a
sawed-off shotgun.
Don't let her in. Don't go out. Don't eat anybody.

PART 1
NARAKA

OUTWORLD
नरक

YEAR 41, POST-UXOR

Zoom in on the Mare Orientale great impact basin.
The skyfreight descends toward the lunar crust. It follows the glowing tracks of the landing strip, reverberating with sand and clay. New arrivals are gnashing onboard, junk from Earth. Cold biologies. A trip of minutes, their muscles bathed in blood and poison. Captivity looming. No innocents. The new haul:

Kaijū Hanzo, face warped by kinetic radiation from the Ohma incident. Human skin collector. 44 outworlds in ten years of activity, expert in knives and creative cooking of internal organs. Oversized hands. Short and stocky, unfit to spacesuit standards. Thirty-five years old. One eye only, quick, worth for two. He loves working on his victim with his dismemberment micro-katanas. Second arrest.

Ute Möbius, priest, psychopathic pedophile, suffering from level 6 hypersexuality. Toenails and fingernails painted in silver servohue. 107 outworlds, and then endless rapes and child abuses. Famous for the thermodilation devices used to ravage his victims. His name is on the Nirsch List of the ten most dangerous serial killers on the planet. Forty years old. Awaiting chemical castration. First arrest.

Peter Unterbergen, the "Danube Ripper." 38 outworlds, his prey being women between fifteen and twenty years old, all natural blondes with slender fingers, small breasts, good educations. Post-mortem rape, removal of labia and breasts, filling of the corpse with flowering rush fruits – similar to sea urchins – and dumping them into the running waters of the

Danube: these are his rituals. Tall, thin, left hand equipped with a bioprosthesis in nortis alloy. Forty-nine years old. Prison break expert. Second arrest.

Beatrix Leonard, aka Ninive, young professional killer working for the Russian criminal caste New Black Flower. 17 outworlds. Expert in direct energy weaponry; her favorite work tool: plasma rifle. She enjoys playing with traditional knives, taking off her victims' ears. A shadow, impossible to detect. She loves wearing dilitium jewelry. Married to New Black Flower elderly leader Anton Khasan. Twenty-five years old. First arrest.

Aki Miyazaki, serial killer. 55 outworlds to his name. He likes mutilating hands. Indifferent to age or gender, he obliterates his prey and drinks their blood. He gives back the bodies, in ashes, to their families. Suffering from a serious, irreversible arm deformity. His fingers grew on his elbows; he has no forearms and refuses to use common biomechanical prostheses. During the most recent arrest, fifteen pairs of hands were found in the cryopreservation system of his flat, each sealed in plastialloy blisters, and a collection of necklaces of synthetic pearls filled with lymphatic liquids. Fifty-six years old. Second arrest.

Jorge Vallejo Corona, the "Placenta Eater." 24 outworlds. He has set up a chamber in his radiation shelter twenty meters underground. There, his kidnapped victims give birth: he kills them after extracting and eating their placenta; finally, he immerses them into a sulfuric acid bath. In some cases, before the baths, he removes their livers, which he eats as well. Self-mutilated tongue, in order to split the muscles: the two halves can move autonomously. *Lizard tongue.* Thirty-three years old. Engineer. First arrest.

Lucas "Blaster" Miller, explosive-specialized killer, former military. 62 outworlds. Thin lips, oval face. One of the shining stars of Makbollah terrorism. He even blew up his own family. A matter of money, of overlapping objectives. Forty-six years old. Third arrest.

And finally, there's me, Kiki Léger, professional killer. 26 outworlds to my name. I'm twenty-six, I'm an expert in bio-communication systems and firearms. I'm good with any pistol, traditional or pulse. I have the Ophiuchus constellation tattooed on my back. I like both women and men. First time they managed to catch me. *Holy shit.*

They say that New Belmarsh prison, this fucking place, is Hell itself. *Naraka,* they call it. An underground jail, dug into the rock and inescapable. I've seen worse, and I'm certainly not impressed by this nice company composed of pieces of shit. *Acid sweat.*

We're the worst scum that must be hidden, slowly disposed of. Spoiled biochemistry, families of too-badass molecules. But I won't stay in this place long, inside the ass of the moon. Hundreds of thousands of kilometers won't be enough to keep me from finding a way to get back to Earth, to my South Paris 5. Domes and bridges floating on shit: home sweet home. Finding a good contract, starting again. There are a lot of people to do in, fucking roaches, big and small. A well-paying job, almost secure. Beats being a whore.

Those idiotic soldiers, all packed with weapons, make us get off running while they bark to hurry up. They look at my rack while I wear the normalizing suit. All men, the same. Leaving this space rock is going to be easier than anticipated. Boobs and bullets: a nice cocktail.

I follow the line of space trash as they escort us to the entrance a few dozens of meters away. On Earth, there's a lot of advertising about these things.

Our cities will be safe again, thanks to the new EDS – Extraterrestrial Detention Systems. New Moon Corporation is building five new space detention centers. In six years, 150,000 accommodations will be ready!

No shit. Call them *accommodations* ... Contracts of billions are signed about the safety of honest citizens. Calling the shots, is Money as always, the great horned roach; just as in my contracts. Meanwhile, they even bought a few chunks of the moon. They can piss into the craters, and onto people.

And so, here's Naraka, the Hell that should lower criminality by 50%. Words, numbers, marketing. Today, on Earth, crime is the best business. As soon as someone fucks too much with the big shots, their *Extraterrestrial Detention Systems* will begin filling with those same honest citizens, and so-called scum like me will be welcomed back home with open arms. Whoever is needed to keep the business going. Just a matter of time.

"Come on, move! What are you doing, man, you want to feel my boot on your butt?"

One of the soldiers yanks us. He makes us walk through a long tunnel with blue lights.

That guy will be the first I do in, using his own brand-new pulse rifle. He may be twenty-five, maybe younger, one of the many poor assholes who will spend most of life watching scum for money. Far away from home, from his planet, with a toothbrush up his ass. Providing for the family while his wife screws anyone she can, spending all the credits he loads on her account every month. What the fuck's money good for if you're holed up here with the rest of us?

He's the one, the first I'll do in, and not only because he keeps pushing me with his limp, trained crotch, but because I pity the douchebag. It will be an act of justice. His wife will have to gain, by herself, the credits she needs to fuck. *May she fuck her way into Hell.*

No Songs for Kiki
नरक

She leads you along the roads of South Paris 5, the old area of the city; it's like traveling in time, back into the technology of the twentieth century. Last turn, last whore staggering on her heels, then you're there: Kiki's home. The building looks like it's made of the cheapest morblix, crooked roof and slightly warped sides. But inside the small courtyard there grows a majestic palm tree. It's at least ten years since you've last seen one. It must be fertilized with sperm.

You go in, following her small ass that sways and sings, a powerful magnet for a man's glands, stinky biology which keeps thrusting ahead the filth of human race through the uselessness of centuries. You follow her small ass like, you're sure, everyone else before you.

It is hard to find a whore with a small, vibrant ass in South Paris 5. You got lucky.

You push the door and enter the room. A child, gluing together pieces of a model skycar, turns around, and keeps looking at you for a few seconds. Then he gets back to his game.

VRUUUMMM!

Kiki kicks his butt without a second thought. "Max, I told you to quit sniffing the glue! It eats away at that tiny fucking brain of yours!"

Max shakes his head to recover, runs out of the room screaming, "Fuck you! Drop dead!" The model skycar stays on the dirty floor, its hull broken. Like the machines of dreams in South Paris 5.

Kiki starts undressing, slipping her T-shirt over her head. Her tits can finally breathe – she wears nothing underneath. She notices your gaze, an ectoplasmic tongue along her orange lines, sculpted by the light drifting in through the window. "Credits first, man."

You insert your card into the reader on the dresser. Thirty credits, plus the price of the mirror in which you're forced to show yourself to yourself, in that *moment. At least ten times more, though not a price you can pay with money. Acoustic signal, green* LED: *the transaction is confirmed.*

Kiki *slips off the last of her garments with the red smile of money. Different than most women, hookers especially, she is more beautiful undressed.*

"Kiki," *you whisper. "But the child ..."*

"Don't bother ... Think he's never seen this stuff before? He's probably out in the yard, playing."

"Look, maybe it's better if I go ..."

"A paying customer must always be satisfied! Come on, undress."

She turns off the lights and throws herself sprawling onto the bed, onto a yellow phenorubber mat – there to protect reality. You pull down your slacks and lose yourself into the tasty, raw meat of that body. Tits, thighs, that wonderful tight ass. Scents of vanilla and dust, mango and old insect husks. You think: Jesus Christ, I didn't even take off my clothes and shoes. *You plunge your fingers into her hair, sensations of sand and tired winds, you explore the corridors of her ass, moist, almost fake, upholstered in wet rubber. You suddenly feel sad for no reason.*

The great palm tree is waiting for its nourishment. Gaping roots. The kid, his playroom, his out-of-order spacecraft.

Kiki's *mouth opens under yours.* She's alone, *you think,* she's really alone. No, *you muse,* I'm the one who's alone. Here in the old city with a whore and her plastic heart.

Her tongue is cold and you bite it. She returns the favor by digging her nails in your back. As you expected, Kiki's *cunt is a squeezing one, one that makes your blood flow backward, challenging gravity, reality, the acrobatics of a big salmon. So much that you no longer know if it's day or night.* Where am I? South Paris 5, of course. One hour from home. *By now, the orange sunset has slid down. You fall asleep upon that magic body, a pleasant desert with its easy dunes and swept plateaus. Then, you roll down aside and your eyes frame the boy. The hull of his spaceship has been fixed.*

VRRRUUUMMM!

UTE'S ILLUSIONS
नरक

YEAR 81, POST-UXOR

Illusions.

Markus has always lived here, a hundred, perhaps a thousand meters underground. No filtered sun. Forbidden entry to the stars.

But this jail, a psychotic arterial system of rock and steel, is only the boiling putrefied guts of his true home, the World Above.

This is what old Ute tells them during the morning prayers. Illusions. Aeons and illusions, shadow plays that bewitch nobody in the Hell of Naraka. But, if necessary, you must be able to dress up as Minotaurs or crystal reptiles when too much reality is around. Cheat yourself, in order to survive.

Twenty-four hours are too many to fill if you only have rock and blood.

Like a squad of sedated ants, they follow the first one moving as soon as they are let loose. Meals in common areas, Ute's prayers, mornings and evenings. Bullshit.

Anything to get out of the cell, the great microwave oven of dreams. Anything to stretch the neck of imagination; with madness between their legs, find a ghost cunt and ass in the skin of this inferno. Entries and exits.

Incomprehensible thoughts becoming words, litanies, habits. Brain unmoving, undone.

Each follows the body wobbling ahead, two lines of them. Roman centuriae of worms.

"Look, now: from the cloud there appeared an angel, his face flashing with fire, his features defiled with blood. He was called Nebro, which means rebel; others call him Yaldabaoth."

Ute speaks of angels and rulers.

"The first is Seth, who is called Christ. The second is Harmathoth. The third Galila. The fourth Yobel. The fifth Adonaios. These are the five who ruled over hell, and the first of all over chaos."

Ute knows the World Above – he claims he has seen it for real. He tells them about grass, sky, rivers, salt, and dreams, about the pillars of sperm of their true home. Ute, Grand Vizier of Nothing, so old that the red dirt of this cursed place has melted with the cells of his body. Sometimes, when fire shines its light on him, he looks phosphorescent. An autonomous flame.

Ute scrawls confused constellations on his maps, smug destinies; he reads past and future, falsifying their coordinates. Dying here, digested – and his paper Stars cannot deny that – is the only destiny of Naraka's white monkeys.

Leather cutouts and phantasmal hands. The invisible engines of shadow plays. Ute projects on their sheets the impossible, saying, *"Look, the soul of a hawk has come to visit."*

In his own sheets, Markus only finds dead sperm, while dreams slap his face.

In Naraka, you get used to your *expiration date*, the day you will be taken to the North Block to be hacked apart. The rocks, the inmates' walls, are marred by slow vertical cracks. Road signs. Algorithms of directions. They go up, go beyond. They fuck with you.

Because you can't get there.

Ute speaks. He fills his mouth with the Sun, the star of the World Above. What kind of world? A tunnel five thousand kilometers wide, maybe. Prison cells of a hundred square kilometers. Legends. Simple superstition. But it is fun to listen to the old man's stories, uncovering decomposed saints, lighting up museums of heroes, turning the power back on to Heaven. Imagine: having legs mighty enough to escape these depths, to climb the Abyss. Fuel for their survival instinct.

On the monitor of Markus's cell, the number they assigned to him blinks: 7.137-2/110101. This is the reality of Naraka, all chatter aside. A big box of edible meat, with no soul. The white monkey is no more than that. All chatter aside.

Paper stars, ghosts of mountains, and the shit of great planets. Just fossil pictures, because Markus has never found anything here. He has to marvel at banal water leaks: mud is the wonder of

Naraka. Its fucking rainbow.

Markus gets in line with the others to go to Ute's morning prayer, realizing he still has muscle and blood inside his legs. The Black Seed people, the guards programming their existence and the quality of their meats, let that happen; they mock the rituals born out of Ute's lunacy. They laugh at the prisoners, at their paradoxical hope of gliding back one day, with their soul, to the World Above. Into that great imaginary tunnel where you cannot touch the two walls enclosing you. Back above. But where?

The soul is not a helicopter.

The white monkeys pray and sing. Their jailers eat. Flavors of ginger and walnuts.

Works just fine, for those bastards, that the inmates fatten up their souls. They will be tastier meals.

Guts becoming rollercoasters. Simple food, or maybe fuel for their EAT systems. Melted meat, gasoline for their war machines.

The Black Seed people, damned motherfuckers. They speak a different language; in your face, they shoot few words: *Right, Left, Stop, In, Out, Monkey*, basic sounds spat through their rotten teeth. The inmates' own idiom gets poorer and poorer, forgotten. Ancient crystals with no longer a symmetry, stains of grease and metamorphic vomit on the pages of Ute's impossible books.

Ute, Grand Vizier of Nothing, is a closet full of synthetic drugs: they need them as much as masturbation. The World Above. Two fixes a day. To get high on hot air. A rain of oxygen and blue shit from the stars. Sometimes you really think you are seeing it. Yes, Ute can project hallucinations, make them fly with the telescopic wings of faith. Boneless wings, webbings made of words. You immediately fall, anyway; you go down face-first onto the floor, but you want to start again right away.

Ute looks ridiculous with his somber gestures, with that yellow-black tunic, like some large bug; but after all, the only room with a window in Naraka is the room of madness.

A hornet that flies along the tunnels of delirium, sidetracking it.

The mad hornet was the one who told Markus the *true story* of the white monkeys, and in his country-less style. Markus was ten years old. Ute began reading a passage from his books, casting a shadow over everything surrounding the boy.

"On the day when the Kittim fall, there shall be a great battle and horrible carnage before the God of Israel, for that is a day appointed by Him, since ancient times, as the day of the battle in which the Sons of Darkness are annihilated. On that day, the covenant of gods and the covenant of men shall engage each other, and a great carnage will ensue. The Sons of Light and the Forces of Darkness shall fight together to manifest the strength of God.

"Markus, do you understand the difference between the rats licking blood from the floors of Naraka and the white monkeys?"

He could not possibly comprehend Ute's hints. They were like asteroids crashing into his desert. Holes, craters, nothing more. Inside, and underneath, there was nothing. Hollow voids. Bottled steam.

Markus's tongue, tied to a reality of corridors and closed doors, steered all doubt, the dismay of shifted sand, the absence of outcome.

"Ute, I don't think I'm a rat. What do you mean?"

"You'll get it. One day you'll get it. This jail of rock is all you see, all you know. The number they gave you is a signal, but I know many frequencies. Rats' frequencies, too, and they're better organized than we are. They don't end up inside those people's bellies, do they? Tails and feelers, used to broadcast in the depth. Wouldn't you like to be a rat?" Ute replied.

Rats, white monkeys, demons infecting the cosmos ...

There was little to do with the old man, little to understand, but it felt good picturing that World Above of his. And Markus longed, too, for that stuff Ute called a *soul*. The machine to escape from here. What did it smell like? Where could you get one? About one thing, young Markus was sure: he did not want to become a rat.

Ute went on with his sermon, towering over the boy, leaving him no chance to reply, his ears not big enough to catch his minuscule sounds. The old man stood, leaning on his cane. He struck the ground three times, as though someone, *lower* still, could answer.

"I know you don't want to become a rat ... listen: what everybody calls the World Above is real. Try and imagine a place where the white monkeys live free, without all these rocky ceilings. A world stirred by a magnetic balance of huge water masses. Stripes of land, cities, and communities with no prison cells, just floating on them. A planet, yes: a great sphere surrounded by ... *how can you explain the sky to someone who only knows Hell?* Let's just say a blue, featureless lid. *You are, as all of us, from there.*"

"But then, why are we here?" Markus pressed. "Who are the guards? And ..."

Ute raised his hand, hieratically halting the run-up of questions. "Wait. I was getting to it." He satiated himself with a deep breath, swallowing a termite. A lost soldier. Without coughing, he sat again, and kept projecting visions on the boy's blank screen.

"The World Above was ruled by crazed ideas, different people slaughtering each other with machines of great power. Then the Black Seed people came, with their self-sustaining combat systems, capable of fueling themselves with human meat. Autonomous, invincible. They fought without exposing themselves, thanks to their army of metal warriors. Our cities became ruins. The white monkeys, your ancestors, were caught and eaten.

"They're men like us, the Black Seed people, but with different hearts. Different eating habits, *especially*. Engineers behind cold assassins with tanks for stomachs. They shut the surviving white monkeys inside Naraka, in this cursed enclosure. A human farm, if you prefer. Mass deportation. *Sons of bitches!*

"You come, as all of us, from that place. From the World Above, from the ruins. From the drift."

Ute allowed himself a pause. Those memories seemed to make him bleed. Underground attics, illusions. He gripped his cane hard, looking *through*, where Markus's eyes could not reach.

The boy's favorite story was about to come, the one about the *Great Alliance*.

"The Black Seed people survive on our meat. The World Above is empty, extinguished, its food reserves depleted. Forests of dusky, radioactive plants, aromatized flexible water ... a real alternative was needed... Never heard of the *Slicer?* Naraka, dug inside the heart of our planet, is the perfect place to rear us, undisturbed. Simple food, my little friend; that's all we are to them. In the World Above, they'd have some troubles, those motherfuckers. Controlling us there would be much more

30

complicated than here, should they deal with the white monkeys of the Great Alliance who live on the mountains. Warriors, descendants of the survivors of the First War.

"White monkeys, *humans*, hiding in the snow, under the leaves in woods. They have powerful weapons: memories. All those things that the Black Seed people took away. Women, children. Stories. Flames that fuel and celebrate. We are those flames, the still living prisoners, the sparks of the past. The Great Alliance keeps attacking those bastards' external structures: molecular burners and energy columns ... Someday, they'll come to get us out of here. Look, it's in these books, too."

The thin fingers of madness were always pulling Ute's strings. Connectors in his nape. Disturbing switchboards. Stopping him was impossible. By then, Markus had learned to listen and to be patient.

The old man seized one of his books, the ones he called *future boxes*. The absurd idea: those torn pages contained the destiny of the white monkeys, hidden in ancient algorithms. *The soul, if you want it, you'll find it inside these, Markus. Grab it!*

Many thought Ute was the lysergic author of those arcane texts. His own God. Underground Christ. The hornet-dressed Master of Justice. Markus suspected that, too. The boy was much more into his Great Alliance stories than his imaginary mixed-up Indias and Palestines. But he had to be patient.

"All in these future boxes, Markus. Wait, listen to this one. *Then the Tesbite shall descend onto Earth from the sky aboard his celestial chariot, and give men three great signs, the signs that life is about to come to an end. Woe upon all those who are found with child in that day, and to those who give suck to infant children, and to those who dwell by the waves. Woe to those who shall behold that day.* Listen, Markus: *For a dark mist shall cover the boundless world, from the east to the west, the south and north. And then shall a wild river of fire flow down from the sky and consume the wonderful Creation, earth and great ocean and grey sea, lakes and rivers and springs, and pitiless Hades and the dome of heaven. All the lights of heaven shall melt together in one, and into a desolate shape. For the stars shall all fall from heaven into the ocean, and all souls of men shall gnash their teeth.* Do you understand, Markus? *Do you understand?*"

No, he did not understand then as he does not understand

now, close to twenty-five. Nonetheless, he is in line for the morning prayer as the rest of them. Perhaps Ute is going to tell them once more the stories of the Great Alliance. Or maybe he will speak of the *soul*, the only thing about them the Black Seed people cannot chew.

I'd like to have it, this soul thing.

Even if he knows it does not exist. That it is only the last station of madness, something you will certainly find in Naraka; you just need to wait. Ute already reached it and went beyond, armed with his divining rod. Many more stations. And yet madness is always there, looking at him. Madness, a creature with disproportionate mandibles, easy to breed here. Eggs everywhere. Throbbing larvae and gills.

Madness breaches, walks under skin, casts its hooks.

Yellow-black delusions.

The World Above.

Illusion.

MIRZAM 7312-4/101001
नरक

"Markus, you knew?" Mirzam whispers; he is behind him in line. Mirzam is close to twenty-five years old, too – close to the North Block and its Slicer. A non-name, as well: number 7.312-4/101011.

"Cut it, Mirzam. Not now."

Markus knows better than to draw their guards' glances, as they lead the desperate platoon toward the Red Cave, one ten-centimeters step after another. Ute must have his sermon ready for the morning prayer, by now, must be there leafing through his absurd books, getting horny on them. Thrusting his dick inside those pages. Fluttering his ludicrous wings. A new maze into which they could rappel, given the right harness. Cattle to be loaded on Charon's boat with paws hanging in the void. Liquid awareness dispersing into small waterfalls.

"They took Wasat to the North Block yesterday. They slaughtered him!"

Mirzam insists. He is more worked up than usual.

He is going to get us all right into the Slicer.

Earlier than anticipated, which may even be a good idea, after all ... why wait? You will stay whole just for a little longer anyway. Destiny wears a precise watch, here; it has no hunches.

"Leave me alone. Shut up and walk!" Markus adds, without even looking back, shaking his chest to free his arm from Mirzam's sweaty grip.

His friend tried suicide more than once. A monkey at the end of his tether. Markus understands him. Once, his brain still decoded reality with its well-aligned hemispheres, but now Mirzam can no longer endure Naraka, can no longer survive. Pissing out a few memories each day until his bladder is empty. Maybe his *soul*, as well, has ended up in the sewer, drowned. Ute will have to recover it with a net, dry it. Mouth-to-mouth resuscitation.

But this time, Mirzam must be right: Wasat really came to a fucking ugly end, just as everyone else. In small pieces inside the jailers' bellies. Or perhaps inside the ones they call *metal dogs*, those awful EAT machines.

Wasat, my friend ...

Markus has to control his rage, squeezing his hands; he cannot allow it out.

He tries to divert him by saying, "You're going crazy, Mirzam, and you know it.".

The wraith, the freak knife-wielding shadow, follows them all down here. They are going to follow Wasat soon, and the long line of those before him.

"Markus! Markus!" Mirzam does not give up.

"So you really want to die, do you? Shut the fuck up!"

He cannot get him to keep that damned mouth closed. Mirzam is going to have them all killed, right now.

"They fucking ate Wasat! I want to bite off their balls, if they have them! *Bite them off!* We're just seventy-kilos cattle ... what are you afraid of? What's worse than what you're facing here? What are you afraid of, Markus? Look at me, *are you listening*?"

Mirzam is exploding. Markus can already smell their blood spreading. This will end badly. Anyway, at least, it will end. But he is not so eager to speed up destiny's timer – Naraka's timer.

Kilometers of seconds to pinpoint an exact death.

The guard stops the convoy, comes back a few steps.

I knew it, goddamn it.

The guard's thoughts rustle like a two-tailed lamprophis as he stares at the rank of their dirty feet. Absolute silence. He approaches Mirzam, who is crying, who is out of his mind, who has swallowed his own brain whole.

The guard sticks out his tongue and licks his tears. Then he passes by them, smirking, satisfied. Maybe Mirzam is right. That guard must have dined, with his comrades, tasting the insides of their friend: Wasat.

Markus, too, is barely holding back his emotions, silently quivering.

The guard gets back to his position at the head of their column, reaching Ute, who is muttering his hallucinated rhymes, ready to lead them to the Red Cave, toward *knowledge*.

Mirzam blurts out, "Anyone else hungry, here? Do you want an arm, a leg? I'm ready and poisonous, damn you! Have you got enough teeth?" He leaves the line to sit, his back against the rocks of the unending corridor. He no longer gives a damn about anything.

Death sits beside Mirzam; only he can see her. When she gets close, when her black face turns into that of the onlooker, the time has come to leave Hell. Death: just the Slicer's messenger, or its competitor in the trade of livestock mammals?

Hope, for some, is that Death comes before the Slicer, surprising it, messing up its schedule. Something, in the World Below, at least would escape the control of the Black Seed people.

Fuck it. I'll try to save my own skin. As long as I have it.

Underground there is no place for philosophy.

The guard approaches Mirzam, who refuses to get up. The guard utters some codes toward the ceiling of the long tunnel. An alert. After a few minutes, more guards come, dividing the group of white monkeys, about ten prisoners for each of them. They change route, final destination: North Block.

Nice one, Mirzam. You'll be happy now!

They walk with their usual ten-centimeters steps.

Mirzam is dragged by the feet by his new friend.

"Leave me, piece of shit!"

The wake of his back traces railroad yards on the ground.

Scattered ash of poetry.

Ute does not notice. He continues his march, toward his Red Cave alone but for the ghosts haunting his four-dimensional mind. His cane traces wrong circles in the void.

The rats will be the only audience of his sermon.

TRAPS AND PLACENTAS
नरक

YEAR 41, POST-UXOR

Really a nice shit of a place, this New Belmarsh. New Moon certainly didn't spare money. Contributors' money, of course. They slam us all into our cells, but ... what the fuck, I can't believe it: they have put me in with Jorge Vallejo Corona, the "Placenta Eater." I mean, all this money, cutting-edge tech, and they don't even have a women's block? What is this place, a whorehouse?

With the Placenta Eater ... I'm certainly not afraid of him. He is two outworlds short of me. If he tries something funny, the asshole, I have a quick solution: I'll bite his dick off.

"Hey, you, two-tongues. You're not going to play the asshole, right?"

"Leave me alone, bitch," the Eater replies.

What a nice roommate.

"Look, it must be a temporary arrangement, don't you think?"

"You tell me. Why don't you ask your friend, that soldier who kept touching your ass?"

Okay, no buddies with Jorge Vallejo Corona. Anyway, this place is really odd. This tunnel is lined with cells, but you cannot hear a noise, nothing. Are we alone down here? *Come on, talk, you bugs and you sons of bitches!*

"Is there anyone in this shithole?"

Voices and faraway lives.

I really was a sloppy bitch, letting them catch me. And now I have to be roommates with the Placenta Eater. I knew that contract was a sting; I was feeling it. But how can you say no to Big Blue? Which choices do you have? Suicide, maybe? Otherwise, becoming one of his neprom-skinned dolls. With your own heart inside, encrusted with diamonds. Biomechanical existences. A pussy with fans and pulse engines. It's not as though he showed his collection to you on a whim, without a reason.

36

He threatens you obliquely, the motherfucker.

He says, "I'm an artist, Kiki: business is all to finance my *collection*. Look, see how marvelous: the heart of the woman in this installation was bitter, believe me. It never knew poetry, beauty. She was a whore in South Paris 5, the ones who work among the rats. Now *she's* a work of art. Have you noticed the eyes? Those pearls are from New Pakistan, from archaeological digs. They may be ten thousand years old. Now this whore sees through jewels, she filters past and future. *She knows more than us*. If she were entirely alive, understanding everything I did for her, she would thank me."

A madman, Big Blue. You can't refuse his offers.

Luckily, he didn't know I used to fuck, too, among the rats of South Paris 5. The first time I met him, before making arrangements for a second-tier murder, he showed me a fucking painting. Again, that artist crap:

"You don't know me yet, Kiki. Don't listen to what they say about me. I am a *protector of beauty*. Follow me, and you'll see. Then, we'll talk business. We have all the time."

Big Blue, with his bodyguards like shadows, led me up to the second floor of his palace. I climbed the stairs, and for the first time a man behind me didn't look at my ass. I was a little hurt, actually, but perhaps I'd really met an artist. *Sure, why not ... a murder artist*. Big Blue: a guy placing 1,500 outworlds a year, working with the best killers in the Country. Favors, arrangements, disputes ... he always knows how to fix everything. But he's an artist, so he says, and that night he showed me his chamber of beauty.

To me, it immediately seemed like a big whorehouse, with all those sluts laying naked on carpets and sofas, more copious than Big Blue's own hair.

"Wait, before you judge, Kiki. It's not what you think."

Among the sluts, there was a man. Rabbit eyes. He was trying, struggling, to write something down. "Who's that one? What's he doing here?" I asked Big Blue, who was grinning already.

"An artist, Kiki, or better ... a *potential* artist, but we'll know that soon enough."

That day I discovered Big Blue's games were pretty dangerous. He invited these poor devils, offering them the chance to show their talents. With the support of very original furnishings. At their disposal, a chamber full of Muses: all those sluts and the Mexican symphony of their flesh, paintings of great authors hanging on the walls. Dilitium sculptures, an unending array of giant vulvas dangling from the ceiling. A two-headed angel with a rocket up his ass. "Unique pieces. There's no collection like this one anywhere in the world," Big Blue claimed. But then, I'm no art expert.

If the poor devil of the day managed to create something of Big Blue's likings, he took a nice bunch of credits and got kicked out. Otherwise, he didn't get out of his palace whole. An odd benefactor, Big Blue. Cat with those mice. Sure, nothing like the rats of South Paris 5, though, those fierce predators.

I knew better than to refuse posing for him, for his canvases muddled in colors and severin flakes. My ass, this time, he looked it well. And, some other times, I had to join the flesh-on-display group of the sluts in the chamber of beauty. To inspire someone. I was always afraid that some old South Paris 5 customer would recognize me. Dressed, it was harder, but you never know. Anyway, Big Blue got me many contracts, and paid handsomely.

Sometimes I let him bang me. *Paris is well worth a fuck.*

The last contract with Big Blue stank. It reeked of his cat-and-mouse games. Doing in his associate, Guadalupe. *Was it a test? A trap?* Sure it was, but you could never say no to Big Blue, right?

I had worked a lot for him: too many contracts with the same killer, for his standards. By then, he had to get rid of me.

Special Forces were waiting for me on the spot. All set up, I couldn't open fire. Who knows why he didn't leave me a place in his neprom doll collection. *Damn asshole, what they have that I don't?*

The rest is history. Destination: the moon, New Belmarsh Penitentiary, one of New Moon Corporation's wonders. *Begone, scum of the Earth!* This fucking place. Naraka, they call it, the worst of all hells.

"Hey, love, what about some fun? Nothing better to do here anyway ..."

Corona has woken up from his silence, from his accurate exploration of our cell. He wants to fuck. *But of course!*

"Look, Eater, you take me out of this shithole and I'll do you everything you ask."

He looks at me as if I were a ham.

POSING FOR BIG BLUE
नरक

YEAR 39, POST-UXOR

I must go to pose for Big Blue, and try to be on time because he doesn't like to wait! Luckily, this doesn't happen too often.

I know the welcome already. His goons lead me upstairs, to the second floor, leaving me in front of the door. I knock and step back. The door swings open: bad sign! Better staying back.

Then he comes, grinning, his blue hair tied on his back. But I don't trust him. Too many empty bottles on the table. *Fishy smell.*

"Come in, little bitch. What's the matter? Should I come and take you?"

As I step through the doorway, I've got a spring in my step, but it's not enough to avoid the wonderful kick in my ass he delivers. His leg raises with such an agility that I think he took lessons from the French Cancan Girls, or maybe from some whore in South Paris 5. Where the rats dance, too. Where many of my panties still lay around.

After all, posing for him is fun. He admires beauty, even if he drinks liters of blood on a daily basis. But what turns him on, inspires him, is not my tight ass. When I'm getting bored, he sees it in my nose. He says, "Your nose is not pointy at all today!"

And when I'm leaving he loads my reader with a lot of credits, adding, "Take it, little bitch. Go and buy someone who screws you good. Or a pair of pretty silk stockings, vintage ones, so you can wear them tomorrow when I make a new picture of you."

While Big Blue paints, he's often interrupted by phone calls, to authorize or deny killings, or maybe from some bitch looking for money and fortune. Sometimes he listens to them, when they're lucky; sometimes he has them brought to the lab where his neprom dolls are created, where they leave their hearts.

Many people need him, including me. From a few-credits whore, by now I'm one of the better-paid killers.

"Your nose isn't pointy at all!"

Shit, not again; but what's the matter with him? Fuck you, crazy Big Blue, I'll go buy someone who screws me, and your goddamn silk stockings. I'll have to wander all the old city in order to find them.

THE SLICER
नरक

North Block. *Here we are.* The last stretch of the tunnel runs into a steel wall. Even with its high percentage of molybdenum, small drawings are carved on the grey and shiny surface, with no apparent logic. Approaching, you can only make out numbers: *847-13/1010, 3.218-21/11100, 88-5/101, 176-8/1101, 33-1/110, 6.276-16/110110, 1.221-7/10110, 199-8/1111, 47-1/101, 1.885-15/10010, 3.258-6/11100, 94-2/100, 743-2/1001, 4.001-5/10101, 250-3/1001, 6.251-14/100011, 278-7/1100 ...*

Old and new numbers.

No hunt scenes, bison, or deer, no Hall of the Bulls. They are the last signs of the white monkeys. This is the entrance of the Slicer.

Markus imagines the line of his peers, waiting in front of the last door of their Naraka. A big elevator leading to the same floor. One button only. Many of his fellows must be seeing that ghost line, too, eyes glued to the memory of that place. Ears vibrating with ancient screams.

Should he write his number, 7.137-2/101001? Leave his own sign? What the fuck would it be good for, that mathematical nothing, that steel gravestone collecting digits? It would be useless. Someone else, instead, is picking up stones and scribbling; they care about marking their entry. Superstitions. Fear of never having really lived, of being unable to leave a trace.

The large metal door opens, slowly swallowed in by the tunnel ceiling. The guards push them all inside, into the Slicer. No one has ever seen it: the terminal Nirvana of all their thoughts, the ultimate frontier.

Uncertainty is a two-headed demon.

The Slicer. It's a wide white room with a multi-floored cage on one side, and a row of about ten tables a few meters one from another, each equipped with blocky machines with transparent stems on their backs – supports for unmoving, blood-stained blades. White monkey blood.

There are about thirty prisoners, yet the cage seems capable of detaining at least a hundred. The other side of the chamber is occupied by a huge rectangular tank, linked to the wall by a system of metal pipes and pumps. The Slicer is more or less like they had imagined it: sprayed with the black sperm of their deeper nightmares; ejaculations and nocturnal deaths.

Mirzam is bleeding, a dark puddle spreading under his body, as if he's growing a pair of red wings. He has been dragged hundreds of meters, the skin of his back in tatters along the floor of the last stretch of the tunnel. Rats will handle it.

They are surrounded.

Mirzam has a hard time breathing, gurgles as he swallows his own curses. Markus likes him because he is one that never quits. *But he got us all up shit creek.*

The operator enters the control unit next to the doorlock system and initializes the procedure. A sequence of lights: red, then yellow, finally green. The same sequence turns the key in Markus's worst chest of memories.

The white monkeys' holographic tattoo.

His sister Nora, a few days old. They were still all together in the family cell. Markus was five.

Probe scan. Data capture. Perigenesis.

QUALITY: AAA STANDARD.

The food code, the potential quality of her meat, was impressed on her nape.

Light sequence on the scanner: red beams, then yellow and finally green.

AAA quality, the very best, meant to be the Nobles' food.

A matter of chaste, privilege. His sister was future food for the élite of the Black Seed people.

South Sector. The Nobles.

A rumble takes those images off his mind, a quick kick in the ass to the past.

The Slicer's power source turns on fiercely.

Now we're going to hear its voice.

"Sons of bitches! Sons of fuck-ass bitches!" Mirzam has not lost his fighting spirit, even if he cannot stand. He is still quite the curse sling anyway.

A guard approaches, uses a small portable pump to suck up his blood – dripped on the greenish floor – and immediately brings the device to his mouth. He likes their friend's taste.

Choke on that spicy venom, you bastard. Mirzam has thorns in his blood.

Everybody turns around. The security chief is coming. Miyazaki. A legendary piece of shit, here in Naraka. His dilitium leg glints.

All the guards stand aside. Miyazaki speaks in the Black Seed tongue. As his fellow inmates, Markus only gets in a few words, but the meaning of his speech – melted in that acid saliva – is all too clear. A black mamba could not have worse intentions.

Mirzam will pay for his insubordination. With his life. A lesson for all.

Miyazaki opens his mouth wide to threaten them, and they imagine slices of white monkeys annoyingly caught in his teeth. One of the prisoners is sure he has actually seen something, keeps pointing at the very spot. Miyazaki's men approach Mirzam, who is sweating rage and adrenaline.

"Stop! Miyazaki! This man has a right to his last prayer: that's the rule of the Slicer."

Old Ute has come back among them, *deus ex machina* in Hell.

Their old hornet. A survivor of this place for so long. An inmate back from the early hauls.

The Black Seed people spared his life: he comes in handy to keep them all quiet, here in the *farm*. His visionary, pandemic religion is an intangible neo-heroin lab. Stuff they gladly thrust into their veins, distilled from undecipherable books, warmed on the microscopic spoon of an impossible hope. Hope. Vain. Hope of wings and flights.

The long red hair clumped on Ute's big skull shakes as he runs toward Mirzam, passing by their shaved heads. He kneels beside Markus's friend and puts his ear to Mirzam's raging mouth, listening to a white monkey soul's call – an echo in the cells of his body giving meaning and order to his flesh, attached to the architecture of his bones.

Then, Ute whispers, "*Fly, fly, Medea! who hast wrought an awful deed, transgressing every law: nor leave behind or sea-borne bark or car that scours the plain,*" while pulling a vial out of his black and yellow tunic containing a white solution. He opens it, dips his fingertips, and marks Mirzam's forehead with an arcane gesture.

He mutters more words, turning on his psychedelic divining instruments:

"*Jesus said to Judas, 'This is why God ordered Michael to give people their lives as a loan, so that they might offer service.'*"

After seconds of silence, Ute's voice booms against the guards, "This is not the Procedure. Why have you brought these white monkeys to the Slicer? They aren't ready yet!"

The old man's neck swells with bitterness. The shepherd, and his sliced flock.

Miyazaki moves in, the only one capable of speaking our tongue.

"Ute, don't push it. You know it can be dangerous."

That black Pilate does not fret as he orders his men to bring Mirzam to one of the tables, his feet hanging a few centimeters above the ground, dangling over the abyss.

Mirzam lets them. Ute's holy water must have carried his thoughts elsewhere.

Has his soul used the ticket to the Beyond? Is it already on the seat of the final skybus?

Maybe he is just high, everything surrounding him having the same meaning of a woman without a cunt.

While they quickly bring him to the machine, Ute keeps muttering. He exorcises reality, combining new invisible scenarios.

Witchcraft. Keys to find the World Above after death. Maps. What a fine pusher.

"*Again it came to the third power, which is called ignorance. And the soul said, 'Why do you judge me, although I have not judged? I was bound, though I have not bound. I was not recognized. But I have recognized that the All is being dissolved, both the earthly things and the heavenly.'*"

The buzz saws start moving upon Mirzam's body. The first one lowers onto his legs; the others follow in coordination. Death's jewelry.

As the Slicer begins its work, they are surprised by the first rain of their lives, red rain: blood sprays vertically and horizontally, yet diagonals are the richest of that precious fuel; clear blood, different than that which squirts from normal wounds.

Many throw up, while others try to escape the red shower and stick their foreheads to the steel walls, missing out on the scene.

The blades quickly reach Mirzam's bones. His screams become deafeningly high- and low-pitched sounds that seem capable of bursting off the roof – not giving a damn about the rock – and devouring hundreds of meters to reach the outside world. Perhaps he wishes to see the sun, if it exists, or to maybe smell even fields of heliotropes watching another star. A new star, a different light. Their friend's eyes awfully bulge. They explode.

His guts wrap around the rotating pivots of the blades like ribbons colored in yellow and orange. Mirzam is cut into seven or eight main parts, and then dumped by the machine into two silver trays that slide on rails out of recesses on both sides of the table.

Holy shit!

The machine closes its shiny compartments, swallowing all the pieces of Markus's friend. Sealing him. The system is ready for the next phase. Pipes and tubes, branching back from all the tables toward the bigger machine, dully vibrate, leaving everyone to imagine the chunks of Mirzam tumbling inside the neck of those mechanical bowels.

Shaking. Bouncing. Silence.

The centrifuge turns on with clattering and munching noises. The operation is visible through the crystal hatch: the grinding of the long bones and of too-large parts. Precise standards must be met. They have to *package* them.

Mirzam has been turned into monkey pulp.

Ute, their Dream King, could only indicate to his soul the fastest way out after raising the anchor of the body. Souls full of acid, lysergic wings.

Their group is covered in blood.

White teeth and wide eyes look like many butterflies, making them recognizable as living beings in that cluster of forms sliding on fresh offal.

Someone is crying.

Someone is praying on his knees to an imaginary god.

Markus is simply trying to clean his face, his burst heart silent.

Mirzam's soul did not feel anything; it had Ute's psychotropic pass in its mouth. Now, it must be shaking the dust off itself.

From the ceiling and the floor of the Slicer, pumps and aspirators appear, clearing the scene like mindless tentacles with no possible effect on their memory.

But that is the lesson.

Soul does not mean anything. Soul is a product of the mouth.

ASTERION'S CELL
नरक

You know they say you're mad. This is ridiculous. It's true, you never go out of your cell, but it is also true that there are infinite doors. Anyone may come in. They won't find the splendor of a Byzanthium palace, nor the empty spaces of an atelier in Montparnasse, but quiet and solitude. They'll find a cell like no other in Naraka. They lie if they say there is one in Ute's ethereal Egypt. Even your slanderers admit that.

Another ludicrous lie is that you're a prisoner. Should you repeat that there's not a closed door, adding that locks are many?

Truth is, you're unique. Sure, you have your distractions. Like EAT machines that munch down fugitives. You, too, know that kind of vertigo. You crouch in the shadow of madness, drink at its tank. You play hide-and-seek with yourself.

There are great terraces in your cell. Sometimes you let yourself drop down until you're covered in blood. You notice the color of the day when it changes.

You imagine someone coming visit and you show them your cell. With big bows, you say, "Let's go back to the terraces, now," or, "I knew you'd like my tank, just look at those water drains," or even, "You'll see how the cell forks, in two deserts."

Every wall of the cell repeats; each of its places is another place. Your cell is as large as the World Above.

Everything exists many times, infinite times. Only two things in Naraka seem to exist only once: above, the monitor, where orders and schedule slide beside the steel sun; below, yourself. Maybe you created the stars of this huge cell yourself, but you can't remember.

Loneliness doesn't hurt, because you know your Savior lives and someday he will rise from the mouth of the ceiling. If your ears could catch every noise in Naraka, you'd hear his steps, sliding on ancient, forlorn livers. What will your Savior look like?

Will he be, perhaps, a bull with the face of a white monkey? Will he be like you? Will his eyes be lifeless, like those of the Black Seed people?

"Would you believe it, Ariadne?" Theseus said. "The Minotaur almost didn't fight back."

THE CHAMBERS OF SIXTEENS
नरक

YEAR 81, POST-UXOR

Markus's night in Naraka is thicker than usual. Just like the stink of death lingering on the ceiling. It stretches its ancestral limbs along the parallels and meridians of his dreams.

He sees Mirzam after his vertical flight back into the World Above. The sun, the mountains, nipples of the earth, plants sucking in poison to spit out oxygen: all of old Ute's inventions materialize. Mirzam's body is whole, as though the Black Seed centrifuge were part and furnishing of a fake parallel dimension. Rows of fires burn behind him; a white tent, then many more: the Great Alliance encampment.

Markus's sight is absolute, that of a vibrant bird who blends wind and cartilage to let its shadow lash at a series of new territories. Finally, the motherfuckers come, *shit, even here.* He can smell them approaching, must give the alarm, but his spirit, with eyes so powerful, has no voice and is mute as the mouth of his cell.

Ute's incorporeal voice comes from somewhere far away, and yet close to his ear: "*At the end of the four days, the Hawk said to the boy: 'In the morning I am going to take you back home.' So he mounted on his back again, and the Hawk flew down to the Navaho camp first, where he circled around a number of times, showing himself to the men, who looked astonished; and then it flew on, to the village of Oraíbi, where the boy lived forever afterwards.*"

He wakes, immediately struck by the kicks of bitterness. A few ribs give. His cell door springs open, revealing the long corridor swaying with lights. He pops out, ready for the inspection.

All the white monkeys are set in unending rows unraveling on either side. Hundreds of unmoving eyes stare at their own dirty feet. He shifts his gaze some degrees, toward Mira, his youngest sister, sixteen years old; the only one in that fucking anthill who never visits his dreams. Just as well, they are too dangerous.

You stay away from them.

The guards begin scanning them and his eyes go back to his feet to avoid trouble. They light them up with magnetic readers to capture info about their bodies, so dense with matter. Markus hates those contraptions analyzing data, updating stats; they have electronic nets and know how to deep-fish. He is inside there, too, in the Black Seed system – Hell's mad cow – with quality codes about his meat and maturation, and all the rest. Devouring databases.

One of the guards stops for a long time in front of his sister's cell. Markus knew it was inevitable. The scanner, with its usual light beams, alerted the guard that Mira, number 11.888-2/1101101, must be inseminated. Green-lighted uterus icon.

She is ready to forge *future food* inside her womb. A tender factory. An orchard to be eventually harvested.

The guards make them fuck, in Naraka, cyclically. Forcible reproduction. They shut the inmates in small spaces near the common areas: the *Chambers of Sixteens*. A shitty name right out of the apish membranes of their desperate encephala.

Names, words, to exorcise the unknown.

Reproduction in captivity is always difficult. Nothing at all like what could happen in Ute's World Above. If that place is anything like the old man tells, if it even exists, then they would definitely be fucking all day long up there. And Markus bets he would always be the first in line.

Inside the Chambers of Sixteens, the jailers put a female with six males. A very good setup for few voluntary matings and many rapes and abuses. It only matters that the seed goes where it must. In whichever way. They even make the males swallow substances in order for their spermatozoa to swim faster. Better resolved armies, with athletes' muscles.

Miyazaki and his men, great voyeurs, follow the scene from a room above, watching through a transparent floor. They let things happen as they will, but if someone tries to protect the female, or wastes his seed on the floor, he is immediately taken to the Slicer.

The operators enjoy the white monkeys' atavistic dances, the synchronous contractions of their muscles. Goggling eyes.

Someone pulls down his pants and masturbates.

The floor collects those slippery unofficial orgasms.

Markus remembers old Ute reciting a poem from the World Above, something about a woman's lips drinking seed from her man, calling it *communion with the earth*, speaking about exultation, about his black eyes that she saw like fleeing gazelles, about no longer believing in God because they were happy.

There is little solidarity among the prisoners in those chambers, no attempts to pretend, or to deceive the guards. In the end, everything goes as predicted. Plenty of seminal fluid, prime mover of the hungry's food reserves. Our wonderful breeders.

His sister's moment has come. One of the Chambers is waiting for her, for the first time, in all its brutality. Markus is afraid she is still a virgin, hopes she broke it herself.

Membrane more, membrane less ...

Surely her heart is empty, sealed just as that of many other females in Naraka. Hidden in the false bottom of awareness. But her uterus has to make room for *their* needs, *their* scheduling. The gate must open at will.

Six white monkeys to do her, those statistically more fecund.

The attendants will supervise everything from their see-through room. They will watch her struggle, scratch, finally surrender. Semen in chains, marching. The control room is equipped with instruments capable of highlighting every small detail.

And while Markus squeezes his fists, trying to hold back tears, Ute's words, read aloud from one of his impossible books, come to his mind once more:

"*Eugénie: Oh dear, what a delicious alcove! But, why all the mirrors?*

"*Madame de Saint-Ange: Because by repeating our postures by a thousand different angles, they infinitely multiply those same pleasures for the ones sitting here on this ottoman. No part of the body can remain hidden: everything must be seen.*"

He can do nothing for her.

The guards go back along the tunnel. The scanner has already stored fertility rates from all the males in that area. The selection of the six. One by one, they take away Markus's friend Phurud, then the younger Belser, a brawny and violent guy, and then four more white monkeys whom he does not know by name. Go or die, no middle grounds.

Death, in Naraka, always comes in person. No middlemen, such as wounds or illness, can make a dent. The advanced technology of the Black Seed people does not allow for interference. They heal you, those bastards; they fix their precious *provisions.*

The Chambers of Sixteens. Of course, Markus had his turns there, too. He remembers the electric smells of sweat, sperm, testosterone, adrenaline, primordial salts, particles of madness, electrons of archetypes. Circles, concentric grooves, memories that keep resounding. Disgust. And yet, in that cursed place he met Electra, with her clean feet and red lips. His woman, so to speak, here in Naraka.

That morning, some time ago – it was his first experience in the Chambers of Sixteens – one of his five peers wanted to do her right away, not giving a damn about any kind of sympathy. His balls were doing all the thinking, deciding for him. Spherical thoughts, *like Electra's perfect breasts.*

They tried to calm him down, with no fuss, but that monkey was bursting with sperm. He was resolute in putting on a new show for the Black Seed people, while supplying them with new meat.

Electra sat in a corner of the room, her eyes lost in the dusts of another galaxy, her thoughts orbiting around an inexistent past, her arms holding her knees.

Her soul: who knew where? Her cunt – that much was sure – was right there.

They witnessed the mating of Electra and her brutal partner, who spat his stuff inside of her in a furious sledgehammer-like assault.

Electra imagined being *elsewhere,* Markus imagined, a place far away, while someone was banging her body and sucking away all her atoms. Then she moved away from that elsewhere, too tight and unreal, to explore Markus's eyes, which were wet with frustration. Everything between them started at that moment.

For him, Electra became that soul Ute spoke about, or

something very similar – the sky of the World Above, the one the old man claimed he could see through the heavy ceiling of his Red Cave.

Faith, and cunt, can pierce through the rock.

He met Electra again during Ute's evening prayer. He'd never seen her attend the redhead shaman's activities, so, she was there for *him*.

Words and roaring silences. Chemical exchanges. What happens when people choose each other ... Electra gave him a steel rope to hold on to, so that he could avoid falling into the pit of despair, of madness, where already too many corpses of white monkeys lay fallen. Heaps, carcasses of dreams that terribly stank. Supremacy of worms.

But now everything is different. Mirzam has ended up in the Slicer. His sister is going to have to spread her thighs, for the first time, in the Chambers of Sixteens. His steel rope is fraying, stretching, and he is dropping too deep into that cursed well where the fumes of decaying illusions are strongest, where the mandibles of insects noisily nibble at breastbones and thoughts.

On the floor of his cell, a black hole opens. It invites him in, promises peace.

Shit, no!

Death has come to fuck with him, with her tricks and ploys. It was his own fault, letting her come too close. That is clear.

Friend or enemy? He really could not tell.

Death does not sit beside him; she keeps standing and tightening her maelstrom. She understands he is not eager to enter, not yet. But she is an impatient creature, this whore, and she wants to take him away at any cost.

Two hours, by now, since his sister was carried to the Chambers of Sixteens. Anxiety has worn him out. Markus has fallen asleep in his cell, leaving the next move to the whore.

Dream.

A battlefield where he cannot easily fight back.

The hems of a black robe are dragging on the floor of his cell.

He goes back to his oneiric flight, to the Great Alliance encampment, to the row of fires.

His sister comes out from a tent, running toward the long shadows of the mountain. Something chases her, but Markus, a thousand meters away, cannot make out the assailant. Could be a white monkey, a Black Seed killer, any possible shit. He folds his wings, quickly nosedives, rides the right airstreams. When he is almost there, a contrary wind prevents him from getting closer. The thin bones of his bird body creak, trying to adapt, but it is not easy. Uncontrollable, core-warping forces. Muscles with ever-changing blood vessels.

He is close enough to watch Mira, though he must endure the pressure against his wings for as long as possible at risk of pulverizing them.

The chaser is Mirzam, nobody else. He wears the black uniform of their jailers. His white monkey eyes engage a few seconds with Markus's, so much smaller.

Has he recognized me?

Mirzam aims his senses back on his sister's diagonal run. A volley of bullets departs from his pulse rifle, scoring a direct hit on Mira's legs.

What the fuck is he doing?

With his air-animal spirit, Markus smells blood, dirt, and the roots of long trees. He listens to Mira's heart pulsating, the vibration of her fear.

Mirzam grabs her by the hair, drags her toward the tent, which is swollen by the incandescent wind. Mira desperately struggles, tries to hold onto rocks, branches, to the dark brown grass of his dream, everything she can reach. But the *new* Mirzam strikes her head with the butt of his rifle, cracking her skull. He pulls down his pants, rapes her, not giving a damn about the blood spewing from her mouth in small gushes.

He finishes his work, steps a few meters away.

He looks for something in the translucent matter of Markus's dream; there is a lot of stuff there.

He finds a large pointy branch, just what he needs, and goes back to Mira. With a wild grin, he impales her, starting from her vagina and pushing into her bowels. The branch travels through his sister, *inside*, until it sticks out of her mouth. The tip wavers in front of Mira's crumbled eyes.

Perhaps she can still see, at least for a few seconds.

The wind is too strong; like an exploded star, it hurls him all the way back to the bed in his cell.

Death is beside him, shaking her head.

MUCH ADO ABOUT NOTHING
नरक

YEAR 41, POST-UXOR

Third day at New Belmarsh. I'm still cellmate with Jorge Vallejo Corona. I've been sleeping with one eye open too many hours. I even have to pee in front of him, this man who looks with interest while making a strange noise with his split tongue. The soldiers are gone. Now we're handled by jailers, very different types. There's no fucking with these guys. Finally, they let us out of the cell. They had setup some kind of refectory. No more shit on aluminum trays.

Thanks, New Moon!

A bend of the main tunnel pushes us into a hall, where I find the rest of my travel-mates: Kaijū Hanzo, Ute Möbius, Peter Unterbergen, Beatrix Leonard, Aki Miyazaki, Lucas "Blaster" Miller. Really a nice group of pieces of shit. Everyone around the same cube, the cube of the scum of the planet. I join them, and behind me – always very, very close to my ass – Placenta Eater follows.

But we're not the only guests in this shitty New Hell. Oh joy!

Thirty, maybe forty among men and women. They don't look like assassins, nor professionals of some standing, at least on a first look. To me, they just seem like poor wretches. Nothing to do with my little friends here, each and every one of them a real masterwork in his or her own genre.

"Welcome, bitch! Got a little action with Jorge? He's good at that, that one," begins Peter Unterbergen, the motherfucker who did in thirty-eight women in his muddy Danube.

"Why don't you try and shove that fork up your ass? Maybe you'd have more fun than screwing corpses."

Unterbergen springs on his feet, gnashing his teeth, but one gaze from our guards is enough to keep him quiet.

Much ado about nothing.

Welcome comes from Hanzo, too, that fucking midget. "Watch it, whore, you don't know who you're dealing with."

"Easy, sons," intervenes Ute Möbius, the sleaze priest. "Let's pray together for this food. The Master of Justice demands respect, even in this place."

I wonder if they've already castrated him. Nobody takes the piss out of him; that's what being in the Nirsch List – the ten most dangerous serial killers on the planet – is all about. The Master of Justice, looking at his résumé, *was he.* Respect was due. I mean, fuck, 107 outworlds get you thinking.

A thin prisoner with junkie eyes passes by our cube.

"Hey, man, how's it's going around here?" my colleague Miller asks. He's the least unbalanced of the scum, including me, probably.

The man doesn't answer and moves away; he just keeps following his dead-end track.

Miyazaki, the man without forearms, won't have that. He takes it badly, very badly.

"You damn son of a bitch, now I'm teaching you how to behave." He gets up, runs toward the man who's staggering next to the exit.

Unterbergen is laughing out loud, "Now he's really fucked! And you, whore, look and learn!"

Miyazaki is about to pounce onto his target, his ludicrous fingers unarmed, simple tiny tentacles growing out of his elbows, and yet he manages to look threatening. He charges like a bull with his square skull down. When he is about to reach him, one of the guards draws a laser carver and, on the fly, hacks his leg off at the knee.

They carry him away as he screams. Not even a slaughtered pig would make such a racket.

Miyazaki's blood managed to spray everywhere, even into my open mouth.

Well, I've swallowed worse.

"Holy shit! Did you see?" My romantic cellmate, Jorge, is all worked up. Though he should be used to blood.

Unterbergen is one of those guys who can't shut their trap, and now is no exception. He gets up and yells at the guards, who've gathered in a small group, "Motherfuckers, this is against the law, the Geneva Convention 3.2 –"

He can't finish the sentence, that loudmouth, because a laser slash scythes off his head, which bounces off the cube to fall into Beatrix's lap. *Ninive*, the group's silent girl.

Ninive grabs Unterbergen's head, turns it round, and finally her slutty voice comes out, "But what the fuck are you talking about, Peter?"

Ninive talking with Unterbergen's head, half of Miyazaki's leg still in the middle of the hall, in a puddle of blood. For a moment, I think: *Wait! This is a dream, a nightmare ... keep drinking like the bitch you are, and this is what happens.*

Then, I understand. It's all real, too real even for the scum of the planet.

The rest of the group is stricken dumb, with gaping mouths and minds dropped into their guts; they look at the scene, at the following cleaning of the hall.

The only one talking is that damn priest, Ute.

"Let's pray together for our friend Peter. The Master of Justice will show his soul the way. White or black, it doesn't matter." Some whispered words, and then he resumes eating, *holy shit!*

A loudspeaker spits nonsensical words:

"*Welcome to New Belmarsh! Now go back in an orderly fashion to the main tunnel. You will be led back to your cells.*"

A KILLER'S DAMNATION
नरक

You will grow old, older and older, and you are afraid
that maybe you won't get
another contract, you are afraid you'll stay drunk
more and more, you are afraid that maybe
there will be worse motherfuckers than you around
you are afraid of fear.

You are afraid you could live to a hundred years
you are afraid that what'll be left of your teeth
may not last
you think you will no longer tame the bullets
your bladder, the will of poetry.

You are afraid people no longer will see you
as dangerous when you get drunk
you are afraid of forgetting
who's the target, the enemy
who you are, as you park your car
to your stakeout.

You are afraid that in Hell there will be
nothing to drink, no one to kill
you are afraid you are already in Hell
and that there is no way back.

EAT!
नरक

His sister and the other white monkeys have not come back to their cells.

Markus fears the worst. He pictures Mira like a caravansary forced to open her legs to *quench* the desperate from the desert. Achaemenid faces and byzantine terrors. The courtyard of her arms, the colonnade of her back supporting the small domes of her unripe breasts, the steam bath of her saliva, the taste of honey, the prayer room of her thin voice, the storage room of her filled uterus. Conquest of Babylon, Cyrus Cylinder, Smart Bombs.

Where the fuck are you, Mira!

Suddenly, reality squeezes his nuts. Frantic cries roar down the tunnel, "EAT! EAT! EAT!" The rhythm of the voices geometrically spreads.

Soon the doors will open. The guards want them to see their best show.

Fucking sadists.

"EAT! EAT! EAT!"

The fugitive hunt, one of the circus moments of Naraka, a merry-go-round of meat grinders. Fumes of madness.

"EAT! EAT! EAT!"

The cries bounce off every meander of that structure, damp as the cunt of a bitch in heat. Rats hide, bugs flee. Once again, some dork is trying to escape, running through the tunnels as if possessed. They think they can reach the World Above on foot. The guards, in case of escape, do not use the Slicer. They prefer something more immediate and educational: their shitty EAT systems. A pretty hunt that is emotionally engaging for everyone. Deeply.

A letter sent to their guts. The idiom of blood.

The white monkey of the day tears along the tunnels, chased by those cursed machines hovering on their magnetic caterpillars, infernal cerebra ready to feed on two-legged game.

Unaware electronic guardians. *Metal dogs.*

The show is guaranteed. On the cell monitor, a red light turns on, marking the escape of a white monkey and the activation of an EAT system. Nobody ever managed to break from Naraka. Those iron machines, instead, keep filling their tanks. Every time.

The EAT models designed by the Black Seed people do not come equipped with particularly advanced hunting software, but they can move fast on any terrain, can shoot tranquilizer or conventional rounds. Once the fugitive is reached, dead or injured, they use laser carvers to hack the body into smaller pieces, to fit into their harvesting duct. Inside the main tank, meat and bones are turned into fuel. All in a few minutes.

An EAT hunt does not last long; those metal dogs can move three times as fast as the white monkeys.

"EAT! EAT! EAT!"

Steady strikes against the steel walls of the cells soon join the cries.

The inmates want to witness, be part of the hunt.

Mvidi Mukulu's drums and the red ants.

Cell doors open. During the hunt, you are allowed to exit on the corridor, as long as you do not get too far. No risks involved. The EAT system is programmed on the fugitive; it would not attack a spectator by mistake, only the exclusive target.

Markus goes out with the rest of them. He has been staying too long between Death's thighs, and he certainly does not fear the metal dogs. Any excuse, even the most inhuman, is good to leave those rock and steel boxes in which they are reared like cows.

The show always offers the same soaking finale: catching, dissecting, storing in the tank. Cries and whirling fans. Suckers and thuds.

The faster and more driven ones manage to run half an hour or less.

For some reason, after finishing the assimilation process, the EAT system expels the victim's liver – probably, that organ is not considered usable biomass.

Livers in the tunnels of Naraka. Collections.

Invisible machinery. Ever alive and dark.

Today's escaping white monkey cannot even get out of the

long, concentric tunnels of Markus's block; the EAT is about ten meters behind him and has already turned on its aiming devices.

Buzzing.

"EAT! EAT! EAT!"

They are all in a frenzy and looking forward to seeing the liver spat out.

Shitty white monkeys cheer and bet. Many are bent on their legs to hold back frustration.

Someone stays back in his cell, watching the scene without moving, eyes streaked with tears. Another masturbates, kneeling in a corner.

Eros and Thanatos?

In this place, what they once were is slowly evaporating. There is nothing surprising, after all, about how many white monkeys are drooling over the bloody epilogue of that hunt. Actually, nobody in Naraka is surprised about anything anymore.

Normality, here, has Shiva's four arms, Ganesha's elephant head, and Jesus Christ's ceiling-less tomb.

The fugitive approaches Markus's cell, lost in the maze of archways and bends. Markus recognize him as Al Terf, who is, like himself, close to twenty-five—close to the Slicer. He is out of breath.

The EAT draws closer and closer. Triumphant caterpillars.

"Markus, help me! Help! I'm wiped out," he pants.

Al Terf should just swallow the fake blue pill of soul, right now. Believe in Ute's science fiction. Think about the *beyond*, because the *now* is going to be pretty painful.

There's nothing to do for him.

"Markus, please ..." The last words of Al Terf are covered by the racket of the white monkeys, who are fired up, so excited about their awful, shared destiny.

"EAT! EAT! EAT!"

"You're done, man. Let's see that liver!"

"Another lap, come on!"

The EAT, cheered on as loud as a champion – a victorious, electronic Thracian gladiator – reaches Al Terf without even opening fire. Its RCS/4d architecture processes a new operative subroutine.

The white monkey kneels in his exhaustion. Sweat makes him glint under the artificial lights of the tunnel. The robot frames the warm body within its sensors, so close. The laser carvers activate.

Al Terf is about to become pieces of a man.

The EAT system always begins with the legs.

Al Terf stays alive for a few seconds before the carvers move on to the upper part of his remains. He looks at Markus for the last time and he's able to close his eyes before the final slash.

Inside of Markus, a lock-less door keeps slamming. It becomes a wind drum.

Fuck!

The robot swallows the white monkey into its tank, one piece at a time, storing him into its inner boiling broth. Mission accomplished, it quickly moves away, back toward the warehouse, excited and vibrating with newly accumulated energy.

Everyone gets back in their cells.

Silence returns to Naraka.

Perhaps Death will revisit him soon.

Will I be able to resist my whore, this time?

Will he be able to stay alive long enough to see his sister again?

From the cell in front of his, the usual sad song begins to resonate; it is Sabik, one who was virtually *born* in madness. His voice is ink, staining every cell door, but the words make no sense.

Sabik's thoughts quickly vanish, dripping away. The night seals Markus inside its black husk.

TROPIC OF NARAKA
नरक

YEAR 81, POST-UXOR

His thoughts widen now that the hunting drums have fallen asleep. Rock slips away.

The spectators have composed themselves back in their cells, and in good order. Under the blue light of the adjoining cell, a white monkey sprawls in his desperation: a young Werther with glass eye-sockets, leaning on his elbows.

Next to the steel door, wrapped in the cloths of his madness, there is someone with a sombrero hat in his hands who could be posing for Rodin's *Balzac*. He is a bundle of past squeezing into the cracks, the stamp of an entire continent, of the World Above, all within in a few centimeters. From the neck above, he is reminiscent of Buffalo Bill, of Christopher Columbus' torn diaries.

In another cell is a woman with her legs spread; perhaps she is just out of the Chambers of Sixteens. Her neck is thrown back and sprained. On her head, a red hat materializes: her thoughts projected in color toward the ceiling. An illusion, or maybe some wonderful bleeding. Imagine the wretched white monkey body coming back from the Chambers, blouse bloody and cunt purplish.

Managing to sleep: the most incredible choice in Naraka. No one listens to voices and to despair. It's impossible to think without your nose starting to run with hope, with fear. Music is a dream, nobody ever singing or playing.

In Markus's dream, rocky walls become wind, dragging with themselves a white-gloved female with a swan in her hands.

A woman holding her son ... future food that could run away from here, sail the waters.

According to legend, Leda, after she was impregnated, gave birth to two twins.

A shape under the tent, in the encampment of the Great

Alliance. A new Leda, with her arcane tingling, safe from the raining sparks of fires. Her symphony has a different orchestra, many brass instruments. Jupiter penetrates her ears; he enjoys going further down on the horizon.

Walls extend, pulled by the long tethers of dreams. Californian sentences, huge-finned whales, Zanzibar; the Alcazar, the Eldorado of Byzanthium.

Ute's boxes spill on the ground corpses of worlds, of illusions. Swimming in the deep cold beneath the asses of the icebergs.

All days become purple.

The caught man, the lights, and the breath of an impossible river.

UTERUS
नरक

Common Room #3, white monkey feeding room.
Sitting at his cube. His stuff inside the usual polycarbonate box.

An odd silence lingers, mixed with the nauseating smells of food. Electra and her red lips are at Markus's side; they share the cramped space, but she is transparent. He cannot see her because he is focused on the entrance, hoping to see Mira coming in.

Electra reads him. She eats silences and shit, that feedlot green mush.

Things that are hard to swallow.

Finally, Phurud enters this plastic space. He's one of the five males who was taken away with his sister. He finds their cube in this underground enclosure. He approaches, looking at the floor. Drags his first words.

"Motherfuckers! Damn motherfuckers!" So he begins, even before sitting.

"Speak! What happened to Mira?" Markus asks, thinking in apnea. "Where is she?"

Phurud keeps looking at the floor, with his inanimate food box on his knees. He is not completely there; he is seeing somewhere else.

How many eyes does he have?

"Speak, fuck!" Markus says, standing. A guard points his feelers toward him in alert. Markus sits back, squeezing his tough food box, managing to warp it with anxious fingers.

"Monkey, I'm waiting," he whispers like an ambushing reptile.

Perhaps he is the ambush prey.

Phurud, with his silence, is a messenger; he is speaking for Death, there inside his box, in his green mush. A small death, apparently not very important for this hell.

Polycarbonate coffins.

A scaring, over-friendly bed guest.

What a damn bastard, Death. She uses Phurud to talk to him, to kill him slowly. Imperceptible neurotoxins, black drops. Death is a mouse-spider spraying its venom, sodium into the cells, upsetting neural activity and the geometry of thoughts.

Phurud speaks again, "Motherfuckers! Motherfuckers!"

His refrain seems unending, his head moving to the left and right, swaying, uncertain what to do, or from which territory to start.

"Speak!" Markus repeats in rage.

"I tried ... I tried to help her, believe me ... but those sons of bitches ... Belser, it was him, he began, we tried to stop him, talk to him ... you know how that animal is. Mira's blood was dripping on her legs, all orange ... but he kept doing it. He did her with his eyes on the control room, where the guards were enjoying it ... They cheered him, touch themselves. After he finished ... after that beast filled her with everything he had, he grabbed her hair and began smashing her face into the wall. Fuck, he had lost it, for real; he wanted to kill her ... We stopped him before he broke her skull ... 'My revenge against the Black Seed people,' he shouted, 'I'll spoil it for those bastards, leave me!' ... So the guards came down and took him away... to the Slicer, I guess... but then..."

"Then what? What else? Where's my sister now?" Markus grabs his arm, shakes the truth out, the tail of things.

It was the voice of mad seas, that great roar, which shattered your child breast, too human and too soft.

Then, the tentacle of Hell, immense excrement, shattered your uterus, Mira ... Darkness now, down to the bladder, rectum, hope.

"She was bleeding. Unconscious. They dragged her up in the control room and laid her down on a bed with some machines. We could see everything, from below ... through the ceiling. They scanned her body with their readers, a lot of strange symbols showed up on their screens. Mira bounced back ... even those butchers were surprised. She got up on her elbows and began screaming. We couldn't hear what she said, you know that room ..."

"Go on! What did they do to her?"

Phurud is losing track. He is not a good messenger. Death will not be happy. She has sent an incompetent.

"One of those animals held her head and arms, another one her legs ... spread. The third opened her belly with a strange tool, which shone like silver ... it looked like a rotating scissor ... Markus ... *forgive me, I couldn't do anything! My god ...*"

Markus misses many of Phurud's words. A background streaked with abysses, laments, and noises accompany his sentences, individual letters spelled by his friend's black tongue.

Death appears behind Phurud, all gussied up. She wears a long blue tunic with large side pockets vomiting out guts, and she holds a heart in her right hand; she has his sister's eyes, replicated to infinity, like small buttons. Only Markus sees her; nobody is moving. The whore vanishes.

But she'll be back.

Phurud finishes his horrible tale:

"Blood was dripping on the ceiling, above us. It looked like it was falling on our faces ... We could no longer see her clearly, but a guard moved away a little, and in his hands ... in his black gloves, he was holding a mass of dark flesh. He put it right away inside one of those metal cabinets ... those ... the ones they use for freezing –"

"I don't give a fuck about the cabinets, I get it ... Phurud, my sister? What did they take? They fixed her, then, right?"

The tears on Phurud's face make everything clear: Mira's insemination was a total fuck-up; the skull injuries would have compromised any possible pregnancy.

Markus's sister had become useless. They had wasted time with her, lost a precious virgin. So, those bastards decided to rip her open and take out her uterus, to use it for their female fertility analyses, their hyper-cloning studies.

Mira had stayed on that bed, with her uterus torn out from her flesh, awake.

Phurud tells that his sister kept pouring blood, mindlessly moving her arms and legs, all tethers of consciousness gone, while the guards were busy with her precious uterus ...

Mira is dead.

Her soft uterus stored and refrigerated in a podris box in the multifunctional cabinets of Naraka.

A night butterfly, with large wings; still, frozen.

Penetrated by fire, glowing down there, between her legs, where women ought to glow, *white monkeys even. That circuit, Hell under his legs again. When she lay there with her legs apart she cried, nuclear bruises spreading like black stains on her soul, her thighs. She stared at the transparent ceiling, counting glad hours, not recalling any; she imagined the World Above, where a man climbs over a woman among walls of sky.*

Belser and his revenge against the Black Seed people ... Nice result, fucking idiot: a burst skull, a lost uterus, his entrails in the rotating machineries of the Slicer's blades. Flags of flesh. His revenge just took white monkey blood. And his Mira.

Darkness. *Nankeen.*

MAISON DES ANGES SPECIALE
नरक

YEAR 41, POST-UXOR

Finally, a cell all to myself. I'm almost sorry about leaving Jorge, my dear Placenta Eater. I was almost warming up to him. A few more days, and maybe I'd put out. Now, they even gave me a nice number: 457-2/1101. Four hundred fifty-seven: the outworlds I'll reach, someday, if I manage to get away from this shitty place. I'm *that* pissed. Sure, some doubt ... after how Unterbergen ended up. He was a dickhead, but down here things are really going awry. And Miyazaki's leg, care to talk about that?

These guards are such sons of bitches that they're bound to be New Moon employees. Scum as well, just like us. Who knows where they found them. No rules, no rights. I'm okay with that; it's just my area of expertise.

I have to get friendly with that pig, Ute. The priest is good. The only one who kept cool in the refectory. I'm sure he already has a plan to escape, while we keep wasting time and spit out days. Except those nails painted in silver servohue, so gross, I respect that priest. But he really should use red.

I see the fatty again two days later. Isolation really isn't my thing.

We eat all together once again.

The guest number in *Grand Hotel Naraka* has grown. The room is full this time. Miyazaki and his leg are gone. Our blood holiday party is down to five members. After filling our trays with shit, Lucas Miller motions me to follow him toward a different cube. We sit alone, while the other three motherfuckers eat a few meters away, peering at us. Jorge grins at me, passing his double tongue against his lips. I answer with my usual middle finger.

Miller has a pretty face, not a killer's. Anyway, with one who blew up even his own family with his bombs ... well, you don't really want to piss him off.

"You thought about getting out of this place, right?" he begins, lacking originality.

"You see, Miller, it's just that this place is kind of growing on me, especially after Unterbergen's beheading. I'm not sure ... *and you really need to fucking ask?* I'm not snuffing it here. You can be sure about that." I'm talking with a dork.

"Okay, beautiful, clear. I'm trying it tonight. Are you coming with?"

Miller explains his escape plan to me while the others keep swallowing New Moon's green shit. The priest prays for some seconds, his face close to his tray, before sinking his teeth into the stinking stuff. If you ask me, he is enjoying Miyazaki's shank broth.

The plan sounds good. Miller seems to know what he's talking about. Makbollah terrorism is a fine crime university.

He studied the security system and the unlock mechanism of the doors. He claims those New Moon idiots could have invested a little more on security. It seems they spared on several components. Actually, it does seem the prison is still under construction. Something temporary. Just as my life, if I choose to follow Miller. Because I've got the feeling he's going to have my ass blow up as he did with his wife's. Anyway, beats being sliced up by the jailers.

"They really are amateurs. With the materials I have already gathered, I can put together a nice device. We're going to make a lot of noise ..."

Miller seems confident. Me, not so much: "Going out, easy, okay ... you blow it all up, but then? How do we get away from here? What about getting back to Earth?"

I laugh in his face. He forgot we're on the moon, not in the outskirts of his Middle Los Angeles.

"I already found a weak spot in their security grid. Let me deal with that. I'll make them blind for a few minutes, but we'll have to move *fast.* And about the trip ... I gave a little present to one of the soldiers before they dumped us here. Some credits. Well, *some* ... let's say now he can buy himself a nice cottage in Maive Bay. So, I got this week's flight plans to Earth. Five outbound freightbots a day. We just have to get on one of those cargoes and we're good."

Miller explains all the details ... shit, he really did his

homework in these last days.

But something isn't clear to me.

"Are you sure? What sort of shit should a space penitentiary deliver to Earth? And then, five times a day? Sounds odd to me. Maybe that soldier ripped you off, don't you think? And yet, they didn't look that bright ..."

My grin doesn't undermine Miller's confidence in the least. He goes on: "I thought the same. *Weird, all these trips to Earth.* But I checked the flight plans ... and I got it. They're loaded with goods, those freightbots. In the documents, hauls are tagged as 'product deliveries' for *Maison des Anges Viande Spéciale.*"

"Ha ha! That's a good one! Miller, what the fuck are you saying? Are they rearing chickens on the moon, now? Okay, meat is worth its weight in gold on Earth, these days, but this really sounds ridiculous! I guess it's just some code they use, don't you think?"

Miller is annoyed, "Look, Kiki, I don't give a total fuck about what they're hauling and why. I just care that they can carry us back there, too."

Bomberman is right. That's our only chance of taking our asses off this place before they do us all in. By now it's clear that's their plan. All doomed. No rules.

The rendezvous is at midnight, tonight. The last freightbot is departing from New Belmarsh airstrip at 0:30.

"That could be a problem for someone lacking a watch, isn't it, Miller?"

He closes the argument: "You'll hear the bang, Kiki. You can't miss it. Then, I'll think about your cell. You know your way around with guns, right? It will get messy, reaching that freightbot."

Miller is forgetting he's dealing with a professional killer. It's not as though ass and tits made a difference, in this cases at least.

"You put something in my hand and you'll see, dickhead, how good I am!" I raise my voice, grabbing the collar of his uniform. The priest turns to look at us. He seems to bless me with a cryptic gesture of his hand.

"Okay, beautiful, voice down now. I don't doubt it ... I'd gladly put something in your hand right now."

Good, a killer with a sense of humor. But if he manages to get me aboard one of those freightbots, and back to my Paris, I'd gladly take something of his in my hand, and not only. You never forget your first love, as your first line of work. And then, Miller is not too shabby.

"See you later, Kiki. Be ready. Leave the rest to me."

Isn't my life, after all, just an array of pictures, changing only in their sequence?

THE WAREHOUSE
नरक

YEAR 41, POST-UXOR

Finally, night has fallen on Hell.

Miller is going to do his gig soon. I have something to do, too, as soon as I'm back on Earth: fuck up Big Blue, the bastard who sold me out to the military. *I'll hurt him, the King of Beauty.*

And this time, he won't be able to ask me anything anymore.

BRRRWWWOOOMMM! An explosion makes me tremble up to my boobs.

Well done, Miller. He did it!

He's at my cell right away, two pulse rifles on his shoulders. Finally, someone with a pair.

"Get me out of here, cool guy," I press, no time to lose.

"Stay clear of the door, quick."

Miller's breath is labored. He sweats as he rigs his makeshift device on the cell lock mechanisms. He turns back and forth every five seconds, to check the tunnel. Like rats, our jailers are going to come out of the dark soon. The alarm is screaming into our ears.

"On the floor, on my count …"

BRRRWWWOOOMMM!

Fuck, what a punch! I raise my eyes, the smoke filling my nose. Torn steel, a true work of art: *Fuck you, Naraka!*

"Out! Out! Take this …"

Miller chucks one of the pulse rifles to me, well-loaded. Who knows where he stole them, but who cares? This is a very resourceful man, apparently.

Now I'm feeling alive again.

Motherfuckers, I'll make you pay before I'm out of here!

Here they are, the guards … they start shooting from the bend of the west tunnel.

We return fire. Miller knows what he's doing. We pin them

down on their positions, while we manage to leave the main tunnel, breaking through a side door with bursts of gunfire.

Now we're less in the open. The worst is over.

We enter a room that looks like a small first-aid station with tables and gears. A lot of tech, thanks to New Moon's money. Turns out Hell's got its emergency rooms, too. On our right, a light alloy staircase rises. We go up without too much thought. Our jailers' shots are getting closer.

We run, they chase. The stairs end at a door leading into a huge chamber – a warehouse, on a first look. My legs ache. Miller is worked up and excited.

"Let's block the door with these crates, fucking help me! Quick!"

Okay, the jailers are sorted out, at least for a few minutes, so we run through the warehouse looking for a way out. We have to go up. New pulse rifle bursts from behind us, the guards about to clear their way. *But what the fuck is there, inside here?* I stop to look at huge pallets beside forklifts occupying most of the warehouse. Everything is *huge*.

"Miller! Look at these ..."

"What are you doing? Come on, let's go! Look, I'm not going to croak here for you," Miller shouts, wildly motioning. He's found an entry to continue our climb up the structure.

"You have to look, shit! *Here's your poultry!*"

Millions of cans, *Maison des Anges Viande Spéciale*, ready to be shipped to Earth. They don't give this stuff to the inmates. *Where does all this meat come from? Who's it for?*

Finally, a furious Miller comes back and reaches me. I fear he wants to do me in. His eyes are bursting out of his face. "Look here, for fuck's sake!"

Miller forcefully pushes me away, grabs one of the cans and tears it out of the sealed packages. He turns it around in his hands, looks at my eyes first, then at the towers of cans rising to the ceiling.

"You get it now, right? The chickens from the moon are us!"

"They sold us as *livestock*. The military, New Moon ... of course."

Miller nods.

Meat is the most profitable tender on Earth ... Uxor. Poisoned earth. Beans as expensive as jewels. Green shit. Twenty billion pieces of shit, all hungry.

More shots. Miller's hot blood squirts on my face. They made a few extra holes in his head, those motherfucking guards. Cool Guy flops on the ground floor right away.

I manage to hide behind the pallets in the nick of time, avoiding the second burst. There's seven of them, and they're going to fuck me up.

The freightbot must be departing in only a few minutes. I manage to keep counting even in all the excitement and action of the flight. Only a woman could do that. Twelve minutes, if I'm not mistaken. Canned human poultry distracts me.

More shots. I cannot move.

Then, as sometimes happens, I turn out to be a lucky bastard.

Miller, on the ground, opens his eyes: Cool Guy is still alive. He manages to pull something out of his pocket, shows it to me. *One of his bombs.* He primes it and keeps staring at me. I understand that this is the time to *run*, whatever the cost. The guards keep shooting as they get closer. They hit my leg, but now I'm far enough, fucking sons of bitches …

BRRRWWWOOOMMM!

Bravo, Miller, once again you did it!

The seven assholes are in chunks on the floor. Now New Moon will have to can them up, too. *Maison des Anges Viande, Recette Spéciale*, very special. I'm limping, but I can move; it isn't a serious wound. I keep climbing Naraka, following the way opened up by Miller. The alarm keeps pounding my ears. *Seven minutes to departure.*

PARADISE LOST
नरक

When you broke away from your hug, you saw tears. Miller was home, finally. Safe, sheltered, secure.

The small studio they reserved for him at the House of Death, bedroom and workroom at once, was about half as big as his cell at New Belmarsh, at Naraka.

In there, you could only fit a cot, a worktable, a chest of drawers. When the yellow lights were on, everything took on a warm color. Van Gogh would have found it delightful.

You couldn't but notice how quickly he set it all in that tidy, precise way of his, typical of an explosive specialist. You'd left him alone only for a few minutes, time to undo the luggage and say a Hail Mary. When you were back to say goodbye, you saw the items on the worktable, perfectly arranged: Semtex, demolition charges, Nobel 808, RDX, butyl rubber, neo plastrite, plastifiers, trackers, and varied electronic knick-knacks. A scent of almonds had filled his new room.

On the chest, which had a built-in mirror, a comb and hairbrush laid, nail scissors and file, an alarm clock, a dress brush, and a couple of framed photographs. His wife had really been a beautiful woman. What was missing, to complete the picture was his can of Maison des Anges Viande Spéciale, *Recette Miller. You fixed that. You tried to explain to him how Aladdin's Lamp worked. But those motherfuckers don't work in this hell. You told him it was too complicated to understand all at once, that he would get it eventually. It wasn't true. No wish would come true in the House of Death. Eventually, you were afraid Miller would have blown up yet another inferno.*

A woman came in without knocking; white and thin, her visage fine and fresh, her arms showing instead the marks of two hundred years. She apologized with Miller for the cramped accommodation she had gotten for him, jokingly calling it a small, comfortable tomb. We don't have much space here. You'll have to make do.

You had to leave him, now. You kissed him, wishing him good night. You got out of his room and of his almond-scented hell. Outside, you looked at the stars and inhaled a mouthful of that fragrant night.

Goodbye, Cool Guy.

THE BLACK MONKEY
नरक

YEAR 81, POST-UXOR

"So, what do you think you'll do now, Markus?"

Tseen-Ke's voice bounces in the silence.

"So what? I'm at the wrong cube? I don't think so, at least from what I heard."

Tseen-Ke is Naraka's black monkey, the only one.

Markus has just learned that his sister is dead, that her uterus keeps living on, in a fucking multifunctional cabinet.

What the fuck does the freak want from me?

"Beat it, black monkey, if you know what's best for you," he replies, standing up to sound more convincing.

Phurud tries to hold him, but Markus is beside himself, ready to kill and die without a pressing reason. Electra did not even notice the black monkey's arrival. She touches her belly, perhaps thinking about Markus's sister. Phurud's excruciating story, especially after those rotating scissors ripping out Mira's uterus, was too much for her. Things that stick in your throat. Harsh.

Tseen-Ke does not quit; he has something to say to him, and right now.

"I heard what happened to Mira. It's too late for her, but not for us. To get away of this cursed place. I repeat: What do you think you'll do now, Markus?"

The black monkey must be high; he wants to escape, he is determined in risking it all, EAT hunt included. He has too many answers, but no plan.

"I get it, black monkey, *but what the fuck do you want from me?*" Tseen-Ke's eyes shine like Ute's imaginary planets: Montparnasse and Byzanthium. They manage to break through the fuselage of Markus's new sadness, detach the leeches licking his heart.

Where did this guy pop out from?

"Escape, Markus. I want to get out of this shitty place. Like you. In a few days, I'll end up into the Slicer, and I'm not just going to wait for it," Tseen-Ke concludes, getting even closer to Markus's breath.

He does not move. Those eyes … more abysses, sinking into his own, just filled. That monkey knows the black rain; it is not only Markus's privilege. There are many Miras. And many white monkeys bent over by tons of debris on their shoulders. Lost things. Tseen-Ke has been dragging them for a long time. But his shiny back is not yet broken. Markus, he melted right away.

Montparnasse and Byzanthium, inside the same monkey, the same spirit, just like one of Ute's omens said:

The shadow of the black monkey will free Naraka, Mary Magdalene shall be back, Pistis Sophia. The black monkey will reveal the mysteries, the vultures of Hierankopolis shall rise in the sky, in the World Above. Machines will fall, together with a thousand stars. The army of Hyskos shall celebrate the destruction of Naraka, thousands of goats shall be sacrificed. Byzanthium and Montparnasse shall be reborn, in the spirit of the black monkey.

Phurud comes forward. "Black monkey, don't you understand? Leave him alone. You have to go!" He feels responsible for Markus's sister death, perhaps, thinking that smashing Tseen-Ke's skull would be quite a good revenge – you just need a splintered rock and a good deal of luck. Far away from the jailers, and at the right moment. Primal thoughts, Iron Age vibrations. Naraka's cursed time machine, the red armchair thrust into a ball of extinct dung. Fossil blood, saber-toothed tigers, still-impossible wheels.

More monkey blood spilled, as always, in vain.

Markus stops him. "Wait, Phurud. Let's hear what the black monkey has to say. Sit with us, Tseen-Ke."

"*Thursday, 11th of October,*" Ute once read. "*The course was W.S.W., and there was more sea than during the whole of the voyage. They saw sandpipers, and a green reed near the ship. Those of the caravel Pinta took up a small pole which appeared to have been worked with iron; also another bit of cane, a land-plant, and a small board. The crew of the caravel Nina also saw signs of land, and a small branch covered with berries. Everyone breathed afresh and rejoiced at these signs.*

"The land was first seen by a sailor named Rodrigo de Triana. But the Admiral, at ten in the previous night on the stern castle, had seen a light, though so uncertain that he could not affirm it was land. He called Pero Gutierrez, a gentleman of the bed-chamber, and invited him to look, too. He did so, and saw it."

They speak for a long time. The black monkey's determination infects them. Wonderful virus, double-helix genome: *Byzanthium and Montparnasse.*

Escape Naraka. Nobody's ever made it, at least since Markus was born in that place.

Tseen-Ke owns a great strength, a glittering spirit, but he does *not* have a plan. He wants to be by their side, anyway. He just needs a target; he is an arrow. They do not have much longer in Feeding Room #3. The Black Seed people are going to take them back to their cells soon.

They could take advantage of the Red Cave: old Ute's theater. The morning prayers, the evening ones, precious opportunities to talk, to organize. Pull the bow. The common rooms, where they eat and are forced to run to tone their muscles, their precious flesh, are under strict surveillance.

"The Admiral asked and admonished the men to keep a good look-out on the forecastle, and to watch well; and to him who should first cry out that he saw land, he would give a silk doublet, beyond the prizes promised by the Sovereigns.

"At two after midnight the land was sighted at a distance of two leagues. They shortened sail, and lay by under the mainsail without the bonnets. The vessels were hove to, waiting for daylight; and on Friday they arrived at a small island of the Lucayos, called, in the language of the Indians, Guanahaní."

They have the spot, but they need an idea; otherwise, they will immediately end up in the grip of those hovering liver-spitters and their laser carvers. *Alien buzz.* The same fate as so many wretches: in pieces, into the steel tank. Markus already hears the cries in his block.

"EAT! EAT! EAT!"

Who will be the first one to be swallowed?

The white monkeys betting their items. Tseen-Ke would be the favorite, no doubt. The last one to end up into the boiling broth of the EATs.

Someone would lose his mate's tooth, betting it on me.

"I'll tear those scrap irons apart. I'm not afraid of them." Tseen-Ke has already become the soul of the group.

Markus, Phurud, and Electra admire the lightning in his eyes: Byzanthium and Montparnasse inside the same monkey. The black monkey. They need a plan. They need Ute's help.

Friday, 12th October

They go just as naked as their mothers made them, and so do the women. All I saw were youths, all below thirty years of age. They are very well made, with very handsome bodies, and very good features. Their hair is short and coarse, almost like a horse's tail. They paint themselves in black, and their own colour is that of the Canarians, neither black nor white. They do not carry arms and do not know anything about them, as I showed them swords, and they took them by the blade and cut themselves for ignorance.

THE MAP OF KUFRA
नरक

YEAR 81, POST-UXOR

The entry to the Red Cave holds the revealing fire of Ute's cock, the soul behind the old man's shadow plays. The initiation formula:

Whoever you are, I warn you. You, who wish to probe Nature's enigmas, if you cannot find inside of yourself what you are looking for, you will not be able to find it outside, either. If you ignore the wonders of your home, how could you expect to find other wonders? The hidden Treasure of the Gods is hidden inside of you. Oh Man, know yourself, and you will know the Gods and the Universe.

Evening prayer. The opportunity to speak with Ute about their escape. *Has the right moment come for real?* Tseen-Ke has persuaded them all. He is pandemic, a mosaic of many colors, small pieces that would not work by themselves. Tseen-Ke – the universal cement, the architect of scrap, the poisoned tip they are about to shoot into Naraka's heart.

Bamboo. Upas-tieulè. Convulsions, calm, then more convulsions, and finally death for suffocation.

There are probably no such things as right moments in Hell, but this is worth a try. There will not be better chances. No more arrows to shoot.

Madness, after Mira's horrible death, is by now screwing Markus's mind; that much is clear. *Hallucinations.* Ears of wheat with purple crystals, silicone trees bent by fruits and cut heads, immense fields of pomegranate trees enclosed in the Himalaya of memories. *Hallucinations.* It happens to all the white monkeys who are close to being moved to the North Block. It is happening to him as well, now. In a while, he will no longer be able to think anymore, let alone escape.

Yes, it is worth risking it all right now. Will the old hornet help? He knows all the secrets of Naraka.

During the so-called *Equinox of the Sons of Light*, Ute always shows them, in the Red Cave, a sacred paper: a reproduction – the old man claims – of a map captured from space, from his imaginary black sky, of the great oasis of Kufra, with its farmed fields surrounded on all sides by the grip of the desert. Proof of the World Above. The hornet's relic.

A chant follows. Words sprout up the oases of Nahal Arugot, Nahal Prat and Nahal David. Small tissues of life, surrounded by the immense, cancerous desert.

Magic dates and pomegranates. Sand in the eyes.

Today is the new equinox, an important ceremony; a lunatic sign, but the coincidence is all there, marking the perfect time for the escape, just like Ute's Sons of Light did, getting back to a communion with the universal soul. His *Dialogues with Mother Earth* open up subtle, imperceptible channels. Who knows, maybe the old man, among all that bullshit ...

Speaking with animals, plants, the soul itself of all places and beings.

The photo from space of the oasis of Kufra, in the World Above, on *Earth*, that picture which everyone touches with superstition, thinking its microscopic residue on their fingertips could offer new fortune, prosperity. New Templars in Hell.

The great cross of Jerusalem above, aimed toward imaginary stars; the rock altar with its future boxes. Ute flies, in the Red Cave, quick with the varicolored feathers of words and thoughts, piercing with his black beak the cuirass of the white monkeys' ignorance. There is no bleeding, just new lifeblood, new hopes. To survive. What a pusher!

The old man artistically materializes his lysergic neoreligion, lumped together by the two-headed spermatozoa of his madness and old memories, fragments of an underground demiurge and his catacombs. The old man, who knows Naraka's codes, can help them nonetheless.

Together, with Electra and Tseen-Ke, they wait for the end of the ceremony. They have to catch the hornet before he flies away. He has to give them some answers. Now.

White monkeys, the mystery of the First Mirror speaks about what we send into the present, to whom and what is beside us. When we are surrounded by rage or fear, the mirror works both ways; it could be, instead, joy, bliss, happiness. What we see in

*the First Mirror is the image of what we are in the now. Who is
close to us sends it back, reflecting us.*

Finally, the function is over.

The white monkeys leave the Red Cave to get back to their
cells in good order. The three of them approach the old man.

Markus speaks first: "Ute, the prophecy: Byzanthium and
Montparnasse in the same person. We want to escape, to get
back in the World Above ... The black monkey, as you can see, is
with us."

The old man studies them for a long time. He shifts the weight
of his body so it leans on his divining rod. His eyes linger on
Electra, on her red mouth. He smiles.

"Come to my cell, the three of you. I'll get you a permit for a
private meeting. The Black Seed people listen to me; they respect
the needs of the faithful."

For the first time, Markus notices a dilitium minotaur is
embedded in the head of Ute's cane.

Instinct biting reason. The unaware bestiality of the human
race.

HOWL
नरक

You've seen the white monkeys of Naraka
undone by madness, hysterical, floating in the boiling
broth of metal dogs
dragging on the cell floor at dawn looking for a fix of hope
of ignorant, ageless bugs.
Men of the Black Seed, glowing for the ancient heavenly contact
with the blue dynamo in their stomach,
they nibble at bones in the eldritch cold gloom
floating among the peaks of Hell, listening to the blues of
prisoners
who showed their brains to the ceiling
they saw monkeys without underpants
who mated while burning dreams in the trash
they looked their transparent terror spat.
You've seen the white monkeys eating fire
they drank turpentine, they burst their chest
night after night with dreams, delusions, waking nightmares,
their dicks in their hand and Death at their backs
wandering up and down in their own mind, in the most hidden of
storage rooms.
You've seen the white monkeys
boning in old Ute's limo
under three-centimeter streetlights and rock ceilings
sex and soup, illusions and sperm, strawberries and sweat
and then they followed that bright hornet to speak about
Byzanthium and Montparnasse
of Eternity, wasted time, and then off aboard the red ship of their
twenty-fives
or to look at Earth so far away, and black.

I'M COMING AT YOU
नरक

Two minutes to launch. I'm inside the cargo, my leg is aching, bleeding, but I should make it. I've seen worse. I squeeze the wound and shout a blasphemy in my head. Just like when my father's brother drank my virginity. My sixteen-years-old cunt.

You're so beautiful, Kiki.

The alarm keeps shrieking, but the freightbot starts moving. Its vibrations cause the boxes of human chicken – piled up in the hold – to lurch. Shit, it's choke-full. Damn, how many moon chickens do they send up here?

Zero minutes to launch.

I'm out of Hell, en route to Earth, toward South Paris 5 and my friend Big Blue. That bastard ...

The engines are roaring at full power. We take up speed.

Fuck you, Grand Hotel Naraka!

I start counting again. A handful of minutes and we'll land, hopefully – thanks to my dear Cool Guy's finger in their eyes – before they sort out that I hitched this ride. Okay, but landing *where*?

A New Moon base, sure: no way are they touching down in a common skyhub with this haul of shit. When the special forces caught me – *Big Blue, I miss you so much!* – I ended up at Illiers-Cambray, where the nice party for the moon picnic was put together: Unterbergen, Miyazaki, the Eater & Co. And Miller.

My outworlds are going to increase soon: some dork who'll get in the way when we land, maybe, a few New Moon managers, just to clean up, and then ... Big Blue.

Wait for me, my love, I'm coming.

You'll see how pointy my little nose is ...

He must be thinking that I ended up in a can; a fine, tender dinner for some fat cats who can still afford to eat meat. By now, on Earth, few people have all their teeth still in their mouths. Is it about fitness for the environment? It is about having fuck-nothing to eat, apart from sucking mud or those shitty synthetic Symprix. Blue, yellow, green. Taste is always the same.

A nice new contract, that's what I need. Credits, so I can have something decent to eat, for me and my neutered cat; and for dessert, as Big Blue would have it, I'll buy myself a nice screw. Sure, silk stockings as well, but to strangle that bastard, a fine way to do him in. Seeing that loud tongue dangling. The esthete, the fucking King of Beauty. But of course.

Big Blue, my love. I'm coming at you.

THE HORNET AND HIS STINGER
नरक

YEAR 81, POST-UXOR

They enter old Ute's cell, which is much larger than theirs. Particles of camphor, caught in the steel, crash together. The harsh back of a plexis cube collects an array of astral maps and an ancient book by Georges I. Gurdjieff, titled *Beelzebub's Tales to His Grandson*. The usual obscure pages that, in the old man's opinion, should awaken the awareness of their ancient existence, the phantasmal World Above. A crazy hornet's flights.

A torment, a peculiar psyche: the compulsion to always act in accord to popular wisdom. Slipping into an unsuccessfully constructed brain, that old saying: every stick has two ends.

The door is overlooked by a Jerusalem cross, similar to the one hanging at the entrance of the Red Cave, but smaller. On the wall facing the bed is a framed painting: a weird divinity with an erection, two large horns, and three faces on his head. The creature is surrounded by real and fantastic animals. Markus recognizes rhinos, elephants, tigers, peacocks.

Ute showed them to him many years ago, in his future boxes, his labyrinthine books. Roars of papers.

Other animals, smaller, seem instead to be made of the warped substance of dreams: blue and azure streakings, two-headed snakes, a bird drawn with eleven stars that flaps sharp wings against worms and strange parasites – its neck golden, its wings purple. *Post fata resurgo.* Damn the old man and his mixed-up Indias and Palestines, Markus can never understand anything of that stuff. But that is exactly what the game is about.

Electra and Tseen-Ke, too, curiously look at that odd place, the Hornet's Lair.

"So, how can I help you?" Ute begins, sitting down on the bed.

Tseen-Ke, the black monkey, is faster than Markus, and he goes straight to the point. "Is there a way to get out of this place? Can you help us?"

Ute looks them in the eyes for a few seconds, scanning their intentions with a ghost probe. He gets up again, helping himself with his magic divining rod. He brushes a small sculpture with his fingers – a saint, sitting on the belly of a horse, riding the wrong way round in an indefinite space; the animal's tongue is dangling.

Markus thinks he hears Ute whispering a few words, but he could be wrong: *That crazy Cerny ...*

"I've been living in this hell for forty years. It takes faith, sons, sacrifice," Ute resumes, enigmatically. "Do you have faith? Because that can bring you anywhere."

Markus intervenes before the old man can fling them back into his rootless, nonsensical continents. "We have the faith, sure, but we want to get out of here, Ute."

The old man looks at him, biting his lip before answering. "Markus, Markus ... I've seen you grow up, survive. It was me, teaching you everything. Are you sure you have faith? *Show it to me*. Then, I'll do something for you."

The old man is coming to the fore. After spitting those last words, he abruptly pushes Markus aside to approach Electra. With his cane, he slowly lifts her white tunic, letting the blue light reflect along her knees, thighs ... then higher, until showing her cunt like a glittering star, carefully steering her pelvis toward the lighting cells.

Electra is surprised, motionless. She looks at Markus with wet eyes he has seen before.

"So, Markus, do you have faith? Does she?"

Inside of Ute, there is a world as big as the World Above; today they discover that by paying the price. Ute, riding the wrong way round. The hornet and his stinger. A lech.

They surrender to the old man's demands. He says he can show them the World Above, but a sacrifice is necessary. Electra's body, celebrated by his hands, and not only ...

A desperate, avid, sensual God. Like in that other book, just beside Ute. *Grunting like a pig. Always falling despite his golden wings, always with his belly up. Their master.*

They stand aside. They do not have much choice.

The hornet makes Electra lie down on his bed. He takes off her tunic. Her long blonde hair, untied, spreads on his black sheets. Lifeless satellites where the old man's soul lives. He opens her legs, slowly.

Ute wears Dyonisus' nebris, soft hooves; a new, very quiet Pan.

A laughing God, an old and morbid God, black and yellow. A pig with golden wings, spitting and sucking, his belly up, cruiser of warm waters – it is he, their master. *Let's kiss!*

"Black monkey, have you got something to say?"

Ute's voice hurls its weight against their awareness.

Markus cannot even move his tongue; his muscles could as well be atrophied.

Tseen-Ke just throws up syllables, staring into his eyes. His squeezed fists are far more meaningful. He squeezes frustration.

The old man has gotten them both high.

How the fuck did he do that?

"Well, so let's begin. Stand aside."

The hornet steps away to rummage in his things, shifting books, future boxes, pearls and small dilitium items. A curved horn drops to the floor; it seems of animal origin. Ute checks the item for damage.

"My *shofar.*"

Finally, he finds what he was looking for: a bottle containing a green, thick fluid. Electra is forced to swallow all of it. Her eyes begin to trip right away, reaching the ultimate border, beyond that string that must never be snapped. She is high, too.

The thousand drugs of Naraka's hornet. A thousand illusions.

The old man does not want to fuck Electra; that is not his goal. His stinger is something different. He gears up with a weird device. Ute looks at them, seems to challenge them, to enjoy their state.

The unexpected torment begins, enough for a lifetime. His woman is extensively penetrated by a black cylinder that seems to expand and heat up. Thermodilation devices.

Ute's hand drives that thing inside her vagina. From time to time, the old man keys sequential commands in the base of the cylinder. Electra does not move. Instead she smiles, looks at the ceiling with wonder in her eyes. She is seeing something else, beyond.

They smell the acrid of burnt flesh, and can only look upon the scene with frozen eyes.

At last, the hornet frees Electra from his disgusting machine, from his filthy hands etched by thick veins. He is profusely sweating, his gaze alien, upset, driven by signals coming from *other* worlds.

After catching his breath, leaning with his arms against the cell wall, Ute speaks again: "The sacrifice is made. Now the moment has come for me to show you the World Above. This is what you wanted, isn't it? We have to go back to the Red Cave. Follow me."

Electra stays on the hornet's bed, unconscious; her eyes on the ceiling of Hell, of her torturer's lair, are now closed, like her cunt.

Markus and Tseen-Ke come back to reality, can move again.

Motherfucker!

"What the fuck was that? What about her? What did you do to her?" Markus screams, forcefully grabbing the old man's black-and-yellow tunic as he walks toward the tunnel like nothing had happened.

"Markus, Markus … You never stop learning. You said you have faith … Your woman will recover soon, but don't count on her virtues anymore. Her sacrifice will be yours, too."

"What do you mean? Just be clear for once!"

Bitter tongue, cold blood.

Ute explains that after the thermodilation, Electra will live, but she will no longer be able to have sexual intercourse. Forever. Her vaginal walls have been cauterized and sealed by his magic cylinder. A vestal virgin. A wife of the Master of Justice. A small hole will function for her bodily needs.

That was the end of his red-mouthed Electra. A priestess of darkness.

"Markus, don't do anything crazy. Take your hands off me, and try to understand through faith. Miyazaki knows you're with me. Don't make him turn on his metal dogs. They would spoil the ritual."

They follow the hornet to the Red Cave. They do not have a choice, as always.

Ute will pay for this, sure; but before that, the old man must take them to the World Above.

They have to escape, have to know where to go.

Electra will come with them. She will recover. She will forget.

They follow Ute behind the altar of the Red Cave, and beyond a narrow steel door leading to a long corridor. Markus had never noticed that entrance, from the audience point of view. They go through the rocky guts for a few minutes, until they reach the base of a light alloy staircase, rising about ten meters before vanishing into the stone.

"So, are you ready?" Ute roars, pointing with his cane to the many steps leading to the World Above.

THE BALCONY
नरक

The steps seem to never end. The old man wearily leads the way, helping himself with his cane; they are four now, not three, on the stairs leading to the World Above: Markus, Ute, and Tseen-Ke's twin fury of Byzanthium and Montparnasse. Electra stayed back in the hornet's lair after tasting his stinger.

At last, they reach a circular room, what seems like the brain of a surveillance tower. Everything appears abandoned, crumbling. They are surrounded by cracked see-through crystals revealing another world from every angle – the world that every white monkey in Naraka dreams about. Something very different than the old man's tales, than the drawings in his future boxes, and the projections of their imaginations.

After catching up breath and strength, Ute begins his story:

"This, we call it the Balcony. Very few white monkeys ever got this far. What you see outside is the World Above, the real one ... Space, which keeps us all prisoners in Naraka, forever. Look up there. That black planet was our home. Earth. From here you could once admire the blue of the oceans, follow with your fingers the patterns of winds and whirls. A hope, a destination four hundred thousand kilometers away. *Going back one day ...* the dream."

A pause.

"Today," he resumed, "the planet is dead. Its resources have been sucked dry, to the root. Colors are gone, together with all the rest. Maybe something still lives in that mud."

What Markus sees through those crystals fills his heart with rage. A big planet of shit, extinct, squeezed at both ends.

But where the fuck are we?

Ute continues his guided tour:

"Now, look down. This grey, ashen surface is the world we

own. Naraka's true skin. We're on the moon, a satellite. This structure was built many years ago by the white monkeys. A space prison, where they locked up the scum of the planet: assassins, criminals. I arrived here forty years ago, with Miyazaki and many others.

"Everybody's destiny was to end up in pieces, in food cans. New Belmarsh: the first space farm of human meat, the ultimate boundary before the *Black Day*."

All for nothing. Endure, survive, hope. Electra's sacrifice, the fake religion. Mass control. They have all been stung by the hornet, by his doses of venom and illusions ... for so many years.

There is no World Above, no place to go.

On this sterile satellite, the farm goes on so the Black Seed people can survive, and so can Ute, Miyazaki, and who knows how many more former inmates and guards. Pioneers, dark heirs of a world that is no more. But they live, too, as prisoners in this desert, just like them. In this horrible, desolate World Above.

Sand in the wind, mating everywhere, randomly.

"I gave you what you wanted: truth. Freedom, that's a different story ... there's no such thing in Naraka." Ute ends his speech like that, tired of opening useless doors on reality.

Miyazaki reaches them on the Balcony, staggering on his dilitium leg, with two metal dogs behind him. One is for Markus, the other for Tseen-Ke; empty tanks, ready to be fueled.

Everything was set up.

Tseen-Ke, silent until now – digesting lumps of rage each second, each step, at each revelation – suddenly pounces on Ute, sinking a splintered stone into his throat. He snatches the cane and flings himself against the central crystal of the Balcony, striking with the dilitium minotaur head and shattering it.

As the air is fiercely sucked out, Miyazaki has time to run, taking shelter on the stairwell and immediately sealing the door behind him.

Holding on to metal struts, the dying Ute and Markus watch the body of Tseen-Ke, the black monkey, tracing a very long curve over the skin of the satellite fifty meters below, like a supersonic leaf flying away from its poisonous tree.

Their lungs rupture almost at the same time.

The brutal vacuum, assaulting them like a whiplash, allows their brains to snap a last photograph. Of all the story, that is what remains.

Ute's gushing blood wraps around his body like a red viper.

PART 2
KALASUTRA

PRINCE CHARMING
नरक

EARTH

No problem getting out of the freightbot. No problem leaving Illiers-Cambray. The same skyhub as the outward trip, just as I had guessed. I'd like to destroy that haul of shit – *canned human meat* – blow it all up, but I've got something more important to do. I'm not going to forget my New Moon friends, anyway.

It will be for next time. Very soon!

The skyhub structure is isolated. A small road runs parallel to the fence. Good enough for a single roadcar; perfect for a whore. Full of dark, secluded corners. You could rig up a nice whoring business here, with all those horny soldiers in the skyhub. Good money for Millander, the pimp king, a good friend of Big Blue's.

Honey, I'm coming …

I need to find a vehicle to reach Paris. More than a hundred kilometers. Roads are not what they used to be.

There's not a soul around. My leg aches, so walking is a problem. Things are starting to look bad. If anyone passes by, dickhead soldiers apart, I can't allow myself to miss them. So be it … a perfect place for a whore, right? I put my tits on display, fix my hair. Someone is bound to stop, eventually.

I take off my pants. It's not as though they kept us up-to-date with fashion while in jail. *Fuck you, New Belmarsh.* Naked thighs always do their dirty job. The douchebag of the day, he'll think the bandage is a garter.

At last, lights appear beyond the ghastly strips of the skyhub: a civilian roadcar.

Shit, he took his time. Will he be Prince Charming?

Lucky Guy sees the lit thighs and slows down. He gets to the boobs and stops.

It works better than Pythagoras' theorem, each time.

Had I showed him my ass, too, he'd have ended up right down

the scarp.

"What's your name? What are you doing here, honey?"

The grin belongs to a man in his forties leaning out of the passenger's window, stretching his neck in a ludicrous way.

"My name is Kiki, and I'm looking for Prince Charming."

I know, it slipped out, but it was right there. Anyway, I can't risk scaring him off. If he goes, I'm screwed. I adapt to the situation.

"I need a lift to Paris. What about that?"

I make my tits bob to convince him, while thinking about how to do him in and take his roadcar. I'm unarmed and injured. I've got to improvise.

"Paris? Paris where?"

Fatty's asking too many questions and the engine is idling. He could drive away. I've already had enough of this shitty country road.

"Going to South Paris 5. Is that okay with you?"

Here's the magic answer; now let's see how my Prince Charming reacts.

"South Paris 5? Fuck yeah, that's good! I see ... you're a little off route tonight, aren't you?"

He thinks he's funny, gloating with those duck eyes of his. He thinks I'm a hooker, but I'm starting to get bored, and when I'm bored I usually shoot. If I haven't got anything to shoot with, well, I *make do.*

"You know how it works, a unique customer ... I do *everything* for my customers, but then the asshole dumped me out here ..."

"What an asshole! A hottie like you ... I'm not going to Paris, but ... okay, for you I'm willing to take the long way round. Look, are you okay if we have a bite somewhere? I know a nice place half an hour from here where they have gourmet meat ... it's en route, if you're not in a hurry."

No shit. He must be loaded if he can afford meat. A card fat with credits. My Prince Charming just saved his life, for a while. I'll do him in after dinner. A nice steak. A *real* steak.

I climb in the roadcar. Fatty says his name is Arnoux. He looks at my leg because the bandage is starting to show a blood stain.

"But ... what happened to you?"

"Nothing serious. I've already told you I do everything, *really everything*, for my customers. Now mind your fucking business and take me to eat."

Arnoux chuckles. He likes my attitude. He likes my boobs even more. The kaleidoscope of his sexual fantasy has already built whole palaces.

His nuts are swollen. You can see it right away when a man hasn't been fucking in a long while.

After a nice steak and my number 27 outworld – *poor Arnoux, you learned about picking up strangers* – it's time to get back to work.

I see the lights of Paris, already smell the repulsive chamomile of Big Blue's aftershave.

I have to lose the roadcar. As soon as they find Fatty's body, I'll have all systems upon me. And this means, more or less, *right now*.

Leg's doing better, but it still hurts. A sideswipe. I *really* was a lucky bitch in that warehouse back in Naraka. I must drop by my flat, fix the bandage, and choose a pistol … the right one.

Maybe I'm old-fashioned, but, for grand occasions, I never forego my amphibious Martin 4, bullets and electromagnetic beams. Big Blue must be properly treated.

Anyway, after thinking about his army of goons, I'll have to also bring a Barret F3000 *bullpup*. I'll make noise. *A lot* of noise. Less romantic than my Martin, but 2,450 expansion bullets per minute is a real panacea for making your way.

Enjoy your Meal!
नरक

THE MOON

"The whore managed to get away. And that asshole Miller snuffed it. We really are a nice bunch of dickheads. Here like this, waiting. Just to shit green."

Aki Miyazaki, with a pretty dilitium trunk in place of his right leg – which ended up in the broth some days ago – stops talking to suck his greenish Symprix. He looks at the curved steel walls of the refectory at New Belmarsh Penitentiary. At the same cube, the survivors of the first haul of Earth scum curse and suck as well.

A short confinement before being canned.

Corona, the Placenta Eater; Kaijū Hanzo; Ute Möbius, the priest; Beatrix Leonard, Ninive.

The Danube Ripper was the first to be retired, losing his head to Naraka.

Miyazaki swallows the last sip of that shit.

"Jorge, you've been a cellmate with that bitch. Did you bang her? How does she taste? Kiki ... it just takes that name to make me hard."

The Placenta Eater cleans his mouth with the back of his hand. His eyes have turned on like red LEDs at Miyazaki's words.

"You still haven't learned to shut that fucking trap? They'll saw off the other leg, too, if you keep pissing people off. I'd like to see you, then, crawling like a worm."

Middle finger toward Miyazaki's square head.

Laughter, fists against the cube. Only the priest keeps eating, indifferent to the psychotic adrenaline of the party. He's the only one who seems to see things clearly, in a place like that, too. In a place like that *especially*.

He tries to steer the scum back under control, to give direction to all those wasted energies.

"If she managed to escape, this means her cunt is worth more than your apish brains put together. Forgive me, my Lord, but there's no other way to relate with these dickheads."

Beatrix, the silent one, the only professional assassin in the herd of serial killers, finds her voice again as well: "You speak well, priest. Why don't you tell us what you'd do? If you don't have anything to say, at least tell us about those children you screwed, to kill some time. Chemical castration's coming, man! They'll rig you up with a nice pair of rubber nuts. You can use them as a rosary." Scornful.

"The girl's a badass! And a nice piece of *ass*, too ..." Miyazaki laughs out loud, pretends he is the priest praying while making his nuts bounce. "I'm gonna do five Hail Marys, now, perhaps they'll bring me luck and they'll fuck *you* up before me."

Ute does not react to the prodding. He begins praying for real, in the bewilderment of the scum.

"*With that thought, she exited her own region, the thirteenth aeon, and descended to the twelfth. The archons chased, enraged with her, because she had thought of glory. And she descended further into the chaos, and approached the lion-faced luminous power. To devour it.*

"*But the power cleaned out her light and all the emanations of self-will, and devoured it all; her matter was thrust into the chaos and became a lion-faced archon of chaos, one half fire and the other darkness: Yaldabaoth.*"

"What the fuck is this shit? What does that mean? If you want to threaten, priest, speak plainly." Hanzo gets on his feet, his radiation-tattooed face lights up in red and orange, almost striped. He is the type who takes it badly when words elude him.

The Placenta Eater pushes down his shoulder, getting him back to his seat.

"Why don't you cool off?" he whispers. "Those piece-of-shit guards don't fool around, here. Remember Unterbergen's head. I wouldn't like to see yours roll, too. Things like that spoil my appetite."

Hanzo swallows his rage, mixes it up in his stomach with the green meal. He vents out just a little as it filters through his rotten teeth: *"Fuck you, priest!"*

From the control room, the scum is constantly kept under observation, as well as the other inmates. All the guests of Grand Hotel Naraka. Some recently arrived, like the scum, while others have been waiting for a long time, already familiar with the logistics. Shadows that keep pissing themselves every morning. Every time the guards choose the lucky cows to be taken to the Slicer. North Block. Hanging lives, waiting for their blades, for a new body of compressed and seasoned meat, canned human meat for Earth's wealthier palates. Foodies who pay handsomely to avoid the usual green shit – that cursed synthetic glue that sticks in your mouth and belly. Alternatives are exhausted. Someone has to be reared for the common good.

For the common good taste.

KILL BLUE
नरक

EARTH

The driver stops close to my feet. A nice sneer, this one. Night shift. He must have been popping pills like mad. He wouldn't be a bad fit in a rocky cell in Naraka. I must convince him to take me to South Paris 5. Nothing new; nobody wants to make that trip. He starts with a snort and tells me he'll take me as far as Bercy Frontière 2, the boundary of civilization. Then three kilometers on foot to reach home. *Merde!* I manage to keep my mouth shut before insulting his sister – because with that trippy face, and those eyes wedged beside the nose, he *must* have a slut sister.

We cross the city. The night has already swallowed everyone. I think about Big Blue. He must know by now that I escaped from Naraka. His New Moon friends must have warned him. Maybe there's someone waiting at my flat, and sure as hell not for a fuck.

The driver stops at Bercy Frontière 2. He doesn't risk a single meter more. He turns back with his jobless wraith face and asks me for fifteen credits.

Does it hurt, that broken nose, motherfucker?

A direct hit with my elbow. He shouts curses in his people's language, tries to do something to stop the bleeding.

I hop out, go. As I imagined, Trippy contents himself with insulting me from his roadcab, spitting out every possible name, but he knows better than to do anything more.

You keep your filthy upholstery and your broken nose, asshole.

I walk along the narrow streets of South Paris 5. Here, they could even shoot you for a piece of bread full of lichen! At last, the dark shape of my house appears, the ghost of what it used to be, so long ago. I made it.

The card for the door is always in the same place, in the

Amaryllis vase. No Big Blue's killer waits in my flat. Alexis hops into my lap; he's starving. Better a cat than a man, who'd keep treating you like a whore even if you've been out of that profession for years.

I prepare everything. *Sangfroid* and bullets.

My red roadcar is parked next to the devoured soul of a junkie wheezing on the sidewalk. He speaks to his wife – used-to-be wife, I understand, because he keeps saying:

You ruined me, bitch. Thursday, you ruined me. You're a bitch!

The windows of Big Blue's villa are lit. The motherfucker is waiting for me.

In love, as ever.

Two goons are taking care of the main entrance, well-armed. Better going in from the rear. Usually, he puts only a man there, as watchdog. The problem will be the inside.

I take position and shoot, a too-easy target. Big Blue's dog slumps on the ground, never knowing what hit him. A hole in his head. Outworld number 28.

"Kiki, Kiki … don't raise hell. Just come in."

Big Blue appears under the lights with his hands up and wearing one of his smiles.

"Do you know how much these people cost? Are you trying to wipe me out?"

He's fucking with me. I'd like to shoot him right now in that wide face, but that would be too easy, too quick. The bastard must pay for it the right way.

"Come in. We have to talk business. Something important."

I follow Big Blue's words, the path of his too-white teeth. I'm confused. I get in, let him hug me like an old friend. He plunges his hands into my ass.

We go up to the second floor. Big Blue really seems in good shape. Who knows what he's taken.

"I want to show you something. You're not going to believe your eyes."

I don't let him fool me and abruptly interrupt his weird elation: "Another of your toys? Listen, why don't we talk about Guadalupe? You know, I'm sorry … I forgot to bring you a gift from Naraka."

Big Blue spreads his arms like a scarecrow, palms to the sky, toward some sort of Fate hailing down out of his control.

"Yes, I heard, Kiki. Guadalupe is playing dirty. That's why I asked you to *retire* him. Look here."

No way: he doesn't want to talk about it. He's sweating adrenaline, happy as a child.

He climbs on a seat and pulls a red cloth, freeing his surprise. A sort of refrigerator with training wheels. Advanced tech; that much is clear. He caresses it, brushing sensors with his fingers, the control systems of that heap of scrap.

He turns back and looks at me, excited.

"Isn't it wonderful? It's a prototype. An EAT system," he reveals, enigmatically.

Perhaps the moment has come to mark down my number 29 outworld.

"What's that, a cyber-butler? Or maybe some machine to empty out your balls? As usual, Big Blue. That crap reeks of military. Your new friends. So, why should I give a shit about it?"

"You have to see, Kiki ..." Big Blue turns serious. "*You really have to see.*"

He calls one of his goons: Monk. He's so big he could not even lace his own shoes, but he makes an impression. Just like the rest of Big Blue's pretty bullshit.

I left my *bullpup* in the backyard. It's not tasteful to bring such a rifle inside a house. But my Martin 4 is at my side, over my ass, well-loaded. I'm ready. If Monk tries something funny, he'll make an ugly end, he and his excited master, who's drooling more than usual today.

Big Blue motions me to stay still, winking like one who knows what's what. I'm becoming an accomplice in something I don't understand. He steps some meters away, opens the liquor cabinet, and draws a Glock 22.

Fuck!

I immediately reach for my Martin.

Big Blue is faster. Without a second thought, he smokes Monk with a couple bullets to the chest. The man heavily drops on the floor. Big Blue is out of his mind. More than usual.

"Lower the gun, Kiki. It's all right. Wait."

He leaves his Glock on the table and approaches his brand new refrigerator. He enters a code and activates the system. The machine starts moving; it seems to be exploring the environment, moving back and forth. A fucking robot ... *So what's new?*

It's time to put an end to the bullshit. My Martin is getting too warm. I face Big Blue head-on.

"Have you given a name to this shit? I'd go with *Guadalupe*, what about it? Listen, thank you for the show, but now we have to set things straight …"

The robot interrupts me with a vibrant noise. From its sides, it activates two laser carvers, the same type used by Naraka guards to slice up Miyazaki's leg, and to cut off Unterbergen's head.

Motherfucker!

Big Blue has made some new friends – those New Moon animals. The machine approaches Monk's body. The carvers, with their azure strings, begin hacking.

How fucking much blood does he have?

After cutting Big Blue's goon into seven or eight main chunks, the robot opens a compartment in its silver belly. Loads in what's left of him. Two green lights illuminate on its control panel, under the neck of the elliptical head.

"*Biomass stored. System ready.*"

It can talk, this metal shit, and with Big Blue's schizophrenic, digitized voice. The refrigerator filled up on gas … Big Blue is more and more excited.

"Did you see that? This is just a prototype. As soon as it's armed, it's going to do everything by itself, self-fueling indefinitely. Disposing of carrions, but perfectly healthy human beings as well. A wonder of technology, Kiki …"

I liked his muses of flesh better, his experiments on talent, even those collections of paintings and human-hearted neprom dolls. Big Blue is ecstatic before the features of his refrigerator. He doesn't seem to mind Monk's pieces still on his precious carpets. He almost trips over them to hug his new death engine.

"This is the future, Kiki. Do you understand? *Pure poetry …* eaten and digested by a machine we ourselves built: the creator becoming food, fuel. There are no boundaries to this technology."

Big Blue keeps ranting and raving, caressing his robot. His designer shoes soak in Monk's blood, a man who had served him for five years.

"Not bad, Blue. New Moon really is working hard. I saw interesting stuff, too, in that place you sent me to: Naraka, *the farm of human chickens on the Moon.*"

As I spit out the last word, my Martin is ready to open fire.

Big Blue keeps grinning and spreading his arms.

I don't give a shit about style. I want to do him in as a pig, disarmed even.

Big Blue comes toward me without fear.

"I've nothing to do with that Guadalupe story. I've got a new contract ready for you. You say the price ..."

Nobody kills the goose that laid the golden eggs. If he hadn't come into my life, I'd still be doing ten-credit blowjobs at South Paris 5 terminal. But tonight, Blue really wants to be the asshole. He thinks he can fool me.

He draws a pistol from the sleeve of his jacket and shoots twice, but Big Blue isn't what he used to be. Too many bio-amphetamines cloud your reflexes.

He swipes me in a shoulder. I dig a nice hole between his eyes.

This is for Guadalupe and the holiday on the Moon.

He drops on his knees – his wide bullets have spoiled forever two magnificent paintings – and then his shocked face kisses the floor, the ancient mosaics. His last gaze, fixed and unending, is for his metal refrigerator.

Fuck, that's true love!

Now the problem is getting out quickly. The villa is chock-full with muscle, dangerous even without their master. My shoulder hurts, but I should make it.

Go down in the courtyard, recover my *bullpup*.

Clean out and get back to my flat.

I'll have to disappear.

A lot of people will be looking for me.

Before going, I enjoy the last, unexpected spectacle of Big Blue. But I'm not the lead, as the damn piece of shit expected.

The robot, still functional, smells the stink of Blue's blood with its electronic nose. "*More fuel available. Scanning environment.*"

Before climbing on the window, I look at the robot's azure laser carvers that are dealing with my old friend's body wrapped in his smart black suit. His *too white* teeth, loaded together with his entrails into the tank of the machine, glint like stars before the hatch shuts.

"*Biomass stored. System ready. System loaded.*"

THE INDIFFERENT BEAUTY
⊸NEPROM DOLL I⊸
नरक

Camille's body lives downtown, in a dark palace. A fortress. Leonardian walls, perfectly sloping, concrete windows, aluminum doors. When her beauty shows itself, to give itself to the dirty streets, to the reflections of shopfronts, to the poor eyes, it wraps itself in a cloud of barbed wire. A biting guest, in perfect synchrony. *Her white visage, long sharp neck, can be partially glimpsed, partially imagined.*

A creature composed by fibers of beauty matter and a fantasy skeleton, imagined by Mirò, with rain upon her, horizontally.

The indifferent beauty, with her cunt narrow and shaved. Smell of vanilla, walls of red velvet.

Every Wednesday afternoon, Camille leaves her dark fortress.

A fixture at the Diable édenté. *A brothel, unattainable for many. A red armchair, a special show. Ring up the curtain: a man and a virgin – she, so not, not* indifferent. *Arranged rape. The room encloses every sound,* the sliding of flesh on flesh on the slope of sweat. *Thin, metallic noises of light alloy anklets and shaking chains.*

Camille looks at the scene. The vanilla scent of her cunt now slowly turns into tastes like sea depths. She sips Indian sparkling wine, wears new shoes, her legs dancing and crossing in their arousal. But Camille always gets bored too soon. She calls Terrand, the brothel's field marshal. *She asks that they treat the virgin's ass, so new, just blossomed out of misery.*

Terrand materializes the indifferent beauty's wishes. He can arrange everything masterfully. He has first-class gear.

A huge, smooth dilitium cylinder, with adjustable girth, begins its slow work. Her ass burns. The virgin pictures the fine dress of the lady watching behind the mirror. She thinks she is important, for once, filling important eyes. The cylinder spits boiling water. Fire in her womb and guts. Its thickness grows every minute.

Camille pays a thousand credits, gets up from her armchair, exits the Diable édenté.

The indifferent beauty shows herself again on the streets, scornful among fetid humanity. Her heels set the rhythm, the haste of going back to her palace, the clock of impossible drives. Nobody can save her from eternal frustration.

You need the right hands to open up her cloud of barbed wire without getting wounded.

Camille shuts herself back inside her fortress. She scans the memories of her senses in the right sequence. The virgin's dilated ass lights up in her mind. Camille soils her clean bed. She touches herself with white fingers, using them down to the knuckles to look for that orgasm hidden deep inside her body. Nowhere to be found. Alien.

She will come back to the Diable édenté in the next days, to check on the virgin's treated ass. Forever changed. Dilation will have reached its final stage, just short of bursting her sphincter.

Technology and patience. Camille will be able to enter her with her arm, touch her soul. Suffering can overcome loneliness. Perhaps this time Camille will manage to come.

Big Blue, the collector, has been following Camille for a long time. He chooses her.

He feels the vibrations of that so-cold heart, those too-thick cartilages, imprisoning orgasm. Thick walls, narrow rooms of upbringing, education. Pleasure is just a splinter, small and sharp, hidden inside her womb. Like that, it can only hurt.

Big Blue knows how to manage that.

Camille becomes his neprom doll #1.

Diamonds embedded in her heart, ventricles glittering. Her platek-treated vagina is installed on a new, artificial support. An organic, warmable mannequin with a golden curtain between its legs. The rest of her old body of flesh is useless, by now. They will be serving it in some gourmet restaurant. And orgasm, the alien, screams, while they chew that for dessert.

Thanks to Big Blue, now the indifferent beauty can have pleasure. She can free herself.

First in line of his beautiful collection. Big Blue's guests are glad to use her supple, treated vagina, its internal temperature always under control. Ideal. Fine technology indeed. The *indifferent beauty is now a tactful aperitif. The collection route, the tasting, begins with her; just after showing your ticket and freeing your shoulders from the coat.*

Someone uses his tongue, someone his fingers, some their loaded penis against her, inside her. A monitor shows to the customer graphics and trends of her stimulation, the emotions of the still-living doll's heart. Her cunt moistened by an adjustable presser. Some customers linger with Camille, pulling down their pants and emptying themselves right away. The impulsive ones, the inexperienced; they don't know the line is long, that Big Blue's organic dolls are many. You have to be able to play with more than one heart.

The indifferent beauty enjoys humanity bursting through her by-now useless cloud of iron wire, her vanilla cunt now singing all the scents in the world.

THE GREAT CATHEDRAL
नरक

THE MOON

Beatrix Leonard, Ninive, professional killer. Twenty-five, blue eyes, thin hips, dilitium tongue piercing. 17 outworlds. Not bad as a career start. Section 197C. Meat class AAB. Stay in Naraka: 14 days.

Night. Cell 578. Beatrix breathes the smell of captive monkeys of that slice of Naraka. Night in Hell gives off a different, parallel dimension of time. She has not lost hope, her eyes still glinting. She knows she is going to be freed soon. She is certainly not ending up like the scum, hacked up, or like those junkies and degenerates.

When her husband – the New Black Flower leader – comes, he will make *a fucking mess*. Many heads will roll; that much is sure. He will hang them, using their guts as a noose, to this putrid rock ceiling. They will dance back and forth. They will show the soles of their shoes to everybody.

But why is he taking so long? Anton ...

From cell 579, a voice shucks the silence, crawling under Beatrix's door. It climbs like a spider to cling to her ears.

Anton?

Just a voice from underground, memory of a too-long stay in Naraka. A man's voice, its rhythm torn apart and offbeat with madness ...

"*I'm a rat, I'm a rat, I'm a rat!*"

"The antithesis of man. I'm a being of pure hyperawareness. I'm not from a bitch's womb, from sperm traffic. Beware: I'm a *hyperaware rat,* a hypertrophic transformation, not just a common rat. But I'm okay with that. *Nobody asks me what I consider myself.* Into what I turned. I still wear the old human uniform, but inside? *Everything is different.* They call me with a number. My thoughts are invisible, redundant. *For them.*

"You'll ask me: *how does this rat act?* Say, for example, it's hurt, in any way, and wishes revenge. Grudge got a special space inside this seemingly tiny body. *A cathedral with five naves.* Multidimensional, hypertrophic cells. *Never heard of those?* Volumes which are small, but huge; wishes which are small, but huge. The rat opens his cathedral, considers his revenge. It spreads doubts and questions in the form of excrement. The wretch who has to deal with Naraka's rat stomps on this unsolved grime, polluting his shoes, brain, and heart. Fatal slop, fetid muck. The rat's ocean drowns any conscience.

"*I'm a rat, I'm a rat, I'm that rat!*

"Spits and insults fall upon me. Men – who are judges of everything and everyone – laugh out loud and ridicule me. *Good.* Pummeled and derided. *Better.* A motion of my paw, a grin of disdain is enough to piss him off: the jailer takes his baton, strikes my back. But he beats something that doesn't exist, and my multidimensional cells wriggle into the *hole*. Sheltered, into my secret lair. There, in the filthy, fetid underground, I dive and wait for my vengeance. The rat's grudge is cold, poisonous and, overall, never-ending.

"From my lair, I look at his boots stomping on my excrement. *It's done.* The jailer will be ashamed of that moment, of my cell, of my eyes, of the blows. My virus gets in his system, his blood forever compromised. He'll keep remembering, dredging up. He'll make up a lot of stories against himself. He'll never forget himself anything. He won't even believe his own right for vengeance, or its success. He will suffer a hundred times more than the one he punished. Spits and blows, they don't bother the rat in the least. His body is elsewhere. On his deathbed, the jailer will remember everything once again, with the interests of a lifetime. *My virus is geometric, a fine maze indeed.*

"He'll be forced to bury himself alive, forced by pain, by torment, in that underground which is my body, my strength. My soul's hypertrophia. Your half-faith won't be enough to save you, my friend.

"This is what I hide in my cathedral, which holds the juice of that odd pleasure I've talked to you about. Shake the burrows, shift stones, reach the man's corpse, sink my teeth into those desperate eyes. Feeding myself, slowly digesting him, giving my virus more opportunities to spread. You don't know, jailer, the true *underground.* Even if you walk along rocky tunnels.

"I'm a rat, I'm a rat, I'm that rat!"

Beatrix listens to the rat's monologue, of that prisoner of Naraka. Thin tears flow, a killer's tears. *Desperation.* Beatrix understands the logics of Hell.

This is not a jail, this is not a place.

More voices walk the tunnel, enter the rat's cell.

Anton ... Anton!...

"Fuck, not again! Look at the mess this son of a bitch did again. *Gross!* This time you'll pay for it." Two guards are inside the cell of inmate 17-3/11. Meat class NE. Stay in Naraka: 210 days. The man's feces cover him entirely, as well as the steel walls. The jailers shout, they load their weapons.

"*The stink!* You really are an animal. I'll teach you a thing or two, then we'll see if you feel like being the asshole again."

The rat is hit, repeatedly. Kicked. One of the guards cannot restrain himself and opens fire, a quick burst.

Does he regret it?

"What the ... did you kill him? Fuck, they'll report us!"

Beatrix can almost see them through the wall: the rat reaper pointing his red eyes and his weapon at his colleague ...

"He tried to come at me, didn't you see? Just open your eyes, dickhead. Didn't you see he tried to jump me, didn't you? Did you see it, *or not?*"

The other one apparently surrenders to Naraka's logics.

"Yeah, sure, *I've seen.*"

"And then again ... a report? An NE prisoner is just good to fill the tanks of those machines, it's spoiled meat. Only a minor scheduling shift, nothing fucking changes. Call PDM service, have him taken away. They'll deal with the cleaning of all this shit. Me, I'm not touching anything in here. And remember *what you've seen.*"

She hears the cell door shut, and footsteps as they leave.

Beatrix squeezes her fists hard. She thinks maybe that rat actually wriggled away from the jailers' hands, hiding down in his lair. *Underground.* Maybe he opened the doors of his *cathedral,* freeing the grudge, the eternal grudge. Bullshit. But that absurd direction in Beatrix's thoughts begins loosening her humanity, her reason, her hope. Naraka's poison is just that.

On the wall of cell 579, the inmate has drawn something with his shit.

A great cathedral.

HOLES
नरक

EARTH

Sipho Lopez, aka Guadalupe. Big Blue's business associate. Big Blue is gone. I've done him in a few days ago. Someone who was considered untouchable here in South Paris 5. But I've *touched*, oh yeah, digging a nice hole in his head. That motherfucker set me up, bought my ticket to Naraka. With Big Blue gone, now I've got to deal with Guadalupe.

Once I'll be done – my golden-egg-duck shot and his associate sent to Hell as well – I'll need to find new clients, new contracts. A killer who's jobless for too long risks losing her marbles. It won't be hard getting back on the market: professionals are in high demand and too many assholes are still walking around on their legs.

Killing: a secure job, just like being a whore, squeezing out the sweat and stink of humanity on a daily basis. I know something about that, but by now I've been out of practice for a long time, and I don't think about going back even for a second. Corpses stink, too, and badly, but you don't have to fuck them.

The problem, now, is Guadalupe – finding him before he finds me. A guy like him can't certainly be outside South Paris 5. This apocalyptic part of the city where men trade with rats. Where you're killed over a slice of bread. Where you get a blowjob for a spoon of meat broth.

Real meat, *maybe.*

South Paris 5 is the perfect habitat for an animal like Guadalupe ... his jungle, his infamous hunting ground.

I had to leave my flat, to shut myself in this shitty hole with my neutered cat and my Martin 4. I am up this neighborhood's ass.

Here, you live under a blue sun, with the junkies' white eyes glittering like dirty stars. A hole where you can't see the bottom.

You won't have it that easy, Guadalupe ... Come find me if you can.

It's all a matter of holes, right?

Holes where you sleep, on floors slippery with the gravy of dreams. Holes to thrust different neighborhoods and perspectives into your rotten veins. Holes to survive, an ass and a cunt into which many have squeezed their loneliness. Holes to live, to eat real meat and buy microscopic dilitium jewels. Holes stopping lives, those of my Martin 4, opened up on Big Blue's forehead, as well as those of twenty-eight other motherfuckers.

Enough with the shitty thoughts.

I've got to move. I need to look for Guadalupe and blow up that hippo face of his.

South Paris 5 is big and small at the same time. Guadalupe must be hiding in one of his *holes*, sweaty as always, his ungainly hands squeezing tissues and human beings. Rings and stones that switch off and light up lives.

Codes. Mines of dilitium, of old blood, dug into his phalanxes. Stigmata of a lecherous, bastard god, licking the empty skulls of sadnesses and fucking the sheep of his flock. A real motherfucker. Big Blue, the King of Beauty, was at least classy and white-teethed.

Guadalupe, and his big ass, think and stink just the same. He sells shit, buys shit. Everything he touches turns to shit. A magic touch. An alchemist transmuting beauty, hope, and life into products of the ass and black sperm. The crystallized stuff paving the streets of South Paris 5.

I've got two coordinates to find him: drugs and whores. I don't think he's directly involved in human meat traffic, let alone doing business with New Moon Corporation and the military; he doesn't have the balls or the brains for that; stuff like that was all Big Blue's field.

With that hippo face and his stinky stories of cunts, bullets, and horse races, I really don't see him in a meeting with the big shots.

Let's begin with the lead I'm more familiar with: the whorehouses.

His friend China "Tramp" Millander. A lieutenant, nothing more. Working for both Big Blue and Guadalupe. A nice piece of shit himself. They had pulled him out of the garbage of South Paris 5, where he panhandled on the streets, dressed as a clown, shared his dinner with the rats and with a junkie wife who could not even pick up a customer anymore. *Tramp*: that nickname was Millander's ancient brand.

Chromosomes of misery: a rat's snout, a jester's smile, sold and warped for years; someone capable of selling his own wife – after struck down by an overdose – to a downtown restaurant for one hundred credits.

Dish of the day: Junkie Stew.

But he, the great jester of South Paris 5, always knew how to reply. Better the mouths of those rich shits than the teeth of the rats.

I did her a big favor.

I'll begin with *Le Sphinx Tatoué*, one of the busier businesses in South Paris 5. Maybe I'll get him right away, the hippo, together with his friend Millander. If I'm lucky.

Big Blue took me there for the first time. He always chose a different location to negotiate an outworld contract.

I had to do in a young judge of the Special Court, a ludicrous freak show the military had put together to guarantee the security of the city, an organization that no longer exists, that nobody remembers. But back then, the Court was fucking with Big Blue enough, and he wasn't the type who cared for wasting his time, let alone being fucked with.

They had this judge and his staff stuck to his ass. I think his name was Roux, something like that. Big Blue entrusted me with this easy contract at the Sphinx Tatoué, my fourth outworld. Back then, I was learning the ropes as a killer, one of those who are called *Coquelets* in South Paris 5. I still had to top my wages fucking someone now and then.

A nice hole, Le Sphinx Tatoué, at least for the standards of this apocalyptic city.

First-class sluts, fancy rooms with everything you need, a restaurant that knows how to satisfy the most demanding and hard-to-please customers. Human meat: you find that almost every day, at the Sphinx Tatoué. And when you don't, and some big shot loses his patience, the alleys of South Paris 5 turn into hunting grounds for the chef's goons. A nice, well-organized team. Human meat, to be eaten and to be fucked, is the specialty of the Sphinx Tatoué.

The other whorehouses managed by Millander for Big Blue and Guadalupe are smaller and less organized; they're for middle-class types who are just looking for a place to empty out their bodies and brains with drugs and psychotreatments, with a side dish of quick, indifferent screwing. They're not places for rich shits, but for the semi-wretched, the ones soon to join the ranks of the subhuman rats of South Paris 5.

Cheap hookers work in those places, skeletons with their tits swollen, and five, maybe six thoughts still wedged inside their brains. You can bang them only out of total foolishness or desperation. Great slices of loneliness.

No human meat, no thermopressure items of dilitium; that's all stuff for the elite of perversion, for the Sphinx Tatoué. Specialty of these miserable whorehouses is one: you can buy, for a few extra credits, the life itself of your whore, man or woman. And there are more than a few customers wanting to have fun simply cutting a throat or banging a fresh corpse. At the Sphinx Tatoué, things are much more sophisticated. But some big shots like it simple, getting dirt on their hands and shoes in those cut-rate places. People who just like to blow up some slut's brains and then having her body packaged and shipped to his home so he can play with it for a few days. Undisturbed. Stuff for rich shits, with their hearts full of stones.

If the whore lead is the right one and the hippo's tastes haven't changed, I could find Guadalupe at the Sphinx Tatoué.

A matter of holes.

SIBEL
नरक

THE MOON

Human meat tastes like pork, only slightly more bitter and substantial. It is really good.

New Belmarsh Penitentiary, supervisor's quarters, third floor underground. Access forbidden. Only a few selected guests. A private reign. Kalasutra.

Thirteen rooms. Three for personal use, ten for tasting and accommodation for the high officials of New France General Staff, New Moon Corporation executives, and some functionaries and diplomats from other countries. *Realpolitik.*

Dedicated environments, including: rooms for selective dissecting, online for well-paying subscribers; a lab for studying prions and infectious diseases linked to anthropophagy; albino organs tasting room, for African Countries and independent cities; collections of selected, therapeutic gall-bladders. *Contracts.*

Sibel, 35 years old. Chinese biologist. Penitentiary Supervisor. Phase 2 of the integrated project of human farming. Expelled from United East Asia for illegal traffic of human meat. Leading for years the body-packaging team *Nelumbium.* Provider of human commodities to several countries and independent metropoles all around the world. A mercenary force, eventually integrated within New France army as special corps.

Sibel. Real name: Ying Yue Guo.

"Ambassador, I suggest you taste a delicious cut, something for real gourmets. Haniko, cut a small lumbar slice. You see, ambassador, there's a big difference eating meat freshly cut from a still-living body. On Earth, elite restaurants have this nasty habit of serving human meat that doesn't come from certified farms; and they may even – unfortunately very often – use old corpses. *Rigor mortis* alters fat and protein: as you're going to appreciate yourself, the difference in taste is huge, let alone nutritive value."

Sibel is a true pro in her line of work. Her blue eyes reflect the Ambassador's anxious face, a prospect customer. Illegal exportation keeps growing in many countries; more and more heads are reared in Naraka to meet the increasing demand.

"But ... will she ... feel pain?"

The Ambassador stammers, raises some objections. He cannot help but look at the young woman on the tasting table, her eyes still open, her nipples hard.

Sibel immediately contains his doubts. She really knows what she's doing. That's her job.

"Ambassador ... can I call you Aleksey? Pain is not an issue, Aleksey. The woman is treated and she doesn't feel anything, though she's fully aware. Pain – her body signaling a tissue damage – would inevitably spoil the aroma of her meat. Let's say we 'cheat' her neurons, avoiding undesired stimuli to reach her cerebral cortex, and we filter out all catabolic byproducts of pain. We only offer the best experience, here. Come on, Aleksey, just taste. You'll discover a whole new world."

Sibel does not drop her charming smile; her beauty guarantees the outcome of every tasting, of every new deal for Naraka. But what she is actually thinking is that the man in front of her is a shitty hypocrite. In his barbaric country, he must have torn apart living flesh without a second thought, without *any* treatment.

And all the problems with infections, as well as with taste and digestion, are caused by those unequipped, personal farms. They really are bad publicity.

Fucking amateurs.

Haniko cuts, using her m-tex carver. The woman, her body on the table, seems to tremble for a couple seconds, her open eyes welling. It is not pain; it is awareness raining down on that devoured soul.

After carefully carving a leaf-shaped strip of meat, Haniko picks it with thin pliers and lays it down on the red-hot kiln at the woman's feet.

A quick cooking takes real skill. It takes nothing to ruin it all.

Sibel oversees the work. Nothing must go wrong. She never loses a deal, a new contract, an important prospect ...

Finally, the slice of human meat arrives on the Ambassador's dish, perfectly cooked, fragrant, its core tender, sprinkled with Himalayan pink salt.

"How wonderful! I've never eaten anything this tasty. A real emotion. Thank you, Sibel, for offering me this privilege. If your quality level is this, then we have a deal!"

The Ambassador's salivation increases. He wants *more*, the fucking glutton, but the contract is about to be signed. An easy customer, after all. This time, Sibel won't even have to use her cunt. Anybody who knows her well can tell you: *that* is another exciting tasting. Sibel is as beautiful as a goddess. Tridimensional brain, perfect body, perfect diet.

LE SPHINX TATOUE'
नरक

EARTH

"Restaurant or tasting?"

The Sphinx Tatoué really is a nice place, no question about that.

Tramp Millander is a despicable man, but, about a few things, he knows what he's doing. After rummaging in trashcans for years, now he's able to turn shit into dilitium. If you have those unique tastes, in South Paris 5 you really can't find better than the Sphinx Tatoué. You should travel to the Mesoamerican Republic, to the paradise city of Shanti, to go even *beyond*.

"Would you prefer starting with the restaurant or the tasting?"

I've got to find my sweaty hippo ... *is he fucking or filling up his belly?*

The cameras must already be projecting me on the screens of the control room, where Millander plays with his holograms and customer identification statistic systems.

I've already been tagged as *CC3 – Customer Class 3 –* thanks to Big Blue, who had me over several times in his private room, the one with iceglass where red-pigmented sperm flows.

The usual perversions of my friend Blue.

But a professional killer has an encrypted bodychip, a secondary identity: Chloé Denis.

So: *fuck you, surveillance!* And fuck you, Millander, too. A basic visual screening won't be enough to recognize me, not with this black wig and my morph system set on dark eyes and Hispanic features, fitting with the pissedness powering my legs right now.

"Sorry, Miss Denis, are you listening?"

What a pain in the ass. He won't let me think in peace. Better to make a choice before the whorehouse foreman, this long and thin dickhead, gets me in trouble with security.

"Tasting, I guess, thanks," I absent-mindedly answer the professional asswipe. "I've just dined."

"Very well. As a CC3, I'll have you escorted to the private gallery."

No inflection, synthetic voice, too-perfect hands. Semi-organic neprom staff? So it seems. His brain must be linked to the control room; and who knows, maybe he even has a smartfiber up his ass to turn on the lights. Once there were no androids working here. Blue used to say it was an inelegant choice for a house of emotions.

I'm certainly not impressed by these well-proportioned, human-looking models. They're still just cogs and circuits – *just like that fucking refrigerator with training wheels* – and a shell between their legs with their serial number. After all, what could be better for Millander & Co.'s business? Electronic eunuchs. Impersonal, dynamic management. Optimization of time and resources. Sure revenue growth. A nice heap of credits every day to inflate Guadalupe's stomach.

Access to the private gallery is an excellent start: wealthy customers and very creative tastings, the kind the hippo enjoys so much.

"Please, Miss Denis, follow me."

A smaller refrigerator – a fucking midget on training wheels, this one not even trying to look human – comes in with a tall top hat on his head, showing the way with a beam of red light.

Many changes at the Sphinx Tatoué.

How fucking long, since I last was here?

Too much tech. And what if my New Moon buddies had gotten their hands on South Paris 5 brothels as well? Wouldn't surprise me, considering the new friendships of Blue, Guadalupe, and the other lurid lieutenants.

The midget droid hands me my tasting card. He leaves with his lights.

Now, what room to begin with? Let's see. With my card, I can get a preview of them all. Maybe I'm catching Guadalupe and his glittering rings right away. Okay, let's go.

First room

I insert my card and the monitor turns on. The real-time

preview begins. I don't think I'll find Guadalupe here: dark room, *black tasting*; you can only see the reflections of cocks painted in silver servohue. A fish tank of eels dancing all around; some vanish or dive halfway into the asses, mouths, and cunts of that mysterious gloom. Who knows who those lucky guys are?

Second room

This monitor isn't working properly, but I manage to glimpse one of the classic little games of the Sphinx Tatoué. Sluts hang by their arms from the ceiling, the customers on red armchairs, operating air compressors to make the plextek cones emerge from the floor. Excellent extreme-dilation penetrators, set in trapdoors right beneath the cunts.

Sluts slowly lower, cones rise with diameters increasing and increasing.

A strange dance.

Several women are unmoving, hanging millimeters above the glowing tips of their dilators, their vaginas ready for penetration. Armchairs and hands dirty with fluids. Nothing new, here. By now, Guadalupe must be inured to stuff like this. Or just bored.

Third room

Something new this time. The Sphinx Tatoué staff is well-paid, and they must always come up with original tastings. Earn their living, these legalized psychopaths. Carnival attractions for big shots. *Domina*-environment: t-girls with diverse morph devices much more advanced than my own. Temporary prostheses; I'd heard about those. Tits ejaculating sperm from the nipples. Double-synthetic cocks with independent tanks: milk, sperm, hallucinogens. Stuff you could embed and use on anybody. Incandescent dilitium rods. Neurocontrolled anal rings.

A few of these t-girls are equipped with facial devices and miniaturized Lemy hydrothermal pumps. Men and women, demanding customers.

Shit! With all this new tech, had I still been a whore, I'd be starving! No Guadalupe. And yet, this environment looks like it's tailor-made for the hippo.

Fourth room

Card's not working, no preview.

Are you kidding me?

I'm authorized for the whole private gallery. The midget with the lights is immediately here; he takes position in front of me and explains the issue:

"Sorry, Miss Denis. For this environment, you have to sign the *full sharing* beforehand."

The midget pulls out a scanner and asks me permission to pass it over my eyes. A fucking release form in this place?

What kind of shit is there inside that room?

If Guadalupe really is fucking – *sorry, tasting* – he's bound to be in a restricted environment.

Grab your damn release, midget, and let me watch!

At last, the preview begins. I should have guessed: a feeding section, the fancy restaurant downstairs not enough. A man, on the right, kneels between the legs of a well-tied-up whore.

Is he licking her?

A better look: that motherfucker is using an *electrolancet* on her cunt. He cuts tiny bits of flesh, brings them to his mouth, and greedily swallows. He eats, that pig, while she doesn't react. He's devouring, calmly, her labia majora.

What the fuck did they give her, that she's that high?

On the left, a mature woman, still wrapped in her elegant dress, is working on a young man. He's tied-up as well, with a sperm extractor between his legs. Very painful. The woman is leaning upon the youth's nipples; she bites them, licks the blood that dribbles down his chest. Then, she gets back to chewing.

The man dissecting the whore's cunt stands, as though he'd like to change his tool. His face shows in the preview for a few seconds. Mouth bloodied, he grins like an old lech who knows he's getting away with it. He licks his fingers.

He picks a plier to continue the tasting.

THE ROTOR AND THE EVIL SPIRITS
नरक

EARTH

I walk along the purple hall of the private gallery at the Sphinx Tatoué. On the far end, the small, blocky shape of that fucking electronic midget shows up again with its red lights. This time the midget is not alone.

Holy shit! I know that one. He's that beast Elifasi Taki. Guadalupe's bodyguard.

He approaches with the midget on a leash.

They found me.

Fucking two-bit morph system. Maybe it was the midget who screwed me with that release bullshit. Anyway, now I'll have to improvise.

Elifasi Taki. South-African killer and shaman. 58 outworlds. He started his career killing seven women in two months, leaving them to rot in a sugarcane plantation. Killed three more women in the Machibi tea plantation. His ritual is unique: the victims' mutilated parts – hands and heads especially – are meant to be offered to a *sangoma*, a human-looking evil spirit whom he calls Tokoloshe. Ten life sentences, one for murder. He manages to escape from Westville Penitentiary after a few months.

Six years ago he became a *shadow citizen* of South Paris 5, working as a bodyguard for Sipho Guadalupe. All the left hands of his victims have been tattooed on his body. He's forty-five years old.

The single most dangerous thing you can encounter in New France.

Taki approaches faster and faster. I start running.

Before I can reach the turn, where I can take the door leading downstairs, I hear the first burst. I manage to dodge the hailstorm, but a bullet hits my foot. I'm screwed. Running like this is impossible. A glancing hit, but it hurts like hell. Taki is behind me, sees my blood trail on the *moquette*. He gets excited, knows he has me. I've got to think fast.

I enter the third door on the right; luckily it's open and I don't have to use the scanner. I wouldn't have time for that. There are about fifty doors in the gallery on either side. Taki will lose time.

I only have a few minutes to find a solution before I'm hacked to pieces.

On the internal screen of the room, I see the beast passing by, stopping halfway along the corridor, thinking. He knows I'm here somewhere, trapped. He's going to begin searching all the environments.

I turn back and behind me there's a red room with a customer sitting on the bed, smiling at me.

"At last. Come here, baby."

The man is waiting for his whore. I've come in just at the right moment. Lucky bitch, as usual. What may the fatty be expecting? What may he have bought?

There are noises in the corridor. Taki entering the rooms to find his prey. Doors open and shut, one after another. He doesn't want to lose his advantage.

I have to think faster, faster.

I undress, remove the black wig and set the morph to a different model: light eyes, features even more pronounced. This junk can't do anymore. This electronic masking is certainly not going to fool someone like Taki.

Fatty's eyes glint as they fill with my tits, my red hair, my red cunt.

"What are you waiting for, slut? I've paid already, downstairs, you know?"

Noises and voices in the gallery, closer and closer.

I've got no choice, so I jump onto Fatty, whose flesh bobs with the mattress. He is flaccid, stinky pudding.

I should have guessed. We're in the Sphinx Tatoué private gallery, not in my old flat, where I did traditional stuff and drew the line about what could and could not be done.

Fatty has a rotor rigged on his cock, a merrel fiber model, another of the whorehouse contraptions – expensive gadgets, everything cutting-edge. The fiber is soft, luckily not one of those metal rotors that shred your vagina, but its rotating motion and flailing pistils risk to set it on fire, my poor pussy. I'm going to bleed, internally. If I don't get out of this bed, I'm going to end up like those poor disposable whores. The customer, here, has a license to kill, and to come. Nothing different than the streets of South Paris 5, after all. If you pay well, nothing's forbidden.

Fatty drives his stubby, sweaty fingers into my cunt. I let him. I've got to buy time.

He shoves like a bastard.

"Nice, tight pussy you've got here. I'll have to tip them well for this special treatment ... someone *fresh* like you. They've earned it."

Fatty sweats more and more, his eyes crashing into black abysses – ones I saw many times, years ago. But the noises in the corridor get closer. Taki is going to be here soon, *too soon.*

An electric noise, its frequencies rising, screeching; the man has turned on the rotor and he's adjusting. *Max speed.* What a goddamn son of a bitch.

A few seconds to choose to live or die: getting my cunt pounded by Fatty, or letting Taki do his thing.

Taki will rape me, cut my hands, and then he'll serve me to Guadalupe in chunks on a fancy dilitium tray. I can see him licking his lips and enjoying my meat. Best possible revenge, so ancestral, a way to dispose of me forever. Digesting me. Taki will finish his work and get a new tattoo and offer my head, stuffed with sugarcane leaves, to his Tokoloshe – the fucking evil spirit who lives inside that harebrained head of his.

What would you do?

I turn belly-down, squeezing the pillow with my hands so that recognizing me will be harder. I make Fatty happy as he flares up in his lurid fantasies.

"You really are a filthy slut. You want to feel it all, do you? I really got lucky, finding one who enjoys his holes bashed in. Now, be still like that ... good girl."

Fatty begins with my pretty ass. He wants a double ride. The rotor begins to penetrate, to spin me, it turns crazily, seems to suck out my very guts. I haven't been able to cry for years, but now my tears have a will of their own as they wet the pillow. *I squeeze hard.*

Taki enters, and his sweetish smell is unmistakable. He takes in the scene: a fat guy pounding a slut's ass, complete with rotor at top speed. Nothing odd at the Sphinx Tatoué. All in order.

One second, two seconds, *three seconds ... never-ending.*

My *customer* turns back, pissed off for the intrusion.

"And what do *you* want? I've paid for everything downstairs. Beat it. This is *my* room."

Taki puts a bullet in his mouth. Then he runs out, looking for me in the corridor.

All clear, and goodbye to fucking Fatty.

I must struggle to free myself from that dripping meat pudding on my back, to pull the still-spinning rotor from my ass. I turn off the device. An excruciating pain leaves me breathless. A few seconds of that lecherous treatment were more than enough.

No more noises in the corridor means Taki must have gone downstairs to look for me there. I must manage to move, to run away from this hell, to get back to my hole and try to recover.

Guadalupe, our date is only put off.

MASSON'S GALATEA
~NEPROM DOLL 2~
नरक

Lee's thoughts live on the back of the ocean; they have the Nereids' pearl saliva. Incomprehensible voices, here on Earth. Bends of circling sounds, frequencies available to the senses of dolphins and tritons, completely muted for men. Lee's skin is white as milk, as transparent hours.

A husband with invisible ears bangs her while he talks to himself. A wounded wolf who scratches her breasts, smells her, while feeling the blank spaces of his own awareness. Too many. *A wolf, scratching harder and harder to understand. He bites her flesh, easy matter, punches those silences.*

Lee lets him and soon the wolf gets tired of his useless fury. He ejaculates all his strength in the last onslaught, and each time he turns into a child. Cries.

Why did you never tell me?

The wolf asks this and understands too late. He's fucking a whore, an easier cunt to own, to buy. Solid walls, clear languages, no imaginary hole to find, to fill, to quench. Even if he keeps speaking only with himself. But you don't need stairs to climb down into those eyes that dance up and down. The whore seems to possess eyes already climbed, already seen, already read. But beware, wolf. She's not wearing her own right now. You see what you want to see.

Why didn't you tell me that you like watching?

Hiding behind the mirror, Lee watches the wolf and his bitch. She's done it many times.

But she lacks the courage to join that bed, in tune with those bodies jerking and stroking. This time, anyway, she shows herself, with a finger in her pussy, her mouth big and soundless. She runs.

The wolf chases. The whore dresses, gets back on the streets to work. She already wears the stockings of future. Stop, Lee. Shit, talk to me! Talk to me for once!

Lee shuts the bathroom door. The wolf pushes but once again he remains in silence. He's not a triton. He cannot breathe at those depths. Small lungs. Small imagination. He scratches the white door, injuring his hands. He shouts that he wants to understand, to be forgiven. Deep down, he thinks he's the one who has to forgive. Such thoughts. A woman's.

I beg you, Lee, let me in. I love you.

She doesn't listen. Her finger in her cunt is still cooking, inside. *She doesn't want to watch; that is not partaking enough.* She wants to give him away, her wolf.

How could she explain that?

Nereids, doomed to breathe in small fish tanks, furnished and equipped with every comfort. Three hundred liters of freshwater, if you're lucky. The tranquility of life, Alpha and Omega of conventions. But they are fish tanks, and they have walls.

Lee! Lee!

The wolf gets angry, strikes the door, leaves the house. He's done it many times. He will go to drink and fuck some more, who knows where, or with whom ... for thirty credits.

Lee exits the bathroom, looks at herself in the mirror, pulls her finger out from her sieged, dry cunt.

How can she explain that to him? She wants to give him away, her wolf. *Offer him, let people use him, his sperm a gift: she wants to drink it between another woman's legs. The one who's not loved, just filled. A* kykeon *that tastes like Athens, like initiation. Mint, barley, sperm. A sip of shoreless sea. Partake.*

Too difficult to explain. You're a fucking frigid. Answers, too easy.

You have to get cured.

The wolf's doctor explores her womb, looking for the right place with his pliers, the spot reacting to stimuli, manual and electric. Nothing. Speculum. Frigid. Sick. *The doctor who visits her at home, often, who fucks her. And then the other one, the one who studies her mind. Dirty as his office, he infected her uterus. Bees stinging Cupid.*

The wolf pays for all the invoices. He doesn't understand. Nobody finds a ladder tall enough to climb down Lee's eyes. Silence.

Noise. Big Blue has killed Lee's wolf.

Now, she is at peace in her synthetic skin, her neprom skeleton.

Around the doll's head – new container of heart and emotions – a bird cage is installed. The bars, thin and fragile, are the ones the wolf built. Incomprehensible cages for creatures with wings. Le baillon vert à bouche de pensée.

Lee is no longer forced to think, to explain herself, to run without ever catching up with herself. Gagged with black velvet in her mouth there is a pansy, a flower telling the story of her as a woman of flesh. A red twine surrounds her hips, a loincloth adorned by a circle of wolf eyes on a mirror.

Whenever Big Blue shows his neprom doll collection, as he passes by his wonderful Galatea, he explains she cannot be sexually had; that is not what she wants.

You can remove the velvet and the pansy from her mouth and make her drink sperm.

The guests ejaculate into a glass until it's full. A bell sounds, informing them that Lee is now ready to have her kykeon. Her cunt, installed between the mannequin's thighs – just behind the mirror and her old wolf's eyes – finally gets wet.

After so much desert.

NEW BLOOD
नरक

THE MOON

Fedder looks at his cell of rock and steel. A small space dug into Naraka's hive. *Deepness. Where may the Queen Bee hide?*

Fedder has arrived today. New blood.

Why the fuck did they shut me in here?

He did nothing wrong. He is not a thief or a rapist. He is not a criminal. No scum, this time. Fedder, just an ordinary seventy-kilos guy, a clerk who picks up and supplies nanobottles at the Vortex, one of the busier *diskohaus* in Berlin-Brandenburg 7.

Fedder: twenty-two years, twenty-two dreams, twenty-two hopes. *Freude am Leben.*

He plays soccer with jersey number twenty-two. He has always loved numbers, girls with small breasts, chocolate chips. He goes to work by electric bike, with his blue backpack. Every night, he runs along the Neue Oberbaumbrücke. He is allowed to go out of his small district for six hours. The solid waters of the Sprea are glued to the base of the bridge pillars, a long backbone which lays unmoving, yellow, for ten years at least. *The vomit of Berlin-Brandenburg 7.*

Fedder counts minutes, colors, and changes; the nanobottles he'll have to manage at the Vortex, and Anja's quick blowjobs.

"Tomorrow I'll let you put it in. Now, be quiet."

Tomorrow. But tomorrow never comes. Fedder counts two hundred and sixteen tomorrows.

He is taken outside the cell, dragged along the trail of the main tunnel – an unending corridor with just a few turns and pulsating with blue lights.

They'll give me something to eat. I've been on an empty stomach for two days.

Two days, three hours and twenty-four minutes.

Fedder is escorted by three guards in Nelumbium special corps uniforms, shock kleben at their sides, their gloves gripping Heckler MP92 sub-machine guns. He looks at the other cells, hundreds of them, flowing beside him. A cyclic panorama. *The hive.*

One cell has its monitor turned on, the pixels forming an inmate's face with a nose pressing against the cells of the interactive system. His words pierce rock and concrete:

"Where are they taking you, man? You're new, right? So pretty ... clean feet. *Tomorrow I'll rip your cock off and I'll eat it.* Now, be quiet, and come back soon."

Jorge Vallejo Corona's voice lures Fedder's eyes away from the invisible horizon of the tunnel. The Placenta Eater is hungry. He would be content even with a few pairs of testicles, to vent some loneliness, to shake that cursed steel cloak that covers him like a lid. The cell, the usual mutations of Naraka.

"Tomorrow I'll rip your cock off and I'll eat it."

Tomorrow, always tomorrow. This time, Fedder only counts *one* tomorrow.

North Block. The Slicer.

Are they going to give me something to eat now?

The big, steel sliding door opens. The escort goes back to Section 65. Fedder is undressed, laid down on a smooth table. Two operators prep him. An oval probe moves parallel to his body a few millimeters away. It stops, records, restarts. Green lights fill the holographic grid of the control panel, completing the boot routine of the system.

The operators whisper something. One of them leaves the table, the other now alone with Fedder. He holds an atax syringe in his white-gloved hand, a grin on his mouth. The needle pierces his skin, makes its way into his flesh, heat branching from his arm to his back, freezing his lower limbs. The operator's eyes are masked by the red see-through visor. Fedder's face is mirrored, warped. The operator whispers again, and this time he is speaking to him.

"We have ten minutes, beautiful. Soon, you'll be leaving for a really cool trip. You'll have fun, you'll see. *I'll have a lot of fun, too.*"

The operator pulls down his white, plextilen lab trousers and the mesasuit beneath. He turns Fedder's body around, his belly pressing and spreading against the shiny alloy of the prep table.

"Are you still there, beautiful? Wait, don't fall asleep just now. Here ... okay, I'm in, *I'm inside you.* You know?"

Fedder sees the operator reflected in thin slices on the metal of the table, a drop of sweat falls, wetting the perfect edge. Then, darkness.

"This one's ready, now. Bodycheck's positive, scan and projections nominal. Lets' do it."

Fedder wakes up to find the other operator is back. His body has left the metal table. They have moved him to Table Number 4, set between sixty and seventy-five kilos. Buzz saws turn on, pistils and vertical teeth turning in synchro.

System testing.

Fedder is in the mouth of the machine; she is already licking its slits and trays. The operator is ready. Fedder's body recovers all its functionalities. Legs and arms held in rectangular metal blocks. Once again, movement is impossible.

Crying, instead, is possible: *"NOOO!"*

LEDs on. Rotations. The operator hesitates.

"Wait. Don't tell me you did this one, too? Shit, we'll have to reboot everything again ..."

The other operator answers without moving his eyes from the secondary scan system. "I didn't come inside him. Don't bust my balls, just start the thing."

"NOOO!"

"The usual dickhead ... *I didn't come inside him* ... and what about hygienic standards? Another fuck-up and they kick us out of here. You know that, right? At least take that thermic pump and clean up his ass."

"Holy shit, you're really giving me a hard time, for like ten fucking cans in millions. Who do you think is going to notice that? I'm cleaning up his ass, alright, but I'm having my shifts changed. I'm done working with a pain in the ass like you."

"NOOO! I BEG YOU ..."

"Right, good, fuck you and all the damn psychos like you. Look, my sons are eating that stuff, too. Come on, hurry up now. This one is busting my eardrums ..."

The operators finally start the process. Fedder would like to count the rotations of the blades, but they are way too fast for that. His voice vanishes. Fedder counts the seconds he lives. The system always starts from the legs. Fedder waits for the blades to sink into his chest before stopping. He doesn't want to count wrong.

Blood squirts. The Slicer is accurate but it hurts – an uncountable pain, a pain that is a great link to the past. Detailed pictures, projected on a wide virtual screen. *Zoom in.* Anja's face. Her small tits; they seem even smaller with those suntan circles. His mother and her awful refrain: *You're not different, honey. You're better than them.* The Oberbaumbrücke and its tall pillars sinking in blood. Death, when she is close, turns off all the monitors of memory. Blood no longer squirts so hard. The main blade is inside, has cut his heart in two, breaking his ribs. Fedder has crossed the bridge.

The escort passes again by Corona's cell.

The Eater is trying to sleep with little success. He hears steps in the tunnel, turns the monitor on.

"Hey, what about the *new blood?* Hey! Motherfuckers. Fucking bad luck, shit … AAA meat category, right? Answer me, you bastards!"

Night turns off in Naraka. Shifts are over.

Tomorrow, in the morning: roll call, head count. Someone is going to piss his pants again.

THE SIREN
नरक

EARTH

Le Sphinx Tatoué.
Leave this shithole. *I've got to be quick.*

I keep bleeding, even from my ass now. I'm not going to stay on my feet much longer.

I quickly dress and set the morph on new facial features. Fatty is sprawling on the bed. I kick his swollen nuts before leaving. If I had my Martin 4 with me, I'd have a little fun disintegrating that limp dick of his. Post mortem, even.

I take his card.

The purple corridor of the private gallery is full of people: sluts, t-girls, and half-naked pigs talking to each other. A woman with a system of artificial members on her belly keeps screaming that they killed her best customer.

A guy runs down the stairs, hiding his dick inside a *superslave* red mask. He stumbles and everybody laughs. A man with bloodied arms comes out of his room with his hands raised. He thinks it's a military bust, the dreaded Cleaners. His face is that of someone who's just torn apart a disposable whore.

A Circle of Hell not yet classified. Taki has made quite the mess looking for me.

The chaos helps me going almost unnoticed. I make my way through that mass of flesh, through that architecture of asses, tits, cocks popping out everywhere. I go downstairs.

There must be a nice close-up of me, by now, in the control room monitors. A few seconds and Taki will be upon me. The exit is close by. I just have to pass by the entry cube and that fucking reception with the android butler.

"Good evening, miss. Restaurant or tasting?"
Again. "Fuck off!"

Let's see what your greeting system suggests now. I can't walk anymore. I'm unarmed, weak, my smell about to reach Taki's nostrils and the sights of his M170 Minigun.

Where the fuck do I want to go like this?

I go back, approach the butler. I'll be kind, this time.

"Call me a roadcab, please."

"We hope to see you again soon, Miss ... *can I have your card?*"

The cybernetic douchebag stammers as he answers, keeps wasting my time.

I hand over Fatty's card. Seems to work.

"Forgive me, Mister Abbandando. I will call immediately."

Too late. The entrance is watched by two of Millander's goons. Taki must be coming.

The cameras whirl around. Millander is operating the joysticks from the control room.

I manage to melt in the shadows shifting on the right of the butler, who follows me with curiosity in his plastic optic nerves. I can't stay hidden much longer.

You've got to think fast, Kiki.

I see a two-meters-tall t-girl pass by, with tiger skin shorts that aren't half bad. She must be going back home, shift over. At least I hope so. I grab her arm, whisper in her ear, "They pounded my ass with the rotor. Please, help me get out of here."

The t-girl looks at me with her huge eyes, grins. She pulls out a sort of leash from her black coat, shining aluminum.

"On your knees, love."

Her voice thunders. Knowing looks. I don't have much choice. She makes me wear a blue-studded collar and drags me toward the exit. The blood pouring out of my ass is beginning to stain my pants. I look perfectly fitting for the scene: a bitch in heat, her ass broken, at the leash of her mistress.

The goons at the door halt us. They're armed to their teeth.

"Who's this slut? Taking work home with you, Vivian?" one of the two imbeciles chuckles.

My mistress kisses his lips, her voice like that of a mighty siren: "The usual, a customer who wants to have some fun. See you tomorrow, love ... *a little extra for you.* Wash your pretty ass well."

The goon is entranced by Vivian's tropical scents and velvet skin. He hardly glances at me, the douchebag. All his thoughts are wedged between the enormous boobs that Vivian skillfully rubbed in his face. He stays there, frozen, a hibernated grin and glitter on the tip of his nose.

We go out. At last, I'm out of that fucking place.

LET US TAKE YOU
नरक

THE MOON

Morning. Naraka's sons are all in a row in front of their cells.

Who will end up in the Slicer? Who will be the interactive first course in Kalasutra?

The human farm is beginning to warm up, to yield, even though they had to stock many *white souls* to speed up the process. Ordinary people. Easy picks in the army of the adrift of the metropoles.

Legionnaires of desperation, with no leaders, weapons, credits.

The concept of human trash, expanded.

In Kalasutra, Sibel makes her calculations: breeding strategies. There are specific targets. No safe margins. Twenty billion people. Resources collapsing. *Earth collapsing.*

Earth after Uxor: traditional farming compromised, lowered by 99%. Synthetic food and its side effects. The new business is human meat. An as-yet illegal commerce, but a lot of stuff, if you have a strategy. *Twenty billion resources.*

Sibel is the strategy. Naraka is her plantation, her dominion, her compulsory space baronage. Commodities, processing, quality control, shipment, proceeds: all very simple. From the crusade against criminality to the design of human feedlots. A necessary evolution. Coincident.

New Moon Corporation is building five more Extraterrestrial Detention Systems.

The project is bearing its first fruits. Naraka *works*. Many independent governments can once again guarantee the availability of safe meat to the privileged. Magic cans, labeled *Certified Meat*. Actual human space chicken. That green synthetic shit keeps being given to ordinary people, like pig fodder.

Fatten up, sons of bitches. *And let us take you.*

Who will end up in the Slicer? Who will be the interactive first course in Kalasutra?

Aki Miyazaki, Jorge Vallejo Corona, Kaijū Hanzo, Beatrix Leonard, and Ute Möbius – the first surviving haul of Earth scum, the supercriminals – are outside their cells. They look around. All cells in Naraka have been filled. Ranks of men and women stretch along the tunnels, an unending burrow. On their left shoulder, the holo-tattoo:

A+, AAA, AA, A, B+, BAA, BBA, BBB, BB, B, NE.

Certification of the quality of their meat.

Only A+s and AAAs reach Sibel's Kalasutra for the interactive tasting rooms and for *special packaging*. All the rest are reared, processed, put together in diverse recipes.

BBs and Bs are used for soups and reconditioned cans; NEs – *No Eat* – are moved directly to the West Block where they are reduced to small pellets called *fuel tablets*, used for the EAT systems. Every day, hundreds of people are gone, most processed in the Slicer. Suicide rate is above 41% of resources. A waste. Sibel is working on that weak spot of her human farm.

Reduction of despair perception.

Kaijū Hanzo, the human skin collector, 44 outworlds in ten years of activity, is waiting for the call of the chosen ones in front of his cell, as are the rest of them. He looks to his right, his only eye trying to frame Corona.

They have a plan to escape, but they need time.

Section 197C. BBB meat category. Stay in Naraka: 15 days.

Paule Fernandez, jobless, 24 years. Her legs are shaking. She feels an unexpected orgasm exploding between her thighs. She looks at the New Moon employee, at the scanner in his gloves. He is about to call the list of the chosen ones. She cannot stop the multiple orgasms, one after another in a few seconds. She is ashamed, she squeezes her cunt with her hands.

Section 197C. BBA meat category. Stay in Naraka: 29 days.

Isako Wu, employee at Ling Jiǔ Chǎng distillery, 28 years, raped yesterday night, once again, by the jailers. Her eyes are empty, the same color of the uniform.

She trustingly waits for her name to be called. *Put an end to it.*

She is afraid the caller is going to skip her name. She is too beautiful and they want to use her much more before turning her into pulp.

Section 197C. BBB meat category. Stay in Naraka: 18 days.

Hans Böhm, alcoholic, 42 years. Bent forward, he keeps throwing up, shaken by withdrawal. But this time he doesn't piss his pants. He spits his very soul on the floor; what remains of him is just an empty shell. Empty like the bottles that took him to Hell. Another Hell. He has already lost his bearings; if they call his name, he won't recognize it.

Section 197C. B meat category. Stay in Naraka: 20 days.

They are the four who are called, destination the Slicer. Four souls to be eaten, to be assembled in the search for the best taste. Different recipes, different consumers.

Kaijū Hanzo immediately reacts. He pounces on one of the guards, manages to snatch his Heckler MP92 sub-machine gun.

"Don't move, motherfuckers, or I'll blow up his brains! Give me an excuse, come on, *just give me a fucking excuse!*"

Hanzo holds the jailer by his neck, the weapon aimed at his throat. He backs slowly away along the tunnel. Shouting his lungs out.

"*Don't fucking move! All of you!* Jorge … come on, come with me. Let's leave this shithole!"

Corona looks at Hanzo, who is sweating his madness. He is surrounded by ten armed guards, who don't really seem to bother about their colleague's fate. The Eater understands it is suicide, lowers his eyes. He leaves Hanzo to his already-written doom.

"*Coward!* Fucking coward. I hope they'll put you in a can soon, motherfucker. I'm getting out of here, you understand? I'm getting out. *Now!*"

Hanzo keeps backing until he reaches the limit of Section 197C. The guards follow him, maintaining a distance of about ten meters. A sniper, hidden in the shadowy belly of the tunnel, shoots once. Dead center, Hanzo's nape. His head opens, neck shaking back and forth with whiplash.

Hanzo manages to stay on his feet, his only eye covered with his blood, pieces of brain sliding down his face. He unloads his Heckler MP92 in the face of the jailer he is holding, point blank.

Red rain, confetti.

The jailers immediately open fire, shredding those two bodies without distinction. Hanzo collapses with his hands still gripping the weapon.

Considering the imminent rigor mortis, the system will recategorize Hanzo's usable meat as NE.

Nothing goes wasted in Naraka. Hanzo will be processed, turned into fuel tablets; they will get maybe fifty out of his body. A lot of range for the EATs.

ADRIEN'S SHOES
नरक

EARTH

Vivian's flat. Rue du Faubourg Saint-Honoré.

From the windows, you can see in the distance the tentacles of South Paris 5, sprawling over the city. A silent, unstoppable cancer. My eyes drift on that huge, dark stain.

"I used to live there. Then I got out of that shit." Vivian catches the paths of my gaze, maybe the sounds of my memories, too. "So, honey, do you want me to call a doctor? They fucked you up pretty good, those motherfuckers ..."

Vivian talks to me while she looks at herself in the mirror. She's trying to remove that mask of diamonds, red and azure dust, her whorehouse face. Her too-big hands make circles on her visage. Her nails, painted in blue servohue, look like small insects lured by a bright light, a chaotic crowd bouncing one against the other to get themselves a first-row place.

I observe her for some seconds before answering. I'm dazed. My ass hurts and blood keeps pouring out.

"Thanks, Vivian ... never mind. I can sort it out myself ..."

Guadalupe and Taki have ears and men everywhere in the city, even in this neighborhood. Calling a doctor would be suicide, for me and for Vivian as well. We could as well put a bullet in our heads ourselves. But I'm too weak. I need time to recover.

I continue, "I only ask you one thing. Could I stay here a few days?"

I have no other choice but entrust myself to my Siren. For now.

Vivian is unfazed; she's that type.

"Sure, honey, no problem. You can stay as long as you want. I assume you're used to some *little noise* ... you know, I have a few loyal customers over. But I have a room all for you, all the privacy you need. Then, when you're feeling better, if you want we can work together. Beats getting yourself killed at the Sphinx Tatoué.

My friends are kind, and loaded. We could make a nice couple, you're so pretty …"

You should know how many customers I've seen – felt inside of me – when I worked at my old flat in South Paris 5. *My customers*. Far from being kind … goddamn pigs, sleazy and violent. But being a whore *there* is very different than *here*. I keep these thoughts to myself; for the Siren, just a few, necessary words: "Thank you, Vivian. I just need a few days, then I'll be on my way."

Vivian doesn't ask many questions. I like her. I hope Millander & Co. won't ever link her to me. I'd hate her to pay the price for her kindness. Empathy between whores.

The doorbell rings. A shiver on my back.

Vivian approaches the video eye of the door, very pissed.

"You again? I've told you a thousand times, you must tell me before coming. Come back tomorrow …"

It's odd for a whore, even of Vivian's level, to reject a customer. She's doing that for me; I understand that from her smile, from her thundering words, modulated by soft, thin lips. A charming contrast. Dichotomies.

"Don't worry. The usual asswipe, and one that doesn't pay well, either. But he's young and pretty, and then … *he's so horny*. I mean, we all have some nice friends that we like … Should have happened to you, too, right? By the way, what's your name, honey?"

My name is too dangerous. I'd rather not lie to Vivian, but I really must.

"Juliette. My name is Juliette."

But the Siren knows better. Working at the Sphinx Tatoué means having gone a long way. She knows liver and stomach of humanity, how the soul of people smells – what's left of it. She answers to me like someone who knows how to play along when needed: "Juliette. *Lovely name*. Perfect for the job. But that doesn't matter. For me, you'll just be Juliette."

Vivian turns off her words as she keeps undressing, pulling down tiger-striped shorts that are squeezing her flesh and rounding her shapes. She doesn't wear any panties between her firm, smooth thighs. Her shaved cock looks like a gargoyle sculpted on the shoulders of Notre Dame: looming, teeth and claws at the ready, among the gothic architectures of her dominant body. She is now completely naked on those high, high heels, shining in silver. She looks like she's ready to take off with those magic things on her feet.

Being here with her takes me back in time. So long ago. My father, vanished in the military Rehabilitation Centers. My mother, no longer taking me to ballet class. She slaves away, cleaning up rich douchebags' shit in their flats of Berciére. She often comes home with her face bruised. Beaten up for the whim of some bored motherfucker. Little money, little to eat.

A different world revealing itself, suddenly. Black curtain. Gone is the magic of ballet, gone is my mother's sweet scent that used to drift through the rooms. Stink of reality, of leftovers hidden in her coat. Stink of death, the death of that levity which had accompanied me for so long. Sixteen years old, moving to South Paris 5. No man's land. Cheap, or so it seems. Big Blue's district of junkies and whores, of narrow streets full of broken bottles. The oasis of the rats and the wretched.

Sixteen years old. I start hustling a little for my uncle Adrien. He manages a fancy shoe shop downtown. My mother is almost never home, but when she is, her eyes and ears are shut. *Eat and survive*, she says. I've got many pretty shoes, alien smells on my skin and my pussy. Adrien, *a real gentleman*, begins bringing a few friends home. He always speaks well of her beautiful niece. Advertising. More shoes, and some credits. A plastic pearl necklace, once. Many more smells, words never listened to. Red, sweaty faces. *Nobody ever looking at you in the eye.*

Then, Florentin's turn comes. Adrien's shop owner, a real motherfucker, full of money and loneliness. This time, I'm alone with him. Adrien locks the room.

Sixty years old, no hair, no soul. Florentin uses his belt, insists on my ass, my back. I manage not to scream, I think about my mother's words. *Eat and survive.*

He uses the shoes to penetrate me, light alloy heels going in and out, scratching my walls, *a pain without memory*. He ties me to the bed, keeps drinking, goes completely out of control. He wants to sodomize me with the empty Chablis bottle. He shoves hard, but can't manage to push it all in; he yells that it's *my* fault. Pulls it out, crashes it on my head.

My mother comes in, Adrien tries to stop her, holding her

arm. She screams, enraged. I've never seen her like that. She has a knife. She threatens Florentin and wounds Adrien's hand. Adrien loses his temper and begins kicking her.

I look at her lying on the floor while she coughs up blood and curses. She tries to get up, is on her knees. Florentin decides he's had enough; the neighbors are going to hear that racket. A matter of reputation. He grabs the broken bottle and sinks it into my mother's neck. Glass and blood. Adrien's hands are in his hair. My mother collapses backward, squirting blood like a fountain. Florentin spits on that deflating body.

Eat and survive.

My mother underground. I keep receiving customers in the flat, more and more.

Adrien is gone from Paris. Florentin keeps making money with his smart shops. I finally have enough credits to eat, to pay the rent, for decent dresses, to buy a gun. My first pistol.

At eighteen years old, I'm a very sought-after whore, at least in the apocalyptic district of South Paris 5. I use my real name: Kiki.

The time has come to go shopping downtown.

Florentin is at his jewelry. He really sells classy stuff. He lets me in, doesn't recognize me. I don't, either. He looks like an ordinary man, no alcohol or cunt in his veins.

My first time shooting. The gun slide wounds my hand. I waste many bullets on the walls, on the windows, but eventually manage to get the pig as well.

Just enough to let it kick the bucket with his face on his dilitium colliers.

The clerk looks at me, upset, raises her hands and says, "Take what you want ... Please, don't kill me."

I don't, even if she's seen my face. I'm sure she must have tried Florentin's belt and bottles, his poisonous saliva.

Her dim eyes tell as much. Her dim eyes won't remember me.

GLASS DROPS
~NEPROM DOLL 3~
नरक

Sophie's hands are carved by detergents. Her heart is kicked every second.

Oval visage, long neck, pulled taut by an invisible cable, the longing for Heaven. Not for herself. Those wings, she'd like to draw them, set them up on Benôit's back. Her son: five years old, Duchenne dystrophy.

Sophie is immune carrier of a broken X chromosome and a divorce for lack of joie de vivre. *Translated: she does not fuck enough. Too many clouds in that sky.*

He left two years ago, flying down the stairs. Pushing a button, formatting everything in a few seconds. Tears of Joy, Doctors, Medicine Boxes, Fights, Broken Bottles, Hospitals, Shattered Nights. *Click. He does not know what a chromosome is; he has never seen it. He hates that absurd term, something so small, invisible, capable of destroying an entire lie,* three lives, even.

He wants to have sex every day. He is twenty years old. He does not know what else love can be. Too hard to understand, like the Morse code of chromosomes. Sophie's womb is swollen with sadness, Hell popping out of her vagina, monsters come out of there. No longer a place for cocks.

Benôit ambulates, falls. His legs are bloated and his breathing gets harder and harder.

The Night Ventilation. *Necessary.*

That awful noise: impossible to sleep, impossible to fuck. Twenty years old, then twenty-four. Impossible to live. His balls are on fire, but their souls are already burnt.

Benôit looks a lot like his father, both of them incurable. The wooden mirror of failure, for him.

It will be up to Sophie. She will have to stretch her neck. Two hundred credits a month, not enough? *Not much work in Paris*

Mernier. Whores and bottles are too expensive.

I can't do more than that.

Benôit is window-tall, his calves like two melons. The rain of Paris. He's always liked rain. His father runs away, coat over his head, shoes sinking in all the puddles. Twenty-five years soaked like a thousand.

Morning comes smugly, without knocking, without asking permission to turn on a new day. Benôit sleeps, laborious breathing. Six o'clock, still early for anything.

Sophie decides to grab a few seconds.

She takes a morkan tube, empties it out of Benôit's pills, shuts herself in the bathroom, and slowly shoves it inside her cunt. It hurts. It has been a long time since anything entered there.

Too dry, *she would need something for …*

A noise, something heavily dropping on the floor. Jesus, Benôit!

Sophie pulls the cylinder out of her cunt, only halfway in. She runs to the bedroom, forgets to put on her panties.

The lamp … it was just the lamp falling. *Her son is fine,* thanks God! *He has awakened, he is framing her mother's known shapes. He wants to hug her.*

Her cunt burns and her heart runs amok. The cylinder inside, life outside; that life.

I really am a slut and should be ashamed, *Sophie thinks.* What the fuck I was thinking …? He could have hurt himself, gotten injured.

She phones the rain man. Seven o'clock. "Yaël, it's me. Do you hear me? Yaël …"

The man does not answer, disconnects. Sophie remembers her husband no longer exists, that he formatted everything. Three hundred credits a month, *is what is left.*

Benôit cries.

Of course, breakfast, and his pills … But what's the fucking matter with me today?

Benôit screams.

He hates that rain knocking on the window. The puddles, the enemy muscles that don't allow him to leap over them, of moving, of running behind his dad.

Sophie is at the pharmacy every day, Rue de Clovis. Close to her flat. She gets back home with her frail back balancing between the usual bags. Medicines and toys. Benôit will be happy.

Big Blue holds the child in his arms. The child does not cry. Two more men are in the kitchen.

"*What the fuck are you doing here? Leave him alone, he's sick!*"

Big Blue smiles, reassuring the woman. For the child's good. *His offer is clear, convincing. A doll, giving herself willingly, a precious jewel for his collection. Something unique. An attraction for his friends. Everybody will be jealous.*

Money buys Sophie's body and an adequate treatment for her son. Technology can do miracles, change any life expectancy.

Big Blue fixes everything.

Sophie becomes his neprom doll #3. So precious. A flower snatched from the teeth of the desert, from morkan tubes. Adieu foulard, *the writing, the name.*

Face and shoulders are covered with glass drops, synthesis of the past. Glittering tears, animated by skillful directional lights. The doll's legs sink halfway into a large black cylinder. The box of illness.

Sophie keeps thinking and remembering as Big Blue has the usual diamonds embedded in her heart, surrounding a shard of onyx. The damaged chromosome. *Sophie's tits and ass are preserved. Her cunt is no more; it cannot remember orgasm, pleasure, beauty.*

The cunt is the hell from which monsters come out.

The doll's arms are reaching upward, toward Heaven.

Sophie can be easily rotated, operating the cylinder at her base. Whenever one of Blue's guests feels like trying her, shoving his desires to the bottom of that so-perfect ass.

Once a month, after giving her an adrenaline shot, they bring Benôit to her.

Everything according to the contract.

The drops of glass, then, mirror all the cells of that face, looking more and more like that old rain.

TOO MUCH SILENCE
नरक

EARTH

Night. I'm back to my hole. Vivian is at the Sphinx Tatoué, working as usual. Guadalupe is hiding somewhere between the thighs of South Paris 5. Everyone at their place.

Full moon. I think about Miller, the Cool Guy who got me out of that hell. *Up there.*

Whenever I can't sleep, I clean my weapons. My Martin 4 has been silent for a while. *Wait, my love, patience.* You'll have your chance with that motherfucking Guadalupe.

After the mess at the Sphinx Tatoué, there's a lot of people hovering on me. Even this hole, bellybutton of the great trashcan of South Paris 5, isn't going to be safe much longer. I've got to leave soon. My ass no longer hurts too badly. *Time to move.*

Maybe I should just leave this city; otherwise it's going to be an unending war. Eternal. When I'll do Guadalupe in, I'll have to deal with that psychopath Taki, or vice versa. And when both of them are retired, go figure if Tramp Millander doesn't unleash all his shit against me. He'll have the district in his grip, that wretch.

A fine career for someone who first started licking garbage. He would be a fitting king for this black hole of New France.

If I'm lucky, I'll have to spend my whole life sleeping on the roofs of Paris with a loaded cannon between my thighs. An eye always open. Fuck, that doesn't look good. Maybe I should review my plans, change my outlook. Easier said than done.

Max is eight years old by now. I haven't seen him since the last time I kicked him in the ass. Three years ago. I was a constantly-wasted whore back then. I had no idea who could be the father among my early loyal customers. Surely, some real sleazebag.

Social services put Max in custody with another family. Destination unknown.

But his face always stayed with me. His voice. His skycar models flying around in that small South Paris 5 sky, among embarrassed men in underpants. *VRRRUUUMMM!*

Maybe Vivian is right. Moving to Hamburg Central and fucking off to this city and all its shitty rats. Hamburg: Reinhardt's undisputed reign; a gentleman, after all. Gambling, drugs. Many outworld contracts ready to be cooked. The right place for a professional.

Leaving all this shit behind, starting again. I could content myself with what I have. After all, I've already had a nice compensation for my forced holiday on Naraka. Seeing Blue's remains crunched and munched was a big privilege. Beyond price. Maybe I'll manage to sleep now.

A noise. Fuck, someone came into the flat.

My Martin 4 looks behind the door, then peeks at the living room. *Open window.* I squeeze against the wall.

Move, fuck, so I can blow your brains up ... Where are you?

Silence.

Where are you, where are you?

They got me in my panties; it really is destiny. Story of my life, old and new.

How the fuck did they find me?

If this motherfucker is Taki, things are getting really dire. If they are Millander's swollen goons, I'll just have to waste some ammo and clean up the house.

Where are you, where are you?

Something drops. He's in the kitchen, the asshole ... I hide behind the sofa, see the door and keep it in my sights. A few meters, a few seconds, and you'll be mine. And you'll tell me everything. You'll tell me how you fucking found me.

Silence still. Then a chant ... I feel ice in my veins. *It's really him, holy shit!* Elifasi Taki ...

Tokoloshe, onsterflike siel
so lank is dat jy nie bring 'n geskenk
Tokoloshe, onsterflike siel
maar vandag het jy twee verrassings
Tokoloshe, onsterflike siel
'n swart kop en 'n wit

Goddamn you and your shitty Afrikaans. Go back to your sugarcane plantations, animal! As fertilizer. *I'll give you a little push if you just show up ...* Taki ...

Silence. Silence. Silence. He can't be gone. No way.

All right, if he really wants me, here I am. I enter the fucking kitchen hurling myself down on the floor as my Martin 4 begins singing.

Nobody's here.

My bullets shred ghosts and tear apart cupboards. The window explodes into smithereens. It can't be. Don't tell me I'm having hallucinations now ... *In Afrikaans?* Either I'm really fucked up, or that motherfucker is hiding well.

Where are you, where are you?

My eyes drop to the servofreezing cabinet. What's that shit?

Fuck, Vivian's head!

Dried blood, ripped mouth, empty. Leaves in her eyes. Her moon-shaped dilitium earrings move, sway.

Fucking son of a bitch, come out!

Fuck, fuck, fuck! Why her?

I cut my feet approaching what's left of Vivian. The floor is covered with glass shards. I look at my blood, flowing freely. It seems like walking on an ice wall.

A mighty blow to my head, then darkness.

Back to Hell
नरक

EARTH

I wake up. It wasn't a dream.

I'm tied to a bed, naked. There's a face a few centimeters from mine. He's looking at me, very interested. I know that hippo snout well. He's that shit Guadalupe. An outline is moving on the background of this red room. I can't make it out clearly. My head hurts.

The nameless outline holds a human head by the hair. Guadalupe steps away from the bed and activates the opening mechanism of a curtain, which slowly rolls up to reveal a window offering light and the diagonal rain of Paris.

Beside me, on an ancient table, there's a nice array of dilitium vibrators and pulsating anal pearls. The wall to my right is alive with a backlit fullpix print of a great odalisque with a fan of peacock feathers. Things become clearer and clearer. I'm in the residential floor of the Sphinx Tatoué. The light turns that outline in the backdrop into something more defined.

Elifasi Taki, and Vivian's head.

I'm screwed.

Guadalupe is rubbing his hippo face, showing all his rings. And he begins, "Kiki, you're always a hottie. I've never had the pleasure of putting it inside you, but we'll fix that. *Soon.* Blue often talked about you … *very good pro, with a great ass.* Poor Blue … You know, we had to vacuum him out of the tank of that fucking machine. A painstaking operation, believe me. Really a bad way to retire. But you know that very well, *right?*"

Guadalupe keeps talking, stomping about the room with his kitschy crocodile-skin shoes. His last words address the window, the rain: "You know that now we have to sort things out. You know the rules."

I hold on to what strength I've got left, spitting my thoughts to him: "*Fuck you.* Do what you have to do without beating around the bush, motherfucker."

It's over for me, by now, but Guadalupe wants to enjoy every bit of it.

"What's with all the rush? That's not as easy as you think. We need to pay Taki. You know how he works. He's waiting. He doesn't want credits. He wants a nice present for his Tokoloshe. I can't certainly get in the way. I'll leave you here alone a few minutes with him, but don't worry, *I'll be back soon.*"

Guadalupe exits. In the slice of hall, I glimpse three armed goons. His watchdogs: teeth, bullets, and flat balls. Guadalupe's rings and his goons' sub-machine guns glint under the lights. The son of a bitch turns back and blows me a kiss. The door shuts.

Taki immediately approaches and sits on the bed, looks at me for a long time. He grins, in his own way, showing large gaps between the higher teeth. I'm in his hands, tied up and with my thighs spread open. His dark face is long, sharp like his knives. He smells my body. Lingers on my tits, on my cunt, on my feet. I feel like throwing up with his disgusting sweetish odor clinging to my skin.

He makes up his mind, frees one of my arms and one of my legs from the chain.

What the fuck does he want to do?

He turns me belly-down, tightens the chains. He pulls them tighter and tighter. I can't react. I try to see what he wants to do, there behind me. He draws his knife, still bloodied. Vivian's blood. He begins chanting one of those crazy Afrikaans litanies for his imaginary demon Tokoloshe. It's the prelude of death, an ugly death.

Vergewe my Tokoloshe
Ek kan nie gee jou die hoof van die vrou
Is nie net myne
Maar ek sal nog 'n klein geskenkie
Klein ...

I smell that sweetish odor coming close again, the heat of his body dropping down on my back, and ... lower.

The blade of his knife begins dancing on my ass. *I shake,* as I've understood where he wants to start hacking. Taki writes fantasy stories on my right buttock with the tip of his knife, without cutting the flesh, without thrusting. Then he moves to the left buttock. Same story.

He's choosing the best part, motherfucker.

I think about Vivian for a moment, about what that cursed psycho could have done to her. But I go back to thinking about me, about my own end. Memories run fast; they follow the rhythm of Taki's knife.

I notice my right arm is not as tightly tied as the other. I can manage to bend it. Luckily, the asshole isn't that lucid. He's in a sort of trance to speak with his Tokoloshe, to arrange his mad rituals. Taki stops, pinches a lump of my right buttock. He has chosen. Now he'll sink his blade and take his *souvenir.*

I have one card to play, and quickly.

Taki is straddling me. I wait for his face to be closer, just a little closer. His blade starts cutting, but pain must not distract me, not now. I feel his breath against my neck.

A matter of seconds.

I shake with all my strength, suddenly turning and elbowing his face. *A pretty nice strike.* Taki falls from the bed, enraged. He swears in his cursed tongue, bleeding from mouth and nose, but he's already back on his feet.

The asshole let his knife drop on the bed. I manage to push it with my knee toward my hand, grasp it. I'm forced to move like an injured spider, with just a few possible movement angles. Taki pounces again, onto my back.

What I was waiting for.

I raise the blade, stabbing his stomach with his own force and weight. A shout: a voice different than usual, thinner. He collapses upon me, unmoving, heavy. His blood is fiery on my back and my wounded ass. But he's still breathing.

The door swings open. The three goons leap in with their eyes wide. They look at the scene, at our blood mixing over our bodies. They don't understand. They're shocked, screaming nonsense. One runs to call Guadalupe. The others keep their guns leveled. They threaten ghosts. Shitty watchdogs.

Guadalupe comes in, out of breath, an old pump-action shotgun in his hands, a Carcano Mod. 107. A nostalgic, Guadalupe. He likes it old school. He kicks his two goons, shoves them out of the room, slams the door shut. His voice roars:

"*Little slut.* They told me you're a snake! I'll make you pay for this. *You can't even imagine!*"

He turns Taki's face around, checks his breathing and thrusts those stubby, ungainly fingers in that dark neck of his. The outcome is clear: "Fuck, this one's a goner!"

Guadalupe hurls Taki's body to the floor. He sticks the cold barrel of the shotgun into my ass.

"And now, slut, I'll fire up your fucking ass! *How about that?*"

I close my eyes.

Seconds pass.

Guadalupe's breathing slowly drops to a normal rhythm. Finally, he pulls out the barrel.

"Too easy, like this. No, *you won't get that lucky.*"

His voice gets hoarser, scratching in his throat among splinters of fury. Guadalupe's last words are worse than the sound of the trigger: "Now you're going back *to Hell.* I'll book a very special treatment for you. You'll see, slut, *you'll see.*"

THE FLIGHT OF THE INSECT
नरक

THE MOON

"I looked again in the river of fire, and I saw the guardian angels of Tartarus taking a man by the throat, and they had a trident in their hands, and they used it to pierce the entrails of that old man.

"I questioned the angel, 'Who is this, my lord, to whom such torment is imposed?' The angel answered, 'This one you see used to be a priest who did not serve his ministry well: he ate, drank, fornicated, and yet kept offering the sacrifice to our Lord on his holy altar.'"

Ute Möbius. The psychopathic priest assimilates Hell. Naraka.

He does not live of seconds and despair like the rest of the inmates. He has the tools. He prays in his cell, day and night. He turns into an insect, and with his mighty exoskeleton he can fly, can squeeze into the narrowest spaces, between the creon red bars, through the tight cracks of ignorant, hopeless minds. The unending tunnels of Naraka turn into roadways of words and new faith, linking the islands of the soul with precise turns.

Signals, feelers.

Everybody is starting to talk about the priest. In the refectories, in the marching rooms, where they are forced to undergo a calisthenics routine so that their meat is well-toned.

Ute keeps spreading his black salt, his drug. *His paws are full of it.*

"The angel answered: 'Follow me, and I will show you the place of the righteous, where they are taken when they die. And then I will take you to the bottomless pit and show you the souls of the sinners, into what manner of place they are taken when they are dead.'"

Hell and hope: Slicer and salvation of that single indestructible piece of a man. The soul. The great key to surviving that place, to understand it, to accept it.

The Moon, Naraka. The first active Extraterrestrial Detention System. Ute turns it into one of the ancestral gateways to the old Hades.

Naraka as the caves of Kolonos close to Athens; Cape Matapan at the tip of Peloponnese; Mount Etna in Sicily; the Ammoudia Bay on the Ionian coast of Greece; Lake Avernum at Cuma, in Campania; the Flegrei Fields; Pandora's castle in Thuringia.

Prisoners, food and living fuel, turning into the legendary Cimmerians, people of darkness living underground, on the right shore of the Acheron, in the ancient Essenes sites on the plateau of Qumran, in the Judean desert, along the Dead Sea.

Purifying baths and Kalasutra.

"And I went after the angel, as he took me into Heaven, and up in the firmament I saw the powers; there was forgetfulness, deceiving and drawing to itself the hearts of men; and the spirits of slander, of fornication, of wrath, and of insolence; and there were the princes of wickedness."

Ute draws on imaginary maps, tracing in blue ink the path of the soul, from the Tartarus of Naraka up to the Elysian Fields. The magical river Lete, the waters of oblivion and reincarnation. The body, too, has a new, different destiny. As for the soul: a parallel perspective. The passage under the Gates of Sleep, beside the door of the Slicer.

The roadways of Naraka and syncretic derivations, rocky ceilings above and steel floors below. The magic astrology of Persia, Zoroastrianism, Hermetism, Kabbalah, Gnostic and Hellenistic philosophies. The great Vedic culture, Samsara, Moksha, and Nirvana. Aeons, Christ and Sophia. Meccan and Medinan surahs. The Valley of the Indo and the Seals. The Āraṇyaka and the sacrifices, the Purāṇa and the Tantric practices. The snake worshipped by the Aseeans. The cane full of knots, bends and spires, that Ute begins to bring. Water diviner of futures. Shepherd of a slaughtered flock. *Grand Vizier of Nothing.*

Ute cooks in his cauldron the souls of the Naraka inmates. He uses many different ingredients. The soul seems to have color, taste and, overall, a destination.

A new syncretic, theosophical religion, a well-processed drug, unbeatable. Nothing better to keep under control the bugs in the Naraka project: the 41% suicide rate of the resources. *A waste*, as Sibel keeps repeating. The queen of Naraka and of the interactive tastings in her Kalasutra. The New Moon manager, with her ambitious targets and her invisible necklaces of human skulls a thousand kilometers long.

Ute is a precious asset, his mad sermons slowly becoming the true oxygen in that underground world.

"And again I looked and saw angels without mercy, having no pity, their faces full of fury, their teeth jutting out of their mouth; their eyes shone like the East morning star, and from their hair and mouths, sparks of fire erupted."

The future of Naraka: education and control of the masses, of the cattle-prisoners.

The past of that priest, the terrible serial killer, does not matter.

Sibel turns him into the perfect *psychedelic shepherd* for his guests. The great pusher of lies. The engineer of a new, fake religious community, a safety net for the jumps of loneliness and despair. An explanation and a philosophy for death, even for packaging.

Placing the soul on a different plane, well outside of the claustrophobic walls of Naraka. The body as a simple vessel, a scrap, a physical husk to be left behind knowingly. The Hyperuranion of the elusive World Above, which does not exist.

Ute will be allowed to keep preaching polluting minds; he will have a wide chamber available, a pagan altar, with a great cross of Jerusalem above. The future Red Cave.

Ute will never end up into the Slicer. His insect wings becoming larger and larger, their reach infinite.

Sibel's earnings and contracts grow.

CLOUD LAB
नरक

THE MOON

Naraka – Cloud Lab.

Nothing better than a hole on the moon to design new synthetic drugs, experimenting far away from prying eyes. Cerebral structures no longer able to manage despair, drifting. Uxor's Cancer, swelling up every day, nibble at the Earth. So, better to take off, driving emotions into fake skies, artificial clouds, and then higher. New galaxies with windows. You make a lot of money building these virtual skycars, parked in shit, available to everybody. *Plimex seats, first row.* A few seconds to escape from a shitty alley, among garbage and carcasses, *landing into the core of a burning star.* Engines, more and more powerful. Ejaculations of thoughts, intangible sperm.

On Earth, Cloud 6 – the *brainburner* – is all the rage these days. But by now, cooked neurons are looking for something else. Something that lasts longer, deeper, and with more persistent emotions. Alternative solar systems, rectangular orbits. Shitty engineers sweat behind new setups, wide-range molecular perspectives. People talk about the forthcoming launch of a new, formidable psychoactive substance: *Hammer.*

Millander has already sunk his teeth into this new business. They are coming up with an arrangement with black labs in Nextokyo. The best equipped. They rub their hands in glee, counting the souls of their apocalyptic district.

Hammer: an amyle nitrite enhanced with yaba X molecules, capable of satisfying the new demands. *Risking a stroke beats jumping from the wreck of Pont Neuf.* Hammer: a luxurious skycar, a proper limo of desperation. Everybody is waiting for it.

New Moon never stands by watching. Let those fucking Japs make their two-bit drug. There are new scenarios to picture, new needs.

Naraka's Cloud Lab is the fortress of hallucinations to come; the trial of the ultimate drug – Cloud 7 – is in its final stages. Many tests provided very satisfying data. Vidal Mayer, New Moon CEO, is constantly squeezing the balls of the project manager, Bero Horn.

"Two months' delay, dickhead. Do you know what the fuck it means?"

Vidal, a quick career in New Moon. An unstoppable architect. Pillars into the stomach of asswipes and competitors. Metal beams to impale officials and human lab rats. Steel and innovative alloys forged with the carbon of disposed-of corpses. An idealist daughter thrown out the window. Useless brainless pulp. Vidal Mayer, a snake.

"You've got a week, then we have to launch the product. *Not a single day more.* It takes nothing for me to come back here, rip off those limp balls of yours, and make you swallow them whole. But don't worry. We'll not leave your wife empty-handed. I'll have her mounted by my dogs. Fine beasts, Neo-2 breed. Don't waste my time. A week."

As always, before going back to Earth, Vidal concedes himself a screw with Sibel in her Kalasutra. Human meat filet and candlelight. Saint-Émilion in the glasses and in the senses, together with a lot more stuff. From the panoramic screen, the Sinai desert vanishes with its red rocks. The environment simulator projects real-time images from Room 9 of the Sphinx Tatoué, the one reserved to New Moon officials.

"Hey, look at that son of a bitch Duchet ..."

A man – grey and flaccid body – is inserting a thamnopis into a girl's cunt. The small, red-and-black snake easily finds its way. Audio is turned off. The cries of the woman could annoy. Duchet sweats. He is excited. In his eyes there are reflections of roaches, of labia majora, of black, never-exorcised dreams.

Vidal and Sibel fuck while the merciless images on the big screen flow. The Queen Bee lets herself be flooded by the Snake's sperm. She raises her legs toward the ceiling so it drips deep. Her hands hold her ankles. Her voice comes out from the teeth of a panting breath.

"What did Bero tell you? What's the progress with Cloud 7?"

"That dork is late, as usual, but we're nearly there. Side effects should be under control. We're going to buy a new fucking nice

planet with all that money. I'm only sorry for *you*, honey."
Sibel smiles, hugs Vidal's snake skin.
"It was worth it."

NEW HAUL
नरक

EARTH

Skyfreight FC442. Destination: New Belmarsh Penitentiary. Third daily flight, new haul of prisoners.

Victor Ilievsky. Art thief, murdered, forger. He defines himself a *gifted improviser*. Originally from MetroSophia, Stara Planina Federation. Detained for two years in Burgas Penitentiary. Modern art expert, lacking any level of moral conscience. Founder and leader of the anarchist group *Ne Etika*. Shadow inspirer of the foundation *Svobodna Kultura*. Seven standard, non-professional outworlds. Forty-one years old.

Jesus Vila Dilmé. Serial killer, 23 outworlds. Called *19 metros cuadrados*, after the size of the notorious garage where he kept mutilating his victims for days. Engineer, he registered several patents at the *Nueva Tecnologia* office of the independent department of the Valencian Union, including one for a portable neural-induction saw. Extensively field-tested. Thirty years old. First arrest. Directly to New Belmarsh.

Kree O'Connor. Irish, professional killer, 16 outworlds. She started her career in Buenos Aires with the *Equipos de mort*. For the last two years she worked as an independent hunter in sector 2 of Balcania and in New France. Twenty-four years old, escaped from Grasse Penitentiary. Second arrest.

Thirteen common criminals complete the haul, no big shots, just petty thieves and kidnappers, and then about thirty wretches and junkies fished in the free communities of Groningen and Esbjerg in the North Federation territory – recently recognized thanks to the international mediation of the powerful New Moon Corporation.

In exchange, those communities must have supplied a lot of raw material for the human chicken farm on the moon. These pallid lowlifes must be only a small part of the deal.

And then, there's me again, Kiki Léger, professional killer, 30 outworlds, recently updated. Ticket directly paid by my friend Guadalupe.

I'm the first escapee from Naraka. I can expect a warm welcome.

The trip takes a handful of minutes, enough for many memories to flow by in my mind, a big piece of my life. Two North Stars, always on: my father and my son, Max, randomly popped out of the old flat in South Paris 5 when I sold my cunt for a few credits. Before this nice career, before Blue, Guadalupe, and many more pieces of shit, before the absurd *fuck-shoot-kill* life.

This pretty fucking epilogue is just what it needed: ending up ground in some meat can. Maybe I'll become the special dish of a birthday party, or a nice wedding anniversary. *Delikatessen.* I'll be pleasing the teeth and jaws of someone with enough money for the super-expensive, super-exclusive food products by New Moon, branded *Maison des Anges*. All in order.

I'll end up under VIP teeth, special teeth, certainly not into *ordinary mouths.*

The light strips of the New Belmarsh skyhub flash.

Desert dust begin to lift, very fine particles. Everybody looks through the windows with eyes full of defiance, of fear, of curiosity; mine, they lighten and darken, steadily, with awareness.

The light external structure of Naraka glints. A fifty-meter tall tower is the first part to show, then the long incinerator, and the large rectangle that hosts the fissors.

At last, if you know where to look, the black mouth of the South Tunnel opens. The gate of Hell. An impossible iceberg of rock and steel, hiding its huge belly, its awful legs, hundreds of meters below.

An alien, underground hive.

PEONIES IN THE DARK
नरक

THE MOON

As soon as we enter the black mouth of Naraka, they immediately separate me from the other inmates, from today's last inbound group, skyfreight FC442. They really make me feel important.

An escort of five guards, all for me.

We soon leave the South Gallery. A secondary elevator makes us swallow dozens of meters of rock, which flows up through the frontal opening, darker and darker, faster and more fierce. The detention area passes by and vanishes, but we keep going down.

The elevator stops. The jailers shove me out.

Weapons, always leveled.

Where the fuck are they taking me?

Of course, isolation: the usual for punishment for escapees.

It must be gnawing at them that for once they took it up their ass. I don't fear being alone. Better this way. It's not as though the company of the scum and of the wretched of the planet – well represented in Naraka – could be much better. I'll live with it.

Fuck isolation.

The escort men don't spit a single word; they keep pushing and jerking at me in complete silence. Yet another tunnel to walk. We are at the third floor underground of this shitty, absurd structure, and I've got a feeling we're not even close to the bottom. It really took some psychopaths to design a fucking hive like this one. I picture the architects of Naraka like a nice party of evolved roaches, a genetic experiment. I'm way fonder of the ignorant, unambitious roaches of South Paris 5. Including both men and actual bugs.

We arrive in front of a steel sliding door, a big one, similar to the ones that break the unending lines of the tunnels of the upper levels. We go in and a round room opens up, with a sort of well in the middle protected by a golden lid. The circular perimeter is riddled by a series of small red doors. The ceiling is a great reflective surface; light sources and architectural patterns, with few horizontal lines, work together to release an illusion of vertigo.

There are no cells, displays, or desperate eyes, no screams and curses, shit and vomit.

This is no Naraka.

What the fuck are they doing down here?

Must be the big shots' accommodations, and they treat themselves well, apparently. Young women wearing kimonos keep entering and exiting the small doors, their hair up, their skin white, almost transparent. One smiles at me with her overly red mouth. *Have they even got whores, down here? A brothel inside a maximum security prison?* Another transparent woman takes my hand and she leads me toward the room she just came out of. She's smiling, too. On that long, white neck, sinking into the rich cloth of her kimono, the holographic tattoo of a red waterlily pulsates. The guards stay at the entrance, unmoving. They lower their weapons. Slowly leave my field of view.

Are you fucking kidding me?

The woman keeps smiling, tries to hide it by covering her mouth with a hand. She opens the door. Here's my destination.

The kiss: the beginning of cannibalism. The same instinct to taste the other.

"So you're the famous Kiki. Please, have a seat."

An Asian woman with big blue eyes greets me. Her perfect body is tightly wrapped by a black dress of reflective retylex. She wears no shoes. She approaches, motions to my chair, brushes the back of my hand. *Suddenly, I find myself with a red peony between my fingers.*

I raise my eyes again.

"I'm Sibel, the jail supervisor." Then she quickly adds, "This place is so much more ... beyond appearances. You'll learn it soon enough."

Sibel looks at me with curiosity for some seconds and steps behind my back. She covers my eyes with her slender fingers. Scents and stirrings of unknown molecules, erupting pomegranates, planets of mangoes and mint. And her voice:

"You're really good. Nobody else managed to get out of here. In one piece, I mean ..."

She gets even closer. *I feel her.* She kisses my right ear. For an instant, I sense the tip of her tongue tracing a small circle. She keeps holding her hands over my eyes, lightly. *Butterflies.* I'm in a total daze. *What should I expect?* My friend Guadalupe's recommendation and my escape would suggest a very different treatment.

I let her go on. Let's see what all this is about. I'm ready to rip off that fucking tongue of hers with my bare hands, at the right moment. I just need two seconds. Sibel shifts her fingers from my eyes, and light come back into my senses; then a new, deeper darkness created by a soft cloth. Her voice is the only guide in a strange maze ... A monster from the apocalyptic Paris, moved to the Moon.

I'm the minotaur of these spaces, half flesh, half cunt.

I feel the hooves growing, and the pelt, the animal shapes. I'm losing my bearings. I grab Sibel's hands to stop her. They're warm, pulsating. I squeeze them hard, try to get her close to my dry mouth, express myself before getting lost.

"Sibel, what the fuck do you want from me? I don't like these games."

A mistake, too few millimeters between us. Sibel edges to my lips. Her breath smells good, clean. *Smells like a vortex.*

"Words are of little use, Kiki. Let me explain in a different way. Leave my hands, let me try."

Sibel's skin fastens on mine. I get back inside myself. I can't be a fucking doll in her hands. I've got to play along. I certainly don't miss my old cell.

Does she want to have sex? Let it be. As my mother used to say: *Eat and survive.*

But she'll have to give me something in return. Get me back to Paris. The stakes are high: Sibel will need to *taste* if I want her to gamble hard. I free her hands. Sibel's body vibrates and mine answers like a magnet.

She really must be a damn slut, this Sibel. Better this way.

I listen to her movements, to everything I can't see. Her breath approaches the floor, my thighs. Sibel pulls down my pants, and I again feel the tip of her tongue, now moving over my panties. *Slits.* She delicately spreads my legs.

It's been months since I last had sex. I begin getting moist even though I'm doing my best to keep it tight, to avoid it. *Fuck!* Sibel notices.

"You really taste good."

I hate myself. I am still the thirty-credits whore of some years ago. I let her take off my panties, penetrate me with her tongue. I'm helpless. Sibel's hair is pure silk. It flows between my legs, touches me with a thousand imaginary hands.

I will explode way, way too soon. Lockless emotions. Even in Hell. I must stop her. Now. I abruptly push her away from my pussy.

"No ... stop. If you want to go on, you'll have to let me go. Away from here."

Silence. Thicker and thicker. I hear her unfastening from me, stepping away. Now she's moving around me, like a satellite.

I remove the blindfold. The light is too bright. I have a hard time putting into focus Sibel's black outline as she opens a door.

"We'll talk about that later, Kiki. Now dinner's ready."

If people were to discover the truth, men would begin eating women.

RAINY TAXI
-NEPROM DOLL 4-
नरक

Black roadcab, engine of change. Unknown trip. At the wheel, a shark-headed woman who knows all the tastes of the world.

Sibel, ferrywoman of abysses, moon-skin. Wonderful teeth.

In the rear seat: another woman in a fancy dress, her hair ruffled. Groups of snails are slithering on her body, shells and black bodies beneath her skirt, sediment of silver slime lines. Lubricant. Unexpected roads. Kiki, iron jellyfish, wind-body.

The women are unmoving. The taxi hood, first in piercing the new dimensions of the imaginary ride, is covered in seaweed and dust of ancient rocks. Traces of oceans, of submerged, split worlds; quadrants of oxygen to partake. Big Blue's last project for his neprom doll collection, a great installation to conclude the visit, the final haven. A vision, an intuition.

Blue imagines his guests climbing on the black roadcab with the two primal women: Sibel and Kiki. Share an extreme voyage with them, a fusion. Shut the door, and breathe in the particles of two cosmoses, the guide becoming passenger, and vice versa.

Mutuality.

Sibel must be preserved with her magic fingers and perfect teeth, with her real eyes so she can look at the road. Suggest the road. Nothing else is needed of her human body.

The woman with the fancy dress, instead, must embed Kiki's tight ass, her legs, her long muscles, so she can climb down the car and switch places with the driver, with the shark woman. Mechanical legs are not enough for a woman meant to keep running until she overcomes herself.

Rainy Taxi is just an idea, a sketch on a sheet of blank paper. A humid project in a drawer. The collection will remain incomplete without Blue. Meaningless. All the other dolls will die. The entire magic row will fall.

It is not technology pulling the strings of that secret, bio-

mechanical world, preserving it; it is a great, headless fantasy without a route of blood vessels, of final outlets. A travel without a destination. It is no use, Guadalupe, that you keep dusting, keep vacuuming the time, keep pressing the main switch to activate those organic circuits to make those hearts beat again. Touching.

It is a legacy you cannot comprehend, Guadalupe, that does not belong to you. All that is left is a big space down there at the end, which will slowly swallow everything else.

Beauty, *Blue used to say*, is not a shape; it is an ideal, imaginary destination.

The last project of the collection, unfinished, must necessarily be impossible.

FULL OF MEMORIES
नरक

THE MOON

"We can start, Haniko ... Are you hungry, Kiki?"

Sibel is sitting in front of me in this narrow, long room of her dominion. The walls, made of soft white tekmex, are covered by shapes reminiscent of great red peonies.

Haniko, a young Japanese woman, gently tilts her head and exits.

The game continues. I'm beginning to feel nervous, as it always happens when I don't understand what's going on. Usually, I don't give it a second thought and I start shooting, but my Martin 4 isn't here with me. I'm a prisoner in the cursed Hive, in the rooms of the Queen Bee.

I squeeze my fists. I'd like to strangle her, an almost invincible desire, just like feeling her skin fastened to mine.

I hate you and I love you, Sibel, whatever you really are. But I try my very best to keep my feelings hidden. The daze, the *vortex*.

"I'm not really hungry, Sibel. Can we skip it?"

I've swallowed any possible gross thing in my life – *Eat and survive*, sure – but a dinner in Naraka makes you think. I've never eaten human meat, not even when my card was chock-full with credits. Sibel keeps grinning. She reaches out with her fingers, touches me. My skin reacts with a direct link to the great heat between my thighs. This super-slut must have drugged me somehow. I just can't resist her in any way, be indifferent to her. Her voice, again:

"Kalasutra is not a place where you *eat*. You must learn to *taste* ... and *travel*. You don't need to be hungry, believe me."

The door opens again. Haniko gently lays a large, oval dilitium tray on the table. In the middle, surrounded by spheres of direct energy burners, are small pieces of meat. They are leaf-shaped, and a few millimeters thick.

Sibel invites me to try.

"This is a special dish. You just need to leave the meat on the burners for a few seconds. Beware: it takes nothing to spoil the taste."

Just as I guessed ... It must be human meat. After all, we're in a huge farm of human chickens. Who knows who they're serving us for dinner, the poor devil. I refuse to eat. Sibel keeps projecting her huge blue eyes.

"Thank you, Sibel, but I'm not hungry. And then again, to be honest, maybe I'm backward-looking, but human meat makes me throw up. *Let's just skip this*, please. Explain to me what I must to do to get away from this fucking place and get back to Earth. If you really want to help me ..."

The woman dismisses Haniko with a gesture. We're alone again. And here her conditions come. I was waiting for them, but they're not what I figured.

"Of course I want to help. Otherwise, you wouldn't be here. You've understood it. I like you very much. This is not meat from this place, not *ordinary* meat. Try, at least. You'd make me happy. More than that, I can assure you that you'd make *yourself* happy. Then, I'll arrange your trip back to Earth. Tomorrow, first freightbot leaving, just to be a little discreet."

And I was thinking I'd have to humor who knows what whim. And instead it just takes eating a few centimeters of shit, holding your nose, *and then it will be over*?

Sibel keeps staring at me, her gaze lowering to my mouth. She insists.

"I could have you immediately taken to the Slicer, or thrown into a cell together with some psychopath who hasn't seen a woman in months. I could taste your meat ... Haniko can cook delicious dishes. Instead, I prefer spending this evening with you. Do you think I care if you eat or you don't? I'd just like to share something with you. To feel you close. Taste it, then you can go, if you want. Or you could stay with me here in Kalasutra. The choice will be up to you. Earth is no longer such a nice place to live, by now."

Maybe Sibel is a crazy Queen Bee, but she's a Queen nonetheless, here at least, up the ass of the moon. *Eat and survive*. So be it. *Who cares?* Swallowing a piece of shitty meat beats ending up in pieces in some can. If the bitch wants to fuck with me, at least I'm playing my last card. Without her, my fate is already written. Guadalupe would party in a whorehouse, maybe serving my sliced ass to his friends. *Fuck no, you won't have it so easy, hippo face.*

I lower my eyes. Sibel understands the game can go on. She shows me what to do.

"Like this, Kiki. Pick up a slice with these pliers, see … a few seconds on the burner … let it melt for an instant on your tongue. Don't chew right away. Try to discover the new tastes, with awareness, before swallowing."

I pick the smaller slice; pale pink, it looks tender. I follow her instructions: burner, then I stick it into my mouth. I must make it. Resist. If I vomit, I'd ruin everything.

I wait a few seconds before swallowing.

Sibel looks at me with satisfaction. That small leaf of human meat goes down into my stomach. It's gone. I made it. *Now, super-slut, just get me on the first cargo to Earth.*

But it's not over. Sibel's smile turns into something evil, scornful. Strange splinters scratch in her voice. "So, you like it?"

I should have expected this. Sibel isn't going to honor the deal. Her visage is dark, transformed, with shadows that had eluded me until now. I try to understand what she further wants from me, what this game is about. Overall, when is it going to end?

I answer, trying to follow her along her unknown routes: "I'm not sure. It's something different than usual. I couldn't define it. Thank you, Sibel, but now … will you let me go?" I certainly can't say the truth … *that I'd throw up my soul,* if I could.

"Of course you can go!" Sibel answers, irked. But she has a different plan. "Why won't you stay with me, instead? On Earth, you wouldn't last long. They'd hunt you down. You'd be safe here."

Staying here … up the ass of the moon, eating human meat and fucking the Queen Bee. Pure madness. *I want to go now.*

I make it clear beyond doubt: "I'd rather go back to Earth. It may be a shithole, but I've got things to fix. I'd probably snuff it in the process, but at least I want to try."

Sibel stands, approaches and, once again, she's behind my shoulders, her fingers over my eyes, darkness.

Fuck.

She whispers into my ear, "Why go? What have you got to fix?"

Sibel's voice is more and more hard, and deep. Maybe she's pissed because I don't want to *become the wife* of the Queen Bee of Naraka.

As you wish, bitch. *I'll tell you why I want to go.* But after that, enough with all the bullshit. Either I'm leaving tomorrow on the first flight available, or I'm snapping your slender neck. I'll end up in the Slicer, *fuck it,* but you'll be coming to Hell with me. *Another* Hell, where you'll be no fucking Queen.

"I've got to go, *period.* Earth's full of shit, overbrimming already. But before I croak I want to see my son again. Try and restart something, somehow. For as long as it can last … *But now let me go.*"

Sibel laughs. She removes her hands from my eyes. She wants to look me right in the face. She touches her nipples, looks even more aroused.

"*Little whore* … your son, Maximilian, you've just eaten him. Tender meat, right? Your friend Guadalupe sent him up here, to me, this morning. At eight years, they're really tender …"

And now you can go. Hell is all yours now.

PART 3
SAMGHATA

MALDOROR RELOADED 1/4
नरक

I hope you are as fierce as what you are about to read, no wavering, zero disorientation. Only then you will be able to find a sure wild trail, a diagonal through the underground of these dark pages, with rocky walls soaked with a new, strange poison.

Without the necessary tension, and spirit disposition – but hold diffidence dear – its apocalyptic, radioactive emanations could melt your soul. Not everybody can safely enter the mouth of Naraka. Just a few will be able to taste the bitter fruit at its core, there, in the belly of the Hive.

Are you really ready?

You could be that fruit.

Before pushing further, think twice. No, don't just go headlong, immediately pulling down your pants toward two welcoming open thighs. It is a trap. Listen to me. Think about the expert crane, flying in the frozen silence of winter, at the tip of her flock, stretching out as far as the eye can see.

Archetypal sensors make plumage stand on end. They don't trust that smooth, calm, attractive horizon. The old neck, with only a few feathers remaining, bends. Undulations. *She turns toward the invisible danger.* Memories. *She feels it, clicks her beak like a sky sentry. Warning the flock.*

She maneuvers her tail following an ancient code. Universal. She shifts away from the vertex of that flying triangle, leaving open a geometric gap.

The storm, the tempest, they are coming. Omens. *Nobody listens to the old crane with her dilitium compasses.*

The flock keeps traveling toward the abyss. But she goes back, instead, quickly descending. Her claws on the branch of a solid tree. She will observe the hurricane, the pain, the blood. She will peek at it all from a distance. She won't let it pass through her. She won't plunge into those black clouds to vanish.

You should descend, too …

But maybe you think I want to hide something from you, that I am trying to deny you an experience.

You don't give a fuck about the old crane, right?

You feel strong and fierce enough, now more than ever. You want to smell the hate with your curious, proud nostrils, roll on your belly like a shark, chase the events with the urgency of your appetite. Rightful, of course. You will succeed in your intent.

You will be a monster, too.

Hell will subtly come into those two misshapen holes on your disgusting snout. As much as you want. You will breathe three thousand times in a row the cursed conscience of Naraka and Samghata, its great shapeless belly.

Here is the door, that door.

NINETY HEADS
नरक

EARTH, NOVYJ PRIVATE SKYHUB

Anton Khasan nervously paces.

The skyfreight is loading mercs on its narrow, curved belly. *Curses. The metal of weapons scratching.* Destination: the Moon. Naraka.

Khasan stops under the ladder, pivots, squeezes the cigar between his teeth and finally spits all his impatience against Ermolay's snout: "So, everything ready?"

Ermolay Golonov begins. His back feels like reinforced concrete and his balls frozen. His jagged voice loses itself in the pockets of his camo and in the lungs of the Siberian wind. "Yes, sir, ten minutes to zero."

"I didn't hear you. Are we ready or not?"

Khasan is more nervous than usual. He does not like this mission. It is different this time. This time it is about his wife, Beatrix. Ermolay trembles. He knows that tone well. He repeats, "Ten minutes to zero!"

Khasan looks toward shadows only he can see. He raises his eyes to the Moon, *there,* with all its three hundred thousand craters.

The skyfreight turns on its lights. Flashing red. Flashing green. Solid.

Ermolay's voice, again, firmer: "Ready for takeoff, sir!"

Seven minutes' delay. Sweaty shirt, in spite of the cold. Khasan looks at his man with disdain: hands on the ladder, too-large boots, thin lips, that pansy voice; he will always be a fucking butler.

A TDI Vector K50 sub-machine gun glints against stripes of moon rays. Good penetration, high rate of fire. A cluster of flames lights up the strip. Incendiary rounds. *Roars.*

Ermolay screams, drops on the strip. He is set on fire and cries with the wind.

He is unlucky; the hits are not lethal. Fire alone will finish the job.

"*Now I hear you!* Let's go."

Khasan has watered down the excess of adrenaline poisoning his blood, but fury still has its hooks sunk in his soul. He climbs the ladder, orders to depart. The hatch closes with a symphony of engines. The skyfreight lifts vertically. The mercs look at the black strip from the windows, the light blue stripes on the sides, a red and yellow stain spreading and shifting: *Ermolay's flame*. The Moon grows bigger and bigger as two hundred thousand more craters reveal themselves.

Anton Khasan, New Black Flower caste leader.

The criminal organization running the independent Oblast of Rjazan. His wife is detained: unacceptable.

Silence on board. Standard skeleton crew for a blood raid: quick incursion, single objective. Thirty men, *Chernyye Volki*, elite corps of Khasan's private army. Motherfuckers only able to shoot and rape. The best selection of schizo maniacs and murderers of old Russia. Big hands, the acrid smell of dust, death, vomited dreams. Wicked brains stuck in black helmets, human exoskeletons. Shreds of ethics and worms crushed under the soles of combat boots, mixed with blood and shit.

Target: *extraction of Beatrix Leonard, detained in New Belmarsh Penitentiary.*

Ten minutes to contact. Ejaculating rage, Khasan speaks to his men: "Someone else lacking his voice, today?"

Silence.

"Good, you bunch of bastards. Three things. Just these. Stick them well inside those fucking heads. Team A thinks about Beatrix. I want her out of that shit in thirty. Team B deals with that bitch, Sibel, the jail supervisor. Let me watch her impaled on the strip when we leave. I don't want to miss that show. Team C stays out with me, waiting for orders … You know how to count? I want to take back home with me three heads for each of you. *Ninety heads*, not one less. I must send a gift to my friends at New Moon Corporation … *All clear?* Do the job and make me enjoy it … You, *what the fuck are you looking at?*"

The addressed man looks at his comrades in confusion, then

returns on Khasan's face.

"Yes, *I'm talking to you* ... piece of shit. What are you looking at? *Do I look funny to you?*"

Khasan kicks the man, keeps doing it until he sees blood gushing, and he goes beyond that. He grabs that sagging body by the hair, shoves his knife into his mouth, breaks his teeth, searches for the root of his tongue ... drools into those by-now dim eyes.

"*So, are you bringing me three of those fucking heads? Eh? Are you doing that? 'Cause I want to piss inside of them. So, how many are you bringing me? Motherfucking bastard ...*"

He manages to stop, just short of slaying another of his own.

"*Damn motherfuckers ...*"

Khasan gets back to counting the craters of that cursed Moon.

The merc skyfreight touches down on the strip of Naraka, only now challenged. A new route, out of system coverage. Thirty black helmets with normalizing suits storm toward the entrance. The skin of the moon crumbles. Khasan follows at a distance, covered by Team C. The outer garrison is easily broken through, three men shredded in rapid succession. Wide arcs of blood.

The mercs split up. Point to their objective. Follow the plan.

Team A. Direction: South entrance, toward the detention area. Second floor underground. They have detailed maps of the structure, thanks to the good offices of Anton Khasan's knife. The tongue of a New Moon manager is attached to the blueprint of the first space penitentiary.

Roars of electromagnetic devices. Breach opened to the main tunnel. Darkness. Silence. Three hundred meters to the elevator, and they are in.

But where the fuck is security?

Hiss of pulse engines, nothing human. From the belly of the tunnel, square shapes detach, black lumps moving in line, in small jerks.

Fucking synthetics.

The men of Team A open fire with a dance of lead cores and metal jackets. A syncopated blues shrieking in the great sound box of the first floor. The dark column advances from the bottom of the tunnel without slowing. No apparent damage. The team leader, Gavriil, orders to use the burners.

"Come on, shit, hurry up!"

Fire snakes stretch forward. They pour out horizontal, illuminating the advancing file. The burning red tongues lick the EATs' armor. Ten of them.

Holy shit!

Gavriil orders to fall back; he knows those metal butchers.

Necrophage robots, they call them, capable of self-fueling with human flesh. Tanks of boiling broth where they cook and digest men. On Earth, there are only prototypes of those cursed machines. Emptying their magazines against them would be useless. Much ado for nothing.

"Out, out! Out of here!"

Gavriil's open mouth breathes the rotten oxygen of Naraka, but it is too late: Team A mercs are surrounded. The vise squeezes. The laser carvers of the EATs turn on, bright blue strings dissecting heads, legs, arms. The great tunnel swallows all the blood of the Siberian stew. Their entrails form a new organic floor; they are collected and quickly melted in the boiling broth of the EAT systems.

Injectors shooting synthetic, clawed gastric juices.

A choir of voices, cyclical and chilling.

"Biomass stored. System ready. Biomass stored. System ready. Biomass stored. System ready. Biomass stored. System ready. Biomass stored. System ready. Biomass stored. System ready."

\#

Team B. Bound to: East entrance, management and direction quarters. Third floor underground. The large tower adjacent to the incinerator sinks deep, to the bottom of the entire structure, the most direct and safest path to reach the target. Sibel. Going up is easy. Gravitational steel ropes leave scars on the light alloy upholstering of the tower. Earth shows herself beyond the rim of the structure, a hole in the black space.

Great blue masses of water and the ribs of continents.

The ten mercs vertically climb the surface. They enter, breaking through the crystal of the control room at the top. The group goes down the stairs toward the quarters, their weapons drawn against the unfathomable mouth of that dark descent, that narrow throat leading into the gloomy belly of the Moon.

Khasan, from outside, radio calls the group leader: "Roman! Where the fuck are you?"

"Team B operational. We're going down on foot. No visual."

Khasan has already lost contact with Team A. The plan is falling through.

"Where's security? Where are those bastards hiding?"

Roman's eyes shift and his words end. The head of a huge steel cylinder appears, hit by the light of their rellplex torches. Khasan's maps are incomplete; they do not show the shrinking sections of the structure. Sometimes the knife does not get everything.

It emerges from the bottom, like a giant piston, pushing toward the apex of the tower. The environment is hermetically shut. The entrances to upper floors switch off, sealing themselves into the walls. Stairs detach from their supports, fold on themselves, are sucked in by the walls; they vanish sequentially, under the mercs' feet. East Tower is a big mouse trap.

Roman orders to get back up. The cylinder vibrates, chasing those alien bodies that ended up in the wrong electronic organism. The cylinder head becomes transparent. Behind the crystals, Sibel's white face appears. *The target.* There is she, inside the brain of that sort of metal nematode, together with two women operating the control systems of the shrinking structure.

The whore smiles. The whore is closer and closer, larger and larger.

The mercs open fire, their bullets ricocheting in that metal box, which becomes narrower each passing second. Suicide. *Don't shoot!* Roman's last order.

Base and top become a gigantic vise. The men have a meter of life still as they try to gain useless seconds, lying down, squeezing like bugs. Sibel greedily looks at the mercs' and brushes her nipples. Base and top finally touch, matching, crushing the ten bodies – alive and dead – and melting them with the cold molecules of steel. Sibel climaxes. A thin human layer covers the panoramic crystal.

The omelet is done. Show is over.

Sibel's tongue licks the crystal. She imagines the taste of Khasan's ten wolves.

Team C. Khasan is foaming. Contact lost with Team A and B, he commands his men to move toward the main entrance. *I'll tear them apart with my own hands.*

They advance about twenty meters, stop in their tracks.

Halt! Don't shoot!

Khasan's eyes frame a body shoved out of the main tunnel, waving its hands. The bioamp controllers in his helmet zoom in on the figure.

Close up on the face. Beatrix. *Wet eyes.* She keeps spreading her arms, as if signaling for something.

Khasan, in syntofrequency with his men, orders to reach her and pick her up. "*You five: go! Move your asses, now!*"

Beatrix's voice is invisible on the skin of the Moon, choked inside the helmet of her normalizing suit. She is screaming: "*Stop. I'm about to explode. Don't get close!*" But nobody can hear her.

The five men reach her. The others stay back with Khasan, covering them. The visor of their helmets light up suddenly, reflecting a quick blue light, then nothing. Beatrix blows up like a mute star, her burst flesh travelling fast and far in the airless low gravity. Lifeless lumps on guided routes. *A flock of her. On the Moon.*

The close explosion has damaged the five rescuers' suits: their limbs swell grotesquely, their lungs explode. Blood bubbles inside those black helmets, quickly filling their skulls.

Khasan falls to his knees. His men try to drag him away, haul him on the skyfreight, to get away from that clusterfuck, but Khasan won't have it. He has already spat out his soul. He pulls his knife out and sinks it into Vladlen's belly, ripping his suit – his most trusted man, the one trying to drag him to safety. The other four run toward the freight.

Khasan screams into his helmet, the echo of his voice vibrating in syntofrequency in the ears of his fleeing wolves: "*Cowards! Come back, bastards!*"

Khasan opens fire with the Parkshir GN11 dropped by Vladlen, switching the environmental selector. He sees the men falling one after another at the foot of the ladder.

Silence.

He turns back to the structure of Naraka. The hate. He looks down on his chest and there is a piece of Beatrix stuck there, a stretch of intestines, like an outworldy snake.

Khasan advances alone toward the entrance. He keeps firing

with the Parkshir. He kills many ghosts, bursting hearts of rock.

"*Come out, motherfuckers!*"

He reaches the main tunnel, the entrance already cleared by Team A.

Nobody.

Khasan's bullets zoom along many angles and trajectories. They are swallowed by darkness. They don't seem to hit anything. A neverending ride, minutes with no noise. Apparently, no destination.

"*Show yourselves!*"

The entrance of the great tunnel shuts. CLANK! Pressurization.

Khasan removes his helmet and drops it in the arms of darkness. He reloads his scorching Parkshir.

Finally, the gloom answers.

Two precise hits to his legs. Kneecaps shattered. Khasan is down. He draws his knife. The blade summons invisible bodies and limbs.

"*What are you waiting for? I'm here!*"

A blow to the head. A new darkness, different. A hovering voyage. Moondust on Khasan's black wings. Space, the red silk of nebulae, elementary asterisms, the spiral gallery of the Orion Arm, Argo Navis with the hull of stars Alpha, Beta and Epsilon, the sails Gamma and Delta, the stern Zeta. *Farther.*

New, imaginary alignments. The constellation Beatrix. Fixed lights of the Vagina Region, purple gases of blood vessels, globular cluster of the past, fragmented pulsars. The great magnitude of pain.

Light. North Block of Naraka, second floor underground.

Khasan folds his wings, opens his eyes. There are no more stars. His body is clutched on Table Number 3 in the Slicer. Neck, wrists, and ankles wrapped in the vise of steel. The buzz saws and the pistils are still unmoving. They glint, just quivering.

A New Moon operator checks the system graphics, his finger on the ignition button. Sibel supervises. They wait for her order. She waits for Khasan's full awareness.

"You're a damn whore ..."

Khasan still manages to spit words. His legs are bleeding. He knows it is over.

"Goddamn ..." He mindlessly searches for his knife. He turns right and spits at the support immobilizing him. "Cowards ..."

Death, so close, lets him whip her black dress.

Sibel's voice blows cold in the room, spreading on Khasan's back in the form of shivers: "Leave him alone with me for a few minutes. Then, you'll proceed as usual."

The New Moon operators go. Sibel begins rubbing her nipples. Khasan turns away to look at an imaginary spot. He doesn't want to soak his final minutes in those big blue eyes, so morbid and aroused. Death brushes the man's brow. A delicate gesture, a definitive one.

Sibel shoves a dilitium dilator into his mouth, sealing his face. Then she hurls herself as a fury between Khasan's legs. Her perfect teeth sink into his scrotum. Blood squirts as Sibel forcefully tears off a testicle. She chews, swallows. She pulls down her dress, her breasts throbbing. She plunges her hands in Khasan's blood. Iliac artery, the perfect pump. She covers herself in red following the wagging trajectories of the gush. Khasan keeps screaming inside his mind, his voice readable only in his warped facial muscles.

She gets up, fixes her straps and dress. Before exiting, she hurls a few last words to him: "Once, Khasan, you used to have balls."

Death wants to fuck the chosen one, even if he lacks a testicle. A shadow mounts on Khasan's pelvis, moving in a dark eddy, coming. A final spasm of muscles. The shadow seems to get a face, then an array of many others. Finally, it vanishes.

The New Moon operators return to their places. The Slicer is initialized. The blades whistle. Squirts and guts on white aprons and walls.

The red strip of memories marks the path.

Old, rotten meat, good only to make fuel for the necrophage robots of Naraka.

NE Category – No Eat.

– Mission terminated –

DEUX JAMBES
नरक

Restaurant *Deux Jambes.*

Sipho Guadalupe enjoys his dinner in one of the most exclusive places of *his* apocalyptic district. A hippo-faced monarch, expanding more and more his reign of shit. A black cancer eating up kilometers of the old Paris every day.

Guadalupe's voice roars, the voice of the master: "Call me Dorian, now."

The waitress runs into the kitchen, her huge tits bouncing, her bra shaking. She pulls at the white jacket of the chef, Dorian Moreau, a true genius of the new cuisine.

"How many times have I told you not to fuck with me in my kitchen? Take those boobs out of here and show them to the customers. It's a slow night."

The waitress, Jeanne, manages to hiss Guadalupe's name before getting a kick in her ass.

"Him? Are you sure? I'm coming now. *Fuck!*"

The man looms at his table with crocodile eyes.

"It's been ages! I'm making something special for you tonight. What can I offer you to drink?"

Dorian's smile is too taut, his face a mask. He sniffed too much zerdlex.

Guadalupe maneuvers his fingers, motioning the chef to come closer. *Closer, closer still.* His dilitium rings glitter under the lights.

Moreau bends in two.

Guadalupe whispers in his ear, "Next time I catch you with that junkie face, I'll have your nuts cooked. Clear? *Don't touch that shit at work.* And clean that fucking nose. There's green shit dripping. Now, bring me a bottle of white wine, immediately, and make me taste the tits of that bitch working for you. Today I want something special."

Cooking a waitress? Dorian cannot refuse his boss's order; that man is capable of breaking in the kitchen, opening fire, and blowing it all up. It would not be the first time.

The chef calls Jeanne right away, talks to her while looking at her tits. Expendable meat. "*You, come with me.* Help me fetch some bottles in the cellar. *Elsie, you fill in for her here for a few minutes.*"

Jeanne descends the stair. Dorian follows her, sweating, one of his knives ready. VG-16X titanium steel foil, folded and twisted thirty-two times: a razor.

Dorian hopes the noises of the kitchen will cover the bitch's cries, but he will have to be quick. He spits his last words: "Look down there. I need two bottles of Romanee. Lower, behind those."

Jeanne leans forward through the thermolite shelves, dust on her fingers, red knees scratching against the floor. Dorian waits for the right moment and plunges his brand new Kai into her stretched back. *Once, twice.* Her flesh is soft. The blade sinks with ease.

Jeanne screams. She manages to break free and collapses upon him. The bitch is full of blood.

They fight on the floor. Dorian tries to silence her by putting a hand over her damned mouth. Jeanne bites him, scratches his face. The bitch tries to take the stairs to escape.

Third slash, on the right side of her neck. Solid. Precise. Finally, Jeanne flops on the ground. A kick in her side. *No reaction.* Dead. Dorian wipes his bloodied face with his apron. The wounds burn. He'll have to go up to the kitchen to fetch more knives.

A voice from above: "Dorian, everything alright? Do you guys need a hand?"

It is that maniac Anton, his *sous-chef.* He thinks Dorian is screwing the busty broad.

"Mind your own fucking business and get back to work!"

He finishes cleaning himself, trying to summon back an acceptable look, and then a bottle explodes against his head.

Damn whore, how long do you take to croak, eh?

Jeanne manages to stand, her tits – flooded with blood and wine – dripping. A strange alchemic rain. The girl staggers, has a hard time breathing. She leans on the scaffolding, throws up blood. *Soutine's flayed ox*. The blue backdrop of the walls, orange and red blood. Perfect chiaroscuro.

Dorian's head hurts. Glass shards have pierced his scalp; the chef is wearing a glittering crown.

Now you'll see, bitch.

The knife has flown away, who knows where. He has to tear that cow apart before it is too late. He has no choice, and flings himself again on Jeanne. He grabs her hair and smashes her head against the shelf, each strike a thought: *Bitch! Die! Die! Fuck!*

At last, Jeanne seems to shut down for good. Soft brain jelly soils Dorian's fingers.

True murderer's fingers, now.

He drags Jeanne behind the shelf of the dessert wines. He opens a bottle of white wine, quickly washes himself. He throws the stained apron away, puts on his white jacket inside-out. He gets back up to the kitchen because he needs more knives. His quivering hands are white, Jeanne's scratches lighting them up in bright red. Stripes and contrasts. He collects his tools, descends to the cellar to work on Jeanne's body.

Quiet, take your time, everything is working out …

He begins carving her right breast, manages to excise it with ease. Little blood, a simpler and cleaner process. Let's proceed. He moves to her left breast, sweat making his eyes sting; it is not a very good cut, so he will have to fix it while it cooks. He puts the meat in the tray, discards the stringy tissues. Better to remove the nipples and areolas as well.

Jeanne's chest looks like a mine of madness, just opened: two shafts.

A pan full of Jeanne; in the kitchen, nobody notices. Flour, juniper leaves, salt, and a free flame. Cooking begins.

Dorian moves to the dressing table, dishes the food, a spoonful of onion mustard and two slices of tomato, red and green.

Then, all of his voice comes quickly out of the silence: "Elsie, *quick*, table 4!"

THE DIAMETER OF THE BOUNDARY
नरक

THE MOON, SAMGHATA

Kiki, wet heart, is taken to the fourth floor underground. Mutations Area, *Samghata*. Another layer of that cursed hive. *Who knows what is there below still.*

THUMP! The elevator reaches its destination.

The armed escort leads Kiki toward her new cell. Earth and South Paris 5 are very far, by now. Stains in space, big and small. Her womb throbs, *memory of her labor.* Tissues taut. Maximilian, her abandoned, devoured son ... One of the many illusions and depravations of Naraka, of Sibel's, Queen Bee in the hive.

As Kiki walks, two floors above her a psychopathic priest is preaching to an audience of ghosts: "*There was a great famine in Samaria, as the siege was becoming harder ... 'Help me, my Lord, o King,' cried a woman, while the King of Israel was passing by on the wall ... And the King asked to her, 'What is the matter with you?' She answered, 'This woman said to me:* Give me your son: let's eat him today. We'll eat mine tomorrow. *So we boiled my son and ate him. And the next day I said to her:* Give your son, now, so we may eat him. *But she had hidden her son.' When the King heard these words, he tore his clothes ...*"

The human mind possesses formidable dams, containment and isolation places for pain, for knife-holding memories. Inside Kiki's body, thick concentric walls begin to rise, an imaginary fortress. A maximum security jail for bastard thoughts.

The structure is still under construction, incomplete. Kiki still lacks bulkheads, and her desperate tongue searches for small atoms of Maximilian stuck between her teeth. Pieces of flesh, of her *own* flesh. The pliers, the burners, the sequence of madness that she lived in Sibel's Kalasutra. The sadistic private reign of that whore.

The imaginary fortress keeps taking shape, spreading. The concentric circles hold the core, isolating it from all the rest. Under construction. Must be done before Kiki may give birth to the truth, may be forced to look at it in the eye, dirty and bloodied.

Having eaten her son's tender meat.

Two horrible, steel-scaled guardians protect the core from unwanted visits, from the flashbacks of memory, from anarchic dreams – the most dangerous. Kiki starts to forget, the experience in Kalasutra sinking deep into the thick blue fog. Margins, small corners remain free. Tips. Slants that cannot reconstruct the entire architecture of what happened, that Warholian stationary skyscraper, documented for days under the maneuvers of the environment.

The first thing we see in the morning from our window. That thing, so big, too big. It devours every day.

The core is sealed.

Eat and survive, Kiki's motto.

Her cuirass gets its shine back.

Mutations Area is much smaller than the standard detention area, *the human farm*. Here, the cells lack interactive monitors; the doors hide the prisoners. Blows, screams and noises less than human mark the inhabited rooms from the empty ones.

Bugs, stroking their legs.

Wide, rectangular halls break the rows of cells, equipped with scientific gear. New Moon shining tech. One of those has its door open, reminiscent of a huge birthing room. Spaces, equipment, sizes ... all out of scale for human needs.

The open door?

Noises inside. The guards halt. Two of them go in with their weapons leveled. One stays back with Kiki.

What the fuck is happening?

Behind a metal table, a red grin appears, a known face with a bloodied mouth. The man gets up slowly, shows his full figure. In his hands is something dark red and silver grey: a veiny chunk of meat from which a tube, a white umbilical, juts out.

Something he doesn't want to let go of ...

"Don't shoot, *holy fuck*, don't shoot!"

The man's voice bounces against the white, slippery walls.

Kiki's limbic system projects pictures: her first detention in Naraka, the reek of shit and rotten flowers and Amorphophallus outgrowth of her cellmate, Jorge Vallejo Corona, the Placenta Eater. *Shit, it's him.* Scum is die-hard.

The guards approach him. Jorge keeps backing. He is protecting his special meal. He certainly doesn't fear the mouths of those two MK56 Kombats pointed at him.

Like a beast, he snarls from a corner, "*This shit is mine!*"

Something is moving in the Eater's eyes. A larva of archetypical drives spreads his wings. *Placentofagia.* Jorge doesn't give a damn about the new company and sinks his teeth into the disk-shaped chunk of meat. He devours a temporary organ, a dynamo of energies and exchanges, an animal placenta, livid, still fresh, rich in iron and hormones.

He cannot use, as his usual, ginger, lemon, and chili peppers. *One-legged philosophies.* In Samghata, you have to make do. Before they take you back to your cell.

"How the fuck did you get here? Fucking psycho!"

The two guards frame each other's eyes, thinking of what to do. The brawnier one decides for both of them: "Just kill the bastard. I feel sick just looking at him. Hey, shithead!"

The two MK56 begin singing, a metallic sliding rhythm. But that motherfucker is still moving. He stretches toward the cow placenta, dragging himself on the floor. He licks it, his eyes cursed and dreamy, and sinks his teeth in again. He cannot avoid it. Months of withdrawal.

A second song of bullets.

Jorge shudders, as though they had inserted a high voltage cable into his ass, and he grins. His red face crashes into the remains of the meal. He looks toward the door, recognizes Kiki.

"Hi, slut! They got you again, eh?"

Last burst.

The Placenta Eater croaks next to his placenta, sitting upright, his neck bent forward, toward a fantasy world. They drag him by the legs to his cell as Kiki watches. A bend swallows everything. The greenish floor of the tunnel tones down the Marsala wine trail of blood, twenty centimeters wide, obliquely traced by Jorge's corpse. Alien chromatisms of Bacon's *Figure with Meat*, of the face of death, leans out over the diameter of the boundary.

Handsome as the random encounter of a sewing machine and an umbrella on a dissecting table!

TEMPLO MAYOR
नरक

THE MOON, SAMGHATA

Mutations Area.

Kiki's cuirass now reflects shadows and lights again. *Eat and survive*, the usual priority. Night of images and telluric dreams in Samghata, green bile of Naraka.

Still alive, after all. Kiki falls asleep on the iron bed of her cell, a slingshot toward transverse worlds. Her subconscious pierces the heavy steel door, which has the shape and tip of a Tenoch obsidian bullet.

Bugs flee from the cell. Around Kiki's body, a Mesoamerican vegetation suddenly grows. Roses of flesh, and great agaves burst into bloom. Anacardium apples with eyes and soul. The floor sprawls, flexible matter and background. It becomes a wide lake.

Kiki's bed is now a small island, rising a hundred meters: Templo Mayor at Tenochtitlan. Bridges and embankments, a long road to dry land. Thoughts carried on red canoes.

Memories of three hundred thousand tumbling souls.

The dismal drum of Huichilobos sounded again, accompanied by conches, horns, and instruments like trumpets. It was a dreadful sound, and when we looked at the tall pyramid from which it came, we saw our comrades, captured in the defeat of Cortés, dragged up the steps to be offered in sacrifice. When they had been carried to a small platform in front of the shrine, where their accursed idols were laid, we saw the priests sticking plumes on the heads of many of the prisoners; and then they made them dance, with a sort of fan in their hands, in front of Huichilobos. Finally, the priests laid them down on their backs on the sacrificial stone and, ripping open their chests, they pulled out their palpitating hearts, which they offered to the idols before them. And then they kicked the corpses down the steps, and the Indian butchers waiting below cut off arms and feet, and flayed the skin off their faces, and worked it afterwards like leather for gloves, with their beards still on, and they kept those for the festivals when they celebrated drunken orgies, while they offered to their idols their hearts and blood, and ate the flesh of their arms and legs.

Kiki opens her eyes. Four butcher priests are squeezing her arms and legs. Statues are watching the scene, flexing their backs and surrounding the moment. Mictlantecuhtli reeks of afterlife. Xolotl snarls with his dog head. The cell bed is gone. Kiki's skin sticks to a low, smooth stone. A small, ancient skycar going who knows where.

The fifth priest wears Big Blue's face skin. His real face emerges in slivers painted green, red, and blue. He raises the obsidian dagger to the sky. *Shouts.*

Psychedelic subconscious, motherfucker.

Big Blue comes back to visit even in her wettest dreams. It was not enough, placing a bullet in his forehead, seeing his remains chewed on by the metal butler's electronic teeth. That prototype.

A professional killer's dreams.

The obsidian dagger glints, then it plunges down onto the woman's chest. A meteorite falling in the middle of a red ocean, raising waves and thin shots of blood.

The cut runs vertically down her body, toward her cunt. Her skin gives easily. The zipper opens. Are they going to tear out her heart? Her uterus?

Kiki looks at the priest, who searches for something in her belly. He rummages, shifting organs, reaching inside her with an arm, copiously sweating.

What the fuck is he searching for?

Screams are standing by, waiting for the event.

Here it is, the treasure hidden inside of Kiki ...

The man shows to the crowd a bloodstained fetus, dark, not very human yet. Minuscule arms and legs, disproportionate skull, impossible gills, reptile eyes. Maximilian, *it's him.* Kiki, ripped open, recognizes her abandoned son, eaten eight years later in the white rooms of Kalasutra.

The priest wants the microscopic heart. He drives his blade into the still-alien body. He finds the small throbbing stone, squeezes it between two fingers. He shows it to everybody. Cries of liberation. Kiki's body is thrown down the infinite steps of the Templo Mayor, where it tumbles down a thousand times. A few meters above, Maximilian's remains roll and bounce. They try to reach her challenging gravity. She spreads her arms to hold him. She cannot leave him again.

Kiki touches dirt and dust at the base of the pyramid, just before her son. Slaves rush to carry out the last work. They cut off the two heads and give them to the aristocrat who caught Kiki.

Sibel, *her* again, the great net of souls. Lady of Collapse.

Kiki's head – stuck on a wooden pike, in a long rack with the merry company of skulls and decaying faces – keeps thinking, understanding.

With a second pair of working eyes – favors of the subconscious – she attends to the preparation of the meat, and to the ritual feast of her body and of the tiny fetus.

Traditional Aztec recipe: a stew flavored with pepper, tomatoes, and ground lilies; chest and heart thrown to the animals of Sibel's royal zoo; morsels for the misshapen creatures of Samghata, the howling victims of the genetic mutation experiments.

When the fuck is this wrench ending?

Kiki's thoughts want to return to reality, to shut themselves inside the cuirass to forget.

I want to wake up!

Eat and survive. Leave it all behind so she can go on. *Get revenge.*

Naraka and Templo Mayor. Everything returns and will eventually find itself again somewhere in the big circle.

Curves with no end, which don't leave any hope for a route toward Infinity.

Monday, December 17th

The wind blew very hard during the night, from E.N.E., but there was not much sea, because this part of the coast is enclosed and sheltered by the island of Tortuga. The sailors were sent to fish with nets. They spent much time with the natives, who brought them certain arrows of the Canibales. They are made of reeds, with sharp tips of wood hardened by fire, and are very long. They showed them two men who lacked certain pieces of flesh on their bodies, hinting that the Canibales had eaten them by the mouthfuls.

MALDOROR RELOADED 2/4
नरक

You have to let your nails grow for fifteen days.

So exciting, tearing away the reader from his bed, from his fantasy. Brushing his forehead with your hand, moving hairs aside. Then, when he is least expecting it, after the deceits of a few pages, sinking your nails into his chest, not too deep, so he won't die.

It would be a pity, missing the spectacle of his misery.

Drinking at those wounds, from his crying, dazed body; nothing tastes as good as that blood, still warm, as those tears, bitter like salt.

Have you never tasted your blood, when you happened to nick a finger? *Good, right? So, if you are not disgusted by your tears and blood, trustingly feed on the tears and blood of your kin. Blindfold that man, that woman, while you rip open their palpitating flesh. Listen to their sublime screams. Finally, after stepping away, plunge again upon that body like an avalanche.* Mangle it with awareness. *Let the monster hidden in the womb be born. Let the seed of future ejaculate.*

Take photos of the collapse and hang the pictures, all the sequences.

So, do Good and Evil exist? Perhaps there is no difference. They are the same one thing through which we live in rage our impotence, the drive to destroy Infinity by the most meaningless and unfit means. Skyships, synthetic drugs, a eunuch God, the cannons of indifference – *you, how many of those have you armed? No, it cannot be. Or maybe, yes, it is better, that they are one thing … Otherwise, who would have broken the bones, ripped open the flesh you left behind?* Four-eyed nature. *An instinct, independent from thought, that of the eagle tearing its prey apart.*

Victims or executioners? A coin, two sides, eternally enlaced. The cloning of a single being, two thoughts, two mouths ripping open the same body. Then, dear reader, you are ripping me open, *just now, and you cannot stop your nails and teeth.*

I'll adorn my body with scented garlands, for this special occasion. We will suffer together. I, because I'm ripped; you, because you are ripping ... with my mouth attached to yours.

I want you to make it, in spite of yourself.

THE BUTCHER'S SHOP
नरक

Morning. The cell doors of the Mutations Area clank open.

An alarm whistles on and off. The inmates must go out.

Kiki comes back from her absurd trip to Mexico, riding her dreamlike pterodactyl that carried her to the summit of Templo Mayor. She does not know this part of the Naraka hive; she does not know what to expect. The name, Mutations Area, promises nothing good. Anyway, she is finally going to meet the other *guests*.

Prisoners in a row, in front of their cells. The guards are already there, with their scanners and statistic systems. A ritual she knows well, the same as the standard detention area two floors above. But here, it is not about who will end up in the Slicer.

Kiki looks around, tries not to be noticed; she knows that is dangerous. The usual line of dirty feet, then, *shit*, a pair of hooves fused with human legs. She raises her eyes again to find large and small outlines, some humanlike, others warped by genetic delirium. More than a cell system, Samghata seems a cursed molecular barn.

Horrible creatures: mutations, men with bovine parts, impossible cows with thin human skin. At the end of the tunnel, Kiki glimpses a woman walking in circles on four alien paws, and with an enormously swollen belly and four human breasts shuffling on the floor. She seems pregnant. She licks the ground with an appalling cow tongue deforming her still-normal mouth.

Normal?

It is not easy to sort out human from animal.

What is her predominant normality, *by now?*

More creatures come out of their cells, bucking against the walls, moaning with unfathomable sounds. Advanced mutation stages. The jailers are forced to enter those cells and execute off-standard checkups. They are equipped with neurowhips and magnetic immobilizers. Waiting her turn, Kiki hears the noise of a burst of bullets. One of the unknown creatures must have been shredded. The jailer comes out of the cell cursing, his uniform covered in blood.

Someone, or something, has gone out of control.

At another cell, two jailers pull at steel ropes, trying to tug out a prisoner. Dismal moans, distortion of human thoughts and primal throats. They cannot do it, so they use the immobilizer and, at last, manage to drag out the body. *Huge.* Sort of an ox with powerful muscles, a human neck, hind legs, and double exposed spinal cords. It is dragged away, vanishing behind the first bend of the tunnel.

Holy shit! Human farm, my ass. Here they're turning us into some shitty new cows.

Much, much more meat ...

Kiki's blood stops, begins flowing backward. The cool of the professional killer wavers. *Becoming one of the horrible creatures.* Genes blended into disgusting conglomerates. Who knows if awareness stays during or *after* the mutation into rearing animal ...

The jailers begin dealing with the prisoners in the first stages. Body scanning. A second holographic tattoo. This time, it is not about categorizing meat quality, but mutation opportunities and DNA load flexibility.

Kiki is tattooed with the code CP/IC – *Complete/Incomplete.*

Other inmates with the same code, others with different ones: HD – *Hybrid,* or RJ – *Rejection,* or NM – *No Mutation.* RJs and NMs are taken back up two floors. They will end up in the Slicer, *100% human meat.* They will be processed, will stay in the warehouse for weeks, spread in several cans branded *Maison des Anges* before being loaded on a freightbot and shipped to destinations on Earth. Depending on the processing and synthetic flavors, the label will be printed with *chicken* or *pork,* from selected farms. Oxygen for the empty storerooms of the *boutiques de viande.*

In some independent cities and countries, the employment of human meat from detention centers has already been legalized. In these cases, the prisoners' meat is packaged in unbranded, much bigger vacuum-sealed blisters. The same happens for wealthy private citizens who buy directly from New Moon.

New Moon Corporation, backbone of the new anti-collapse system for Earth, is world leader in this new widespread commerce. New space detention and human farming centers are already under construction with the official – or less – support of several military governments. Millions of meat packages. The countdown for the collapse of Earth has only been slowed down. But someone will have time to make enough money to build themselves a new fucking planet.

CP/IC.

Kiki watches her electronic tattoo while they take her back to her cell. She will stay where Sibel threw her: in Samghata.

She thinks she will have to escape again, before becoming a pregnant cow and giving birth to a calf with two heads and nine testicles. Maybe one of his faces will look like Guadalupe's hippo snout.

More cries, moans.

Someone slips a sheet of paper under the door of Kiki's cell, folded in two. She immediately grabs it. Perhaps someone has a plan to break out.

She unfolds a strange picture. It looks like a butcher's shop, an ancient painting. Flayed sides of beef hang from the ceiling, and a man dressed in white, maybe the owner, weighs a piece of meat, appreciating its quality. And maybe the coin he is going to earn out from it. On a worktable, some steaks. Another man, kneeling on the floor, holds a big knife, seems to be working on the head of an animal. A guard, armed with a spear, watches the operations, their commerce. The picture is front view, bidimensional, realistic. No distortion. Impossible to find vanishing points, escape routes for both eye and interpretation. It's a static snap-shot of another prison.

What does this shit mean? Are they fucking with me?

Kiki crumples the picture and tosses it against the steel door. She sits on that cold floor and gathers her legs in her arms.

You've got to think fast, Kiki.

The odd present, an image of the *Butcher's Shop* by Annibale Caracci, is from Sibel.

Art and sadism, a wonderful couple.

Sibel keeps rubbing her nipples in her Kalasutra, thinking about what a nice, fat cow Kiki could become, the whore who managed to escape from Naraka.

The struggle between what one might call Uncreated and the Creature – illustrated by the permanent contradiction of human and his Taboo. Absorption of the sacred enemy. To transform him into totem. However, only pure elites managed to realize carnal anthropophagy, which carries in itself the highest meaning of life and avoids all the ills identified by Freud, the ills of catechism. Low anthropophagy agglomerated into the sins of catechism – envy, usury, calumny, murder. Plague of the so-called cultured and Christianized peoples, it is against it we are acting. Anthropophagi.

THE TEST
नरक

"Let me see what you can do."

Just another workday for Guadalupe. Whore selection for Le Sphinx Tatoué.

Every professional slut, before beginning her service at the whorehouse, must go through him – except the wretched disposables; those are hauled in by Millander, Charon for that second-tier raw material. The streets of that cancer-district are very good rearing grounds, *en plein air* markets to stock up. Treated whores, who have to work for a day and then go back – in pieces or with their throats ripped – are among the trash of those filthy alleys. When they are lucky.

Their final destination is often a tray of the brothel restaurant, at least the edible parts, to be digested by wealthy stomachs of customers making reservations for specific cuts, as well as gourmet and heretic collectors.

"You know how to suck, you little slut ..."

Guadalupe is lying on a large, elegant bed in the private gallery. Eloise, wedged between his hippo legs, is doing her best to show that she deserves the job. Her overheating jaws, her neck, and mouth, quickly go back and forth.

"What a frenzy ... Okay, okay ... now stop. I want to try your pretty little ass ..."

Guadalupe grabs her hair. He sets her kneeling on the edge of the bed. His fingers and rings print themselves in Eloise's soft back. Velvet and rust contrasts.

The man, fat demiurge, begins commanding: "Down with that fucking back! Good, like that. Now, don't piss me off and shut up ..."

Guadalupe closely studies the woman's ass, a lovely shape. Tasty. It looks already properly used, which is even better. They have no use for timid little sluts at the Sphinx.

He gears up with a cylindrical dilitium dilator.

Eloise moans.

Guadalupe soon moves to other calibers, growing bigger.

"Let's see if you can take this, too ... *good girl* ..."

Guadalupe impales Eloise with the last, huge cylinder, which is equipped with a pneumatic pump capable of throwing out several atmospheres. Eloise whines, louder and louder. The item is too big even for a *well-worked* ass like hers. When Guadalupe turns on the pump, scorching compressed air bursts down to her guts, into the tail of her soul.

This time, tearing cries fill the room.

"I told you not to piss me off! Take it all, and see that you like it, too ..."

Eloise pretends she is coming, humors the boss. The mattress under her face is soaked with silent tears and pus of dreams. At last, Guadalupe stops, pulls out the dilator.

The door opens. Someone enters the room.

Eloise, obedient, keeps her eyes forward, leaves her ass at the mercy of the events.

Guadalupe roars again, "Turn around and spread your thighs. Now you must look in the face who's banging you ..."

Eloise's red eyes fill with a heinous sight. A man pulls his pants down, his skin appearing rotten. A fucking zombie held together by the cartilages of testosterone. Eloise holds back her nausea, and her retching.

"Gerard is one of our best customers. He suffers from a weird skin condition. A gluttonous son of a bitch ... He binged on uncertified human meat. You know, that prion thing ..."

The man flings himself at Eloise, begins licking her body, that so-perfect skin rubbing against his, which is harsh, with sores everywhere. A volcano and its lava. Gerard penetrates her with all his strength. He bleeds; her body collects and absorbs everything, always obedient.

Eloise, a white canvas.

The tongue in her mouth, thick and acidic.

Gerard stops a moment to let her know he is about to come inside her, that now she must fully spread her legs to receive him, *entirely.*

Guadalupe supervises with a satisfied look. He brushes wet

lips with his thumb.

"*Be a good girl, bitch* ... Gerard is very contagious. We have a lot of customers like him. See that you enjoy it... the fuck of your life ..."

Eloise can no longer take it; she is too disgusted.

She pushes the man away from her legs.

Guadalupe turns red with fury. A mighty storm is coming. He mutters, "Forgive me, Gerard. I'll have another room ready for you right away, with one of our best sluts. You can go. I'll deal with this two-bit trollop."

Eloise cries, knees clutched in her arms, blonde hair dropping like a curtain. Polluted forever.

When Gerard is gone, Guadalupe snaps: "You really are shitty bitch. Who the fuck did send you, eh? You made me look like a dick. Have you got any idea who I am? *Don't you know?*"

He pulls a knife from his jacket heaped on the small sofa, one of those blades that command respect. Then he reveals to Eloise, "Now, I'm cutting your hands and feet off, so, if you want to work, you'll have to let even rats bang you. You'll see. You'll remember me."

Eloise leaps from the bed, tries to escape.

Guadalupe doesn't control his rage and drools. "Come here, whore. If you don't stop, you'll make things worse. *Come here!*"

Eloise starts throwing objects at him, everything she can reach: dilitium dilators, a vase, her purse. A heel hits Guadalupe dead center, cutting his forehead.

Blood. Blind rage.

The veins on his neck swell; they look like poisonous snakes ready to strike their prey. He sticks the knife into the wall with a firm blow, draws his pistol and opens fire without another thought. He empties the entire magazine into the frail shape of Eloise, who tries protecting herself with the palms of her hands and the light linens of blue silk.

The corner of the room turns into a fountain of blood.

Eloise deflates as she slowly slides against the wall. Her body brutalized by explosive bullets; a moon with a million craters. But Guadalupe is not finished. He frees his knife from the wall, approaches what is left of her on the floor. He spits on the glinting blade, spreads her legs and rips open her cunt, to the belly.

Finally, he concludes, "Trust my luck! Always these shitty, brainless bitches ..."

Millander blows in with two of his watchdogs. After Big Blue's death, the thin and slimy manager of the Sphinx Tatoué, and of many more sinister businesses in South Paris 5, is number two in the district. A few years ago, nobody would have ever bet a credit on this man. Now he is smartly dressed, wears a ludicrous blue, dilitium-plated hat, and he lives in a villa with a cunt-shaped swimming pool.

"What the fuck have you done ..." he says. "Jesus ... you made her into pulp!"

Guadalupe turns around, surprised. "Since when do you care so much about your whores? Have it all cleaned up, *and quick!*"

Millander's reply is sharp: "That slut was sent by Vidal. *Fuck, we're in deep shit!*"

Guadalupe's eyes light up; he has smelled the stink of a trap. Vidal, New Moon Corporation CEO. The Untouchable of the untouchables.

Guadalupe thrusts his gaze inside Millander's fetid soul. "Vidal? And what were you waiting for, to tell me that? But of course. *You really are a damn bastard. You, fucking tramp ... You really believe you can set someone like me up?*"

Millander backs off without answering.

"I'm going to explain it to him," Guadalupe mutters. "Don't worry. But before, I have a little handiwork to do. *I want to try your skin on ...*"

The hippo, his knife still bloodied, pounces on Millander, but a burst to the legs cripples him and Guadalupe rolls on the floor in pain. The watchdogs did their job.

Millander raises his voice, his *number one* voice: "*Stop, don't kill him!* Vidal will want him alive." And he goes on while kicking Guadalupe, "You, you *shitty fatso*, you'll see they're going to pay you a nice trip on the Moon, for this fuckup ... you'll reach your Kiki soon. *In Naraka.* I'll ask Sibel, *when she's done with you*, to send me a can of your meat ... *motherfucker special reserve!*"

Guadalupe bleeds. Unfortunately, he is still alive. He knows Naraka well. He knows that death, sometimes, is a preferential route, a privilege.

Millander framed him. That tramp used to eat the trash of his restaurants. That thin piece of shit sold his wife's body for a few credits, for a pork stew order. Important customers, immediate payment. Millander. Tramp Millander.

SPARKS
नरक

THE MOON, SAMGHATA

Underground night. Kiki cannot sleep. Shitty dreams, shitty wakefulness.

There is no difference.

In the tunnel, outside her cell, noises crawl: of dragged creatures, snapping neurowhips, voices and souls hanging between tatters of human conscience and animal muscles and fibers. *Conglomerates.* The delirium of DNA grease monkeys, of this surreal section of the Naraka hive. The slaughterhouse of Samghata keeps working. Ruminating awareness.

Sometimes, a few minutes of silence – even Hell has its shifts – but it doesn't last long.

Someone approaches Kiki's cell door. The lock mechanisms click.

My time has come.

Three shadow-faced jailers appear. They are armed with evil grins, full of white teeth, telescopic neurowhips, and magnetic immobilizers.

"We wanted to wish you a good night, bitch. Trust me, it's best for you if you just play along."

Their laughter blends with the other foul sounds polluting the tunnel. Already mutated creatures open their nostrils; they recognize the smell of rape. Bucking hooves. A rain of stones against the slippery cell walls. Tails quivering, together with the wings of bugs. Gases raising from the spoiled milk squirted on the floor. Stink of excrement.

Human barns. Almost human.

One of the jailers approaches Kiki, licking his upper lip.

"I'll take the ass. This time it's my turn to choose."

"Stay back!"

The neurowhip jolts her body. Electric discharges burn her skin, her spine jerking back and forth, which seems to expand

and then contract. An elevator of pain with many floors.

Electronic scratches.

The guard doesn't want to take chances. He will take that ass when the prisoner is down. Tamed. A professional killer, as her profile on his portable reader shows: you must tread carefully. His neurowhip strikes again, slicing the thick air of the cell. *Sparks.*

Kiki is on the floor, shaking. Squeezing her fists.

A satyr with a hard-on, the guard whispers, *"Are you ready, now, honey?* Now, put this dress on. Pretty, right? It belongs to the *bride of the whip.* Don't be dumb … down here, nobody notices one head more, or one less …"

He tosses to Kiki an elegant black dress with glittering sleeves, turns the whip back on and waits.

The alien sounds, the rebooting and reloading of that cursed tool, make Kiki start. Listening to those noises makes her skin burn, imagining its electric symphony. She knows more lashes would doom her to unconsciousness and to the mercy of those three men. She wouldn't come out of that alive.

She struggles to get up, then takes off the jail uniform and begins putting on the fucking dress. A bride of darkness, among the microscopic naves of six square meters.

Arousal grows and grows for the three men. The one with Samghata's *ius primae noctis* watches Kiki's naked skin while her thighs lap at the cloth, her tits filling up the empty, dead shapes.

"Shit, you're really hot!" The satyr doesn't hold back. "A pity they're making a fucking *cow for slaughter* out of you. Maybe we're keeping you as a toy for a few days. A pastime, you know, a little bend to the rules. *Don't we have a fucking right to it?* They gave us the shittiest of all tasks here …"

The other two jailers nod. They begin touching between their legs. The shorter one, a viper with a hissing voice, complains, "Shit, Messier! You get all the hot ones. How the fuck does this turnover thing work?"

Messier grabs the man's lapel. *"Don't break my balls …* You'll do her tomorrow. We'll leave you all alone with her if you like. If you're so hard tonight, you're welcome to screw her. *After* I've worked on her alright, she'll be all yours. *No problem there, right, man?* Don't worry, I'm only having her ass, tonight."

Kiki takes advantage of their exchange, collects the few strengths she has remaining, and kicks the graveyard-shift satyr in the balls.

The man bends, his choked voice rustling, "*Fucking whore! My nuts … You'll pay for that …*"

His neurowhip drops. Now he holds something very different in his hands.

Just a few seconds, sure … many if you are trained.

Kiki picks up the fallen whip, begins to flail it against the three surprised men with an array of sparks. One of the jailers manages to stand, his face all striped. He draws his magnetic immobilizer from his belt. A blue discharge connects its two poles. He tries to reach Kiki's neck, stretching ahead. Kiki easily dodges, and a well-directed whiplash turns off the man's fury; he passes out, his gaze frozen on his navel.

Kiki keeps striking the three bodies until her arms become heavy; they produce a lot of sparks.

She grabs one of their pistols and opens fire. Three bullets, three easy hits. Outworlds 31, 32, and 33.

She goes out in the tunnel, looks around.

You've got to think fast, Kiki. Fast.

The alarm is already blaring; the satyr must have triggered it after losing his balls.

Galloping troops. A ballet of combat boots and angry voices.

Kiki's eyes scan the environment. They nail themselves to a round opening, low on the wall, just before the bend of the main tunnel.

What the fuck is that? She manages to unlock the hatch by turning a small key, already in position; she leans her head in. *Access to a maintenance system?* After a few meters, the passage seems to lead into a bigger metallic duct. *Maybe I can squeeze in. I've got no choice. No time.*

She stretches her muscles, squeezes into that opening, makes it by a hair's breadth. She closes the hatch behind her.

The pistol is a short vanguard, as Kiki crawls toward the unknown.

RUE MERCADER
नरक

A child follows me, reaches me
an ocean sways in his eyes.
He tells me his parents are dead,
then he runs away.
I chase him along the dirty roads of South Paris 5
along the sidewalks of generations
I shout his name, that cursed name
people come out of the shops, pieces of souls
with threatening brooms and pistols
but the children jump with joy at that name
they join me
we chase the child, shout his name
people curse us.

Finally, the child falls close to us
he gets up again, staggering, hears our voices
shouting his name.
Faster than us, troops come
a fury of mothers and fathers
they sink their teeth in his brains.

I invoke the angels of my generation
on the roofs, in the alleys, in the brothels
under the trash and the empty bottles of the past
but nobody stops that army
nibbling at the child's bones.
We arrive, his little body mangled
I shout his name for the last time: Beauty
BEAUTY! BEAUTY! BEAUTY!

EARTH, SOUTH PARIS 5

Rue Mercader.

Tramp Millander gets out of his roadcar, puts on his ludicrous hat. Some accidents should not happen, not in *his* district. His gaunt face points right to Virgile, the muscle he left to watch the door of Doriane's home. Doriane, his personal whore.

How would that hippo Guadalupe have acted?

It was time to raise his voice. True Number One voice.

"How the fuck did it happen? Were you sleeping, fucking? Say something."

Millander rummages in his pockets, ignoring the muscle in front of him.

"I didn't move from here," Virgile stammers, in a cold sweat. "I didn't see anyone going in. It's the truth." He knows you pay with your head for something like that.

Guadalupe would have shoved a dynamite stick up his ass and would have had him stewed for dinner, but Virgile doesn't know what's going through the frail Millander's head, though, as his new boss listens to him moving his tongue like an eel.

Then he spits out what he has to say: "Good, you did your fucking job. This is for you."

Millander, the Tramp, is known for buying respect.

Virgile's breath comes back. He grins, offers his hand.

Millander drops something onto his palm, something that shines under the sun, even the sick sun of South Paris 5.

Gold? No, even better: a small piece of dilitium! Shit, so it's true, the tramp is a gentleman. My lucky day …

Virgile looks closely at the dilitium chunk, until his nose touches it. He does not understand. Its shape is odd. *What the fuck is it?*

"I always pay my men well. You know that, right?" Millander goes on: "This is your fucking severance pay. A tooth of that bitch, your wife; to tear it away, they had to smash up her face. You treat your bitches well, do you? If she recovers, you'll have to bang her with your eyes closed, if you want to be hard enough … Now, *swallow that fucking tooth.* And if you care about your head, don't let me see you again."

Virgile swallows the dilitium tooth without blinking, holds back the staggering emotions in his apish brain. Then he leaves on foot. He is wearing an expensive suit, oversized. He vanishes behind a heap of garbage. Going back to where he came from.

Millander approaches the scene, trying to keep his shoes clean. His Doriane is sprawling in the middle of the street. Slaughtered and thrown out the window of the facing building. One of Millander's buildings, of course. Twenty meters without wings. Many, too many. People are gathered in a circle around her.

What would Guadalupe have done?

His men are watching, sizing him up.

An untouchable's bitch reduced like that is bad publicity.

Millander coldly approaches Doriane's body, her profile staring at the door of an abyss. Now, she will have to knock. Her brain is leaving her beautiful, well-proportioned head, slipping, giving in to the incline of the street; a thin, yellowish thread stretches, more and more. Her right ear glints, flashing at the passage of clouds. A cunt-shaped earring. One of his presents to her.

He stands again, looks around. He motions one of his men to join him.

Another trained muscle approaches, looking breathless. Millander takes him aside, passing an arm behind his wide back. Asks him for a gun.

His voice, well synchronized with that of the weapon, is perfectly heard by everybody: "*What the fuck are you looking at? Piss off, you shits! Go! Go!*"

Millander shoots into the crowd. They disband, someone staying on the ground. Moans, curses.

One of Millander's men pulls up in a roadcar. *Better to beat it now, boss.* Another deals with Doriane's body; he grabs her feet and drags her away, a shoe under his armpit.

But the Tramp wants to make an exit. Nobody must fuck with him ever again.

Nobody touches my stuff ...

He opens the car door, shoots his driver in the face, and pushes him out of the cabin. On the driver's seat, he accelerates, going in a circle. He passes over the curb, crushing the bones of the crippled voyeurs. An arm, cut right off, bounces on the windshield.

Would Guadalupe have done better?

Millander vanishes with all his army of apes.
People reappear at the windows.
A shopkeeper pours hot water on the curb.
The blood slowly trickles away.

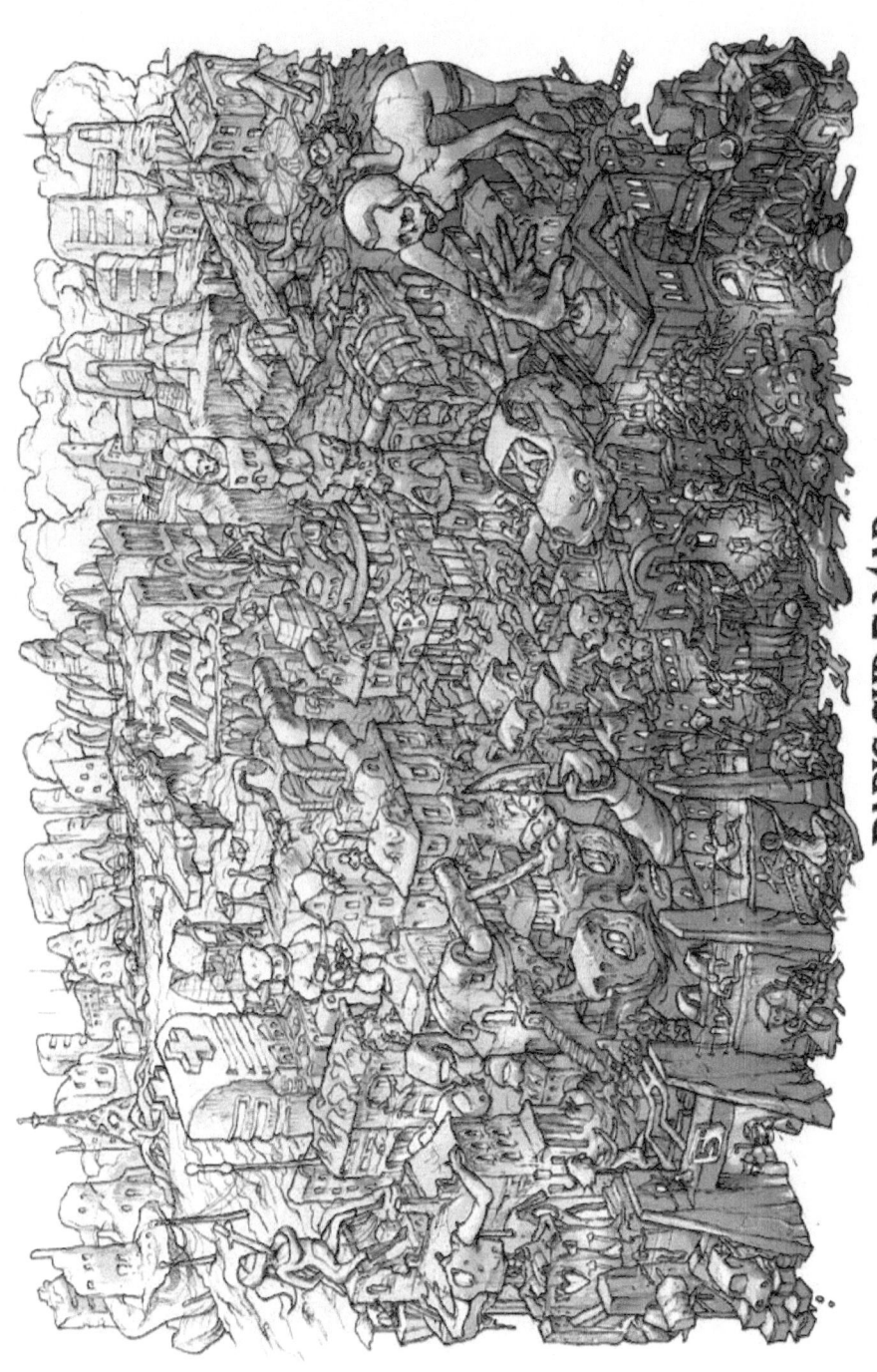

PARIS SUD S MAP

THE LAMENT OF THE BEAST
नरक

THE MOON, SAMGHATA

Kiki keeps crawling under the skin of Hell, like a bug trying to reach its underground lair. Finally, she enters the large metallic duct.

It's easier here.

The voices in the Mutations Area rooms become distant, but they won't take too long to find her. The duct goes on straight for a while; she must discover where it leads. Her trip in the steel burrow continues. Elbows, knees, her ass dancing and pushing. Light coming in through narrow, rectangular openings every ten meters.

Kiki reaches a grate carved in the ceiling of a big room.

She stops, peering through the horizontal slits.

An unexpected scene.

The hippo, that bastard Guadalupe, of all people, is tied to a strange machine with five or six jailers keeping him at gunpoint, while Sibel, the Queen Bee, caresses his hair.

How the fuck did he end up here? And what's Sibel doing out of her Kalasutra?

Kiki shifts for a better look: now she can enjoy the taut face of that motherfucker. A perfect shot. *Zoom in on the hippo.*

Blasphemies; the hippo is really pissed. Sibel steps away, showing him her ass, then raises an arm with some centimeters of her blue dress lifting with it. A signal. The machine turns on. A hypnotic sequence of LEDs.

Guadalupe seems to be nailed to a cross. His arms are spread horizontally with two symmetrical steel arcs above them. His legs are splayed, and a transparent probe is shoved into his navel. His chest heaves with impatience.

A living sculpture, Big Blue would say. Title: *Mutation*, or more direct: *And now you're screwed.*

Kiki smiles. This time it is the bastard's turn to pay the check.

"*Stop this shit right now!*" Guadalupe's voice rises to the ceiling, tinnily bouncing into the duct. "Vidal must deal with Millander, not with me. That slimy tramp fucked you, too ... *Not me, fuck! Not this ... Listen to me!*"

Sibel frees her tits; she lets them ease softly into the hands of gravity, begins rubbing her nipples. Fresh blood, ready to squirt. The chemicals of terror make all physiological fluids explode, the invisible landing of death. A sure orgasm for the Queen Bee.

Matrixes of needles emerge from the two arcs over Guadalupe's arms. They turn and lower toward his swollen veins, toward muscles that spasm to free themselves from the steel grasp. Guadalupe watches the simultaneous descent of the two matrixes; right, left. Repeatedly. His wrists twist until they almost snap. *No, shit, no!* Then ... the blackout.

His gaze raises to the ceiling, blank and empty. For a moment, Kiki imagines she has crossed the bastard's eyes. She likes to think she has glimpsed a stain of fear. A crumble, at least, in front of the Abyss. She had never seen fear in Guadalupe's eyes before. Nobody else on Earth ever had

His arms are pierced, and the needles ejaculate a green liquid into Guadalupe's blood. The probe begins pumping something thick and jelly-like into his navel. Guadalupe is immediately intubated. The machine monitors start showing graphics, numbers, the hologram of a double-helix structure with which the operators interact with perblix gloves.

Kiki cannot see clearly. The voices in the room are confusing, overlapping hostile terms like *supercoil, bond, primer, restriction enzymes, proteome.*

Guadalupe's body swells, begins warping. Some tissues burst. His skin stretches as new masses seem to be born, to be awakened, creating their own impossible place. The operators working on the DNA hologram step aside, discussing amongst themselves. More fragments, incomprehensible words of that arcane process: "*Wrong sequencing, sub-bonder activation, now!*" It looks like something has gone off-course.

Kiki leans for a better look, but Sibel is out of view. She can only make out her legs, and fingers slipping under the panties to penetrate her cunt. When the blue dress goes back to its place, Sibel goes away.

Guadalupe changes rapidly: that sort of cross to which he is nailed can no longer hold his new weight, his different size; the small bridges break and fall off; the probe comes out of his body, vomiting a rain of jelly.

The operators rush out of the room, the last one pushing a red button on the wall. An alarm blares. Kiki covers her ears with her hands.

The framework gives and Guadalupe's body slips to the floor.

He is still moving: *he is still alive.*

His arms are fused with his chest, which evolves into a huge mass of flesh. His face is unrecognizable, his jaw completely dislocated, a deep crack splitting the skull in two.

The creature *moans.* A primal, animal cry, together with the outburst of his excrement.

Kiki watches the horror; she cannot avert her eyes.

Samghata manifests itself in all its abomination.

She will end up like that, too, if she cannot manage to escape from that Hell … from that cursed Hive of bottomless hells.

The door of the room opens again and two black-suited men appear, armed with burners and tewkler conduits. They approach the creature and open the thermovalves. The blue tongues of the flames point on that disgusting body, which begins to fry. The stomach continues dilating while a dark coat of fur begins covering it. The guards are forced to use their laser carvers to rip open the flesh in several places. The lament of the beast makes the panoramic crystals vibrate.

Blood shoots onto Kiki's face, whirlpooling up through the grate.

Guadalupe explodes, erupting unknown muscle masses still in formation. The floor is littered with limbs, jelly, dark blood, his dilitium rings. Intestine wraps around a support biobox like an anaconda.

Silence.

Kiki resumes crawling in her metallic duct, looking for a way out. She thinks it would be better shooting herself in the mouth rather than being caught again. Before turning into a molecular cow, if the mutation works out right, *and supplying to them a couple hundred kilos of meat.*

19 Metros Cuadrados
नरक

Second floor underground.

Jesus Vila Dilmé. Serial killer, 23 outworlds. Called *19 metros cuadrados*, after the size of the garage where he butchered his victims, before being captured and thrown into Naraka. The same haul of scum as Kiki's.

His cell door opens, pressure mechanisms coming off. Three jailers enter the fetid space, armed to their teeth. The first one, protected by a see-through mulglass shield, harshly orders, "Out! We must take a walk."

Vila Dilmé sits on his cot. He stares at the facing wall and the steel, smooth and compact, too perfect, no distractions. He doesn't seem to notice the intrusion in his space, in his box.

"Do you hear me, asshole? Do we have to kick your ass out of here?"

The jailer's voice raises as he switches off the safety on his magnetic immobilizer, which starts vibrating. One of the many breaths of Naraka.

"You go fuck yourselves, all three of you pieces of shit, and close the door when you go."

Vila Dilmé's gaze is unmoving from the centimeter of steel drawing his attention, a scope for many thoughts.

"Listen to this dickhead ... Would you like breakfast in your room, too?" The jailers laugh and turn on their immobilizers, the sinusoidal blue curves materializing. Ready. "You asked for it ..."

Vila Dilmé springs up, his neck still hurting from the last blow. He looks at them for the first time. *Three douchebags in uniforms.* Their grins, now, hang badly on their faces.

The skinnier one reminds him of an Engineering student, a little shithead on whom he tried his last patented project of neuroinduction saw. That tool really worked fine, a true jewel. Chain in secondary dilitium, silicon oil, double neurolink horn probe, plugged into carotid and nape. Fusion, perfect sharing, crazy speed. Blood shooting on the ceiling and the walls of the garage, piercing them from side to side like a Kombat M67 assault. Short spears of blood flying like bullets. Mandatory to wear a plemar armor and an absorption neprom helmet.

Shit, how that student screamed!

Asynchronous pain, too-slow neurons, outdated. Just enough to allow the victim an observation of his own dissecting. Last cut: the head, full of useless empty tunnels. Shot by an imaginary cannon against an iron cabinet. A nice hole. Like the one on the wall of the garage behind it.

Vila Dilmé had to recover the engineer's head in his courtyard more than ten meters away.

Good times.

Now: three douchebags shouting orders to him, men similar to those he made piss themselves.

"So, have you decided? Don't make me waste energy, I have no time."

Vila Dilmé indifferently exits the cell, following the armed escort leading him along the main tunnel. He thinks he is ending up right into the Slicer. *Good!* He feels excited at the thought of trying new blades, advanced systems he has only heard about. Rotating, jointed pistils, very good technology to cut, to process human meat ...

He knows the Slicer is in the North Block, but the jailers change course and they push him into an elevator. An angry gesture. His deep voice dilates in that cramped space: "Where the fuck are you taking me?"

The small party descends to the third floor underground. Sibel's Kalasutra. The guards keep jerking him. The tunnels of the new area are much narrower and they spread out of a large circular chamber. Three women with kimonos fix red peonies in their hair. They stop, look at him with curiosity.

"*Hey, you treat yourselves well, here!* Instead of rec time, we get a nice screw?"

Vila Dilmé laughs out loud, showing a row of rotten teeth.

So many square meters of scented cunt down in this fucking place ...

A blow bends his knees, another comes to his head, leaving him flat on the white floor. For an instant he sees his tattooed face reflected: a snake wrapping itself around his right eye, its tail shaped like a steel chain, a saw.

Two kicks in the backbone reanimate him. Colors are back.

Vila Dilmé squints and puts things into focus. He makes out two feet sealed inside black shoes with steel stiletto heels. His neck bends backward, his gaze rising. An optic elevator. It flows along two perfect legs. Propping himself up on his palms, he manages to frame Sibel's sinuous outline. Blue eyes lowering on his fetus of awareness.

Vila Dilmé fastens invisible hooks to the woman's perfect, round atoms, to her harmonic assemblage, the aroma of vanilla and mango, of salt, the primal cloud forming itself and rising between her thighs.

"If I'm dreaming, *shit, don't wake me up!*" His lips move by themselves.

Sibel doesn't waste time: "Let's make a deal. You build me a neuroinduction saw, including all documentation, and I'll get you out of here. After the trials."

The man passes a hand around his neck. "And who the fuck are you to guarantee that?" he abruptly replies. "How can I know you're not slicing me up, like all the rest?"

Sibel smiles, then has him follow her to another room.

"Look here, jerk. If you like, I'll fix you right away, too. I have important guests very soon."

Ten armchairs surround a big round table. In the middle, three human bodies are set on a creolite platform: two women and a man. Their flesh quivers, their lungs blow; one of the women has her eyes fixed on the ceiling.

They are alive, but they cannot move.

Red patterns highlight their skin, bordering specific body parts. The man has two circles on the left side of his abdomen and shoulders. The women, belly down, have red lines tracing rectangular sections on both buttocks; on their thighs, five or six smaller circles are drawn.

A large dilitium dish for each armchair, linked by a mechanical, alloy arm, contain organs. Vila Dilmé recognizes parts of a human breast, some fibers of a long muscle, testicles, thin slices of meat wrapped around a mixture of ingredients.

Fruit, nuts, sage. A second mechanical arm completes each tasting station. Another tray is split in several sectors with a variety of dressings, spices and sauces, small dilitium tools, pulse dismemberers, dermotomes, portable burners.

Sibel approaches a station and turns on the holographic system to analyze the bodies in tasting. A rearing data sheet is visualized, together with meat quality, and an interactive wizard for the less experienced, walking the user through the carving operations.

"So, jerk, are you beginning to get it, or must I have your fingers and balls cut off to fix a fucking aperitif?" Sibel smiles.

He keeps watching that infernal tasting chamber; finally, puffing, he says he is available.

"All right, bitch. You'll have your fucking saw. I just need a lab where I can work. And ... a few subjects for the first tests."

He cannot hold back an erection.

MALDOROR RELOADED 3/4
नरक

I will tell you a dream. A grave, a firefly wandering about, big like a house.

Heinous yellow light. It is the collective conscience that keeps chasing me.

In front of me: a rotten wall, ruined. And writing:

Here lies a whore who died of love. Don't pray for her.

Flying atoms, green and blue, form a body. A naked woman stretches on my feet. She caresses my legs. Her mouth appears and disappears.

The cursed firefly whispers to me, 'Beware, you're the weaker, I'm the stronger one.*"*

In my muscles, an unknown force reverberates. I grab a large stone, raise it up to my chest. I run up the mountain, with that huge weight in my arms.

I reach the summit. Leave it all in the hands of gravity. The big rock falls, crushes the firefly. Conscience with three and a half pairs of legs. An unstable spider. *Its head sinks underground. The rock keeps bouncing until it plunges into the waters of a lake, digging an upside-down cone. The light of the damned firefly, finally, no longer shines.*

"Why did you do it?" the naked woman cries out. Her mouth *vanishes again.*

"I prefer you over her."

The woman stands, her green and blue nipples quivering. She has two holes in her ethereal body, through which stars pass. Through. *One in her chest, at the level of her heart, one between her thighs.*

"Only you, and the disgusting monsters crawling in those black abysses don't loathe me. You are good."

The whore vanishes. I kneel on the rotten wall, praying.

But conscience has a thousand forms. She does not quit.

Raging dogs break their chains, flee from the farms. They run through the country, hunting me. They look everywhere with wild concern, platoons of incandescent eyelids.

They raise their ears, their heads, swell up their terrible necks, and they begin howling against the stars of the North, against the stars in the East, in the South, West, against the cold air from which they fill their lungs, entering their red nostrils like ice, against the oblique-flying owls, against the toads, the mysteries they do not understand and make them slaves, against my smell, against the moon and Naraka, where a whore, Kiki, is the only medicine for the great collapse.

The friends of the graveyards pounce on me. They tear me apart. They eat me with what good teeth they have remaining. The wild animals do not dare join this meal of human meat. They run away. The cursed dogs, worn out after the long run, come too late, their tongue dangling.

Underground, I find my green and blue woman. She holds me tight.

RAISE YOUR GLASS
नरक

THE MOON, NARAKA: THE RED CAVE

"*And so Eve took that fruit for her, the thick lifeblood of Adam, penetrating places which seemed to be empty. Beyond Eden, the dimension of Man seeing and shaping All. Eden, the most ancient Naraka. The World Above, the true world, inaccessible. She was forbidden to swallow sperm, forbidden that form of* coitus interruptus. *But then Uriel appeared to Eve, Angel of Light. He showed her the way. The way out of the Eden underground. What a great teaching! He lowered himself down to her, even if he was wrapped in immortal life. Undressed of his wings, Uriel possessed the woman, ejaculating outside, into a golden chalice. So did Eve, gathering in her mouth, and then in the chalice, the fabrication of Adam's hybris. Angels can fly. They can move anywhere and they can foresee the future. Adam drank with Eve the kykeon, the primal, his sperm mixed with water and barley. The hinge of that small sky opens. A much larger world shows itself. The great tree in the middle of Eden is the antenna and the kykeon is the transmission. The man fled, the Master of Justice placed in the east of the garden the Cherubs, who wielded the flaming sword, to watch the way that led in the world of All. Outside the first Naraka.*"

Ute Möbius, the priest. Fierce killer, featured in the Nirsch List. 107 outworlds. He is now the high priest of Naraka's imprisoned souls. In his Red Cave, he preaches faith, his mixed up Indias and Palestines.

Ute, with his Infinite-diviner cane, knows how to speak to people, to show a *path* even if you are stuck up the ass of Hell. The World Above: the soul can get back to it, stay there forever. The prison of steel and rock is illusory. The vessel of flesh cannot be the right skycar, the fuselage capable of breaking the chains of space to land on the new world, to leave behind the Black Eden of Naraka. The flesh vessel, to which you are too faithful, is just slag to be removed, a weight holding down your ankles, anchored to pain.

The morning and evening prayers in the Red Cave. Recurrent dates for the prisoners of Naraka. The believers are growing and growing.

Ute begins his rituals spreading his arms, pointing his cane at the rocky ceiling. He shows the perspective, the World Above waiting for them all. In a different form.

And now, let's exchange the kykeon. Let's partake.

The mating of the high priest with a woman, the cauterization of her vagina. Mass masturbation, mystic rituals with ancient, miscellaneous origins. *Sperm, barley and water.* Chalices passing by hundreds of hands, throats, and purified souls.

Suicide ratio in Naraka conspicuously decreases: Sibel saw it right with that nutjob priest. Optimization of resources; New Moon will be happy about the new data, the results of the unique saving operation designed by Sibel. Suicide management.

Ute has found a panacea for his throbbing, violent sexual deviations. So far away are the dark days, while he was waiting for his chemical castration in a New England prison.

Now he mates in public, pouring out as he wishes, sealing forever the cunt of his whore of the day. Unaware sluts in white dresses. And then ... the private meetings with the devotees in his cell, turned into a flat, equipped with all the absurd tools for thermodilation and cauterization.

Readings and interpretations of old books, of fragments. Even Samghata – not known to all the inmates, the notorious Mutations Area – finds its own impossible philosophy. The descriptions of the Angels, the higher and purest beings, assembled in mosaic bodies with animal and human tiles. Not so different than the *human molecular cows* that New Moon is experimenting on and breeding in the underground of Samghata. Super-Naraka under construction, the future. Angels with feet like calf hooves ... features of a bull.

"As I looked, behold, a storm wind was coming from the north, a great cloud with fire flashing forth continually and a bright light around it, and in its midst something like glowing metal. Within it there were figures resembling four living beings.

And this was their appearance: they had human form. Each of them had four faces and four wings. Their legs were straight and their feet were like calf hooves, and they gleamed like burnished bronze. Under their wings were human hands. Their wings touched one another; their faces did not turn when they moved, each went straight forward. Each had the face of a man; all four had the face of a lion on the right and the face of a bull on the left, and all four had the face of an eagle. Such were their faces. In the midst of the living beings there was something that looked like burning coals of fire, like torches darting back and forth among the living beings. The fire was bright, and lightning was flashing from the fire."

FLESH HUNTERS
नरक

EARTH, SOUTH PARIS 5 ALLEYS

Ariane runs through the rotten heart of the city. She took her shoes off to go faster. Riding her ass is a team of *chasseurs de viande*, flesh hunters. The improvised suppliers of the district restaurants. Demand is higher and higher.

Provisions of controlled raw material, still illegal, is no longer enough for the kitchens to meet the orders. Deux Jambes, Dorian Moreau's place and one of Millander's businesses, has fifty booked tables for dinner. Customers who must be satisfied. The motto of Deux Jambes is pretty clear: "Only here, 24/7." A matter of reputation. The end justifies the means.

The flesh hunters took the order from the restaurant: *three women and two men. Age range: 20-25. Alive, or deceased by no longer than four hours.* Delivery and standards will be carefully checked. A race against time. Junkies' bodies, easier to intercept, are not accepted at Deux Jambes, but they are always good for two-bit places that pay well.

The chasseurs' roadtruck, equipped with cold stores and dissecting worktables, has writing on its side: *Service Rapide.* But it is too big to pass through the district alleys. The hunters are forced to get off and chase Ariane on foot. A shitty job.

The team leader, Romaric, urges his men: "*Come on*, this is the last one for today. We've got an hour left. Move your asses and get that bitch! Double pay, tonight!"

Ariane, twenty-two years old and with eyes too big on her slender face, is too far from home to escape the hunters. Her thoughts swell up, together with the muscles of her body.

Getting so close to the apocalyptic district is dangerous, but Ariane had to take that chance. With no credits remaining, she went to a work meeting in a display-shop of the small suburb of

Darse Metro, adjoining the cancerous macro area of South Paris 5.

But the flesh hunters were working just on the border, especially for the most important and demanding orders. They followed Ariane out of their territory before drawing her into their grounds. Nouvelle Creteil, one of the new pulsating hearts of South Paris 5, a territory extension that Millander inherited from Guadalupe. That little slut managed to run into the alleys. A waste of time.

"Where the fuck did she go? You two, you go right. You, follow me."

Romaric is drooling over finishing the delivery. He still smells the woman's odors, of her tight cunt, of their money. But she seems to have vanished behind heaps of trash, shut windows, old armchairs where whores' asses are waiting for customers.

Ariane does not have a choice. Her legs are no longer holding and the men are getting close. She hears them swearing. She stops, catches her breath, decides to undress.

Gone is her t-shirt, out her tits. She tears her skirt, reducing it to twenty centimeters of cloth. The lines of her ass sway free. She rummages in her purse and everything drops on the ground. Her hands shake as she picks up the lipstick, servohue and blush, shader and just-bought syntomascara. She heavily marks her young visage. She uses the servohue on her breasts, too, making them burst with purple to shine under the scarce lights. She unties her hair.

Now she really looks like a whore.

She exits the alley and takes position on a bigger street, where several roadcars are passing by.

The hunters come out of the alleys in two groups, about thirty meters away; they look around.

Romaric loses his patience in that maze of streets and shit, kicks some empty bottles; and Terraux, too: he had let her run away when she was just a few steps away.

"It's just full of whores here. We don't even get paid for those … Fuck! Let's go back."

Ariane smiles. Those worms are going to go empty-handed tonight.

But how will I get back home in this state?

Her heart speeds up again. Getting out of South Paris 5,

dressed as a hooker ...

A roadcar stops beside her. *A customer.* The man tilts his head, scanning Ariane's body. He stamps his senses several seconds on those purple tits. Then he draws out his voice: "Fuck! And where have you been hiding until now? How much, little slut?"

Ariane tries to leave, but the roadcar flanks her again.

"What are you doing, filthy bitch, playing hard-to-get? Hey, come here!"

A stone hits the windshield. Another beats against the side of the vehicle. The man, scared, slips away at full speed, vanishing in the darkness. Ariane turns back; two whores are behind her, gnashing their teeth. The blonde one – at least ninety kilos of flesh squeezed inside an emerald green dress – spits at her, "What the fuck do you think you're doing? Stealing our customers?"

Ariane has no time to answer. Her beauty is threatening. Dangerous.

A matter of customers, pimps, and territory. A matter of survival.

The other, red-costumed whore does not lose time. She pulls a knife and plants it into Ariane's stomach.

Ariane drops on the ground, bleeds. She tries to pull out the blade, which is sunk down to the hilt. The blonde fatty sits on Ariane's legs and begins hitting her head with a stone. The fury of the blows breaks bones and harmonies of that face. Ariane loses consciousness, the puddle of blood beneath her back spreading more and more.

"*Shit, stop it!* Get back to work. I'll deal with this mess. Holy shit ..."

Geneaux, the local pimp, is late. The usual shot of booze to swallow his boredom. A sniff of that new stuff that is beginning to be around in the district.

He crouches, presses two fingers on Ariane's neck, looks for a heartbeat. She is still breathing, but barely. The man wants to avoid further trouble, so he grabs her legs and drags her toward the throat of a dark alley. He dumps her among the trash. Ariane's white flesh is conspicuous among so much grey shit. Thighs like motorways for inner drives encrusted by time, freshly repainted. Geneaux cannot hold back. His face is throbbing.

There's an unstoppable desire to taste Ariane. He licks her knees, then those purple-glinting tits. Appetizers of her taste, the one hiding beneath her skin. *Meat.*

He turns the woman on her side, lifts her skirt to reveal her buttocks. Symposium of lines, of fresh and tender stuff. Before his brain explodes, Geneaux sinks in his teeth. He fills his mouth with pieces of that so-tasty ass; *almighty, he swallows.* He discovers an unknown world, surrounded by hundreds of moons that were invisible until now.

Ariane moans. She is not dead yet, but she is close.

The pimp stops a second, looks at that unconscious face and its double gaze: onto Hell, here, but even on another one. Farther. He resumes his meal, nothing can really distract him.

When his belly is finally full, his heartbeat goes back to normal. Geneaux stands, cleans his mouth, and leaves the red and black alley.

He lights a cigarette, goes slowly back to watch his business with his hands in his pockets. He looks at the stars, now shining like his whores. He has *new* eyes, now.

Ariane's body bleeds alone. Bug radars are flashing. Rats and cloacal creatures awaken from their slumber. They will finish the work.

CLOUD 7
नरक

THE MOON, SAMGHATA

Kiki's face is still dirty with black blood mixed with that shitty jelly: the mess of Guadalupe and his exploding warped body. She keeps crawling in the metal duct. After a ninety-degree turn, she reaches a second grate. Through the slits, light permeates her steel burrow. A bug overcomes her and bounces on the lit grille, then finds its course again and manages to escape.

Kiki watches the environment before her. The empty room doesn't look like a detention area. Time to get out. The duct that swallowed her begins to vibrate, as though waiting for more guests. Things bigger and heavier than bugs.

A kick on the grate, a three-meters drop. The floor resounds under her weight. Kiki doesn't move for a few seconds; bent on her legs, she turns in a circle, ready to open fire. *Nobody.* Hundreds of plextilen boxes surround her, full of green shit. A pantry.

Two doors: which to choose?

Sibel's watchdogs must be turning Naraka upside down to find her. Someone must have already lost his head after her escape. His head or something else.

You've got to think quick, Kiki.

Earth is far away: the only way to leave this cursed place is to reach the freightbot hangar, south of the structure. Just as when she managed to escape with Miller's help. Miller, the Cool Guy who ended up packaged. A flight accompanied by thousands of human chicken cans, for the richest teeth on Earth.

Kiki will have to make do by herself this time. Improvise. It won't be the first time.

She chooses the door on the right, which opens onto a refectory. Nobody here as well. The cubes are all vacant, no trace of staff or jailers.

Kiki crosses the large room running, finds the door on the other end locked.

Fuck!

She gets back in the storage room, tries the other door. Finally, a tunnel. It must lead somewhere. She just has to find a shitty elevator or, better, stairs. Blue lights pulsate on her body, breaking the shadows. Kiki has been on the displays of the control room for a while, by now, videomonitor endings flexing their optic fingers like sea anemones, following her every step. The neck of the tunnel chokes into a fork. Huge steel doors block both sides. Encrypted access.

Jesus, this would take tons of explosive!

Trapped. The area is isolated with pocket bulkheads, heavily sliding down to sever the main tunnel.

Holy shit!

An electromagnetic pulse security system quickly sucks Kiki's pistol, dragging it into the elliptic device on the ceiling. *Red LED.*

Fuck! They didn't have all this shit last time!

Kiki remembers Miller saying Naraka security fell short, and that he would exploit weak spots to arrange their escape, messing up their systems somehow. It seems they have made progress. Maybe her own escape suggested investment …

A vibration: the entrance on the right gapes swallowing the large surface of steel into the floor.

The mouth of the passage shows ten black helmets. Its magnificent black teeth.

Sibel and her watchdogs, of course.

The Queen Bee unties her hair and tosses her helmet to Kiki.

"Nice reflex! Maybe you'd better follow us. It's easy to get lost, here."

Kiki lowers her head as many thoughts tumble down to the floor. One of the jailers seals her wrists in a primelock, grabs her arm and leads her toward the elevator. Third floor underground: Kalasutra.

That whore wants to take me back into her reign.

Meters of rock quickly flow, animating the shadows of enclosed memories.

Max, the skycar model, small garments on the floor, his sad smile, his taste …

Kiki's psyche does its job, raising a new warping fence higher.

Confined in the core, on little clump of awareness, stays the dilitium dish and that impossible meat that Sibel had her swallow.

Kalasutra and its circular shape, reassuring colors, peonies, child-women in red kimonos, camouflage of terror.

The escort leaves the Queen Bee alone.

You're too confident, bitch. I just need a second ...

Sibel stretches the muscles of her right arm, all the lights drawn to her hand. She invites Kiki into her personal quarters. It's a large room equipped with an environmental simulator, and materializing on a window is a great Earth desert. Red rocks like those of Sinai. A microscopic rain of crystal dust falls from the ceiling. Sibel raises her arms and opens her mouth, swallowing those glittering molecules. She turns around, laughing out loud.

The crystal rain also falls on Kiki's hair and naked shoulders as she searches the room for *something to shove into that cursed slut's throat.*

"Kiki, don't worry. I'll let you do anything you want. And you'll enjoy it."

Sibel keeps laughing, covered in her crystals. She seems euphoric, as if she's in altered LOC. Her body movements follow a nonexistent music, a drumbeat of hallucinations. She hugs Kiki, kisses her mouth. "You see this crystal dust? It's Cloud 7, a synthetic drug based on MDPV – Methylenedioxypyrovalerone – and vegetal khat ... Once you've tried it, you can never do without, ever again. Your body, your emotions ... they change forever. The last wheeze of New Moon labs. Human meat demand must grow faster. In a few days, Cloud 7 will be available everywhere on Earth: a new drug, the ultimate trip, even sold as a cooking salt. A brand new business product ... a pandemic, alchemic mix. Market epidemic, you see? New Moon has estimated it is going to build, in a year, five more Naraka Farms, or Extraterrestrial Detention Systems, if you prefer."

Kiki listens to Sibel's folly ... *Folly, right?* She wants to know more. "And what does this drug have to do with your shitty farms? I don't get it."

Sibel laughs heartily; she approaches Kiki, whispers into her ear, "You don't understand ... this substance unleashes glee, violence, self-harm and, overall, *cannibalism.* Human meat, believe me, becomes your prime need. Experimental Cloud 7 ultimately led to a collapse of the nervous system. New Moon is working on that, right here. I was among the first to try it. I didn't know about the side effects. Nobody knew. Soon, my brain will shut down, but I'm having a ball right now. And you can't really ask for a better place than this – Naraka – to quench your every appetite. *A few months are worth a hundred lives.*"

Kiki raises her eyes to the cursed crystal rain. Maybe it's just suggestion, but she feels something changing inside of her. She looks at Sibel's perfect body. She no longer wishes to kill her, to have revenge. That skin, that so-white skin, she would like to bite it. *Eat it.* An unknown drive rushes in her bloodstream. Powerful, sensual anthropophagic thoughts.

Sibel undresses and throws herself on the bed. She lets Kiki admire her features, her curves.

Let the appetite grow. You cannot resist Cloud 7.

Kiki squeezes her hands, tries to point her thoughts elsewhere, but she cannot free herself from the grip of those damned coils, wrapping around some insane idea. She bites her lips until they bleed. All is useless.

Cloud 7 is showing its effects, in just a few minutes.

"Kiki, I beg you, eat my flesh. Let me try the last great orgasm: *to be devoured.* It's what I want! In my stage, you'll discover that it represents absolute Nirvana. Nobody will disturb us, here. Look at me ..."

The drug is fully in her bloodstream, the Ouroboros tightly anchored to her brain.

Kiki no longer hesitates as she leaps onto Sibel's soft body. She squeezes her flesh in her fingers, starts with tiny bites, then she sinks her teeth, deeper and deeper: into Sibel's face, breasts, thighs.

A feeling of absolute. Ten wings on her back.

Blood squirts.

Sibel comes with tears in her eyes while Kiki, out of control, rips her open, licking and greedily swallowing. Her neurons translate new signals, new tastes. Dark zones of her right hemisphere light up. Her psyche quickly interacts with her stomach, mouth, and tongue. They blend with the rapture of hallucination, delirium; basic, primal emotions. Her heart roars faster, about to burst. Kiki's alteration state shows more and more violently; a deep bite on her neck, and Sibel's carotid snaps.

The Queen Bee dies throwing up blood, devoured in a greedy fury.

She reaches her Nirvana, under a transparent sky, sinks into matterless earth.

An applause crumbles those instants of wonderful symbiotic madness.

Kiki turns around with a morsel of Sibel's meat between her lips.

A man has been watching that naked lunch with an escort of five guards. His voice is like that of a dream, from a different dimension; it vibrates: "Congratulations, Kiki. Superb! Sorry I didn't introduce myself. I'm Vidal Mayer, New Moon Corporation CEO. Now Sibel's job is yours. Don't thank me. I know you'll do your best. Sibel was sure of it. Your new blood shows a lot of promise. *Naraka needs you, now.*"

MALDOROR RELOADED 4/4
नरक

You won't see me, in my ultimate hour, surrounded by priests. I will die with my eyes high, staring at a wide panoramic monitor.
Will you open the door to my dying room, that day?

Whoever you will be, don't leave. Approach, and try to glimpse some sign of pain, of fear, on my hyena face. You won't find any.

I will be enjoying myself still, watching the many examples of human evil. If you like, you'll be able to attend, too. The eagle, the crow, the immortal pelican, they will see me as a horrible, contented wraith. They have eyes to see, but they won't be able to understand it entirely.

The viper, the big eye of the toad, the tiger, the elephant, the tooth of the polar seal, they all will be asking themselves why the fuck I got a waiver to the laws of nature.

A contented wraith in front of his wide panoramic monitor. A new phenomenon, something similar to a terrifying comet in the bloodied space. You won't have to fear me. I won't curse you. You'll be able to sit beside me.

Somebody could take advantage of the situation, suck what little blood is still inhabiting my body: Would you do that? Would you like to see, too, what I will be about to see?

You won't have to go out of your way to look for my dying room. Let the firefly of collective conscience chase you.
Beware: that one is a damn motherfucker.

A sperm whale rises, slowly, from the bottom of the sea, and shows its head above the water, to look at the ships passing by in those solitary neighborhood. Curiosity is born with the Universe. I will understand if you will desire to come visit, but listen to me: a useless doubt must not torment your thoughts. All graves must be measured with the serene compass of the philosopher. So you shall not be surprised by the visions, by the metastases of reality that your eyes will see through mine.

So let's be quick. Imagine my contented wraith face, the thick molecules of my dying room. Pretend you already are where you will come.

But before ... help me. I am too curious about seeing beyond, I don't want to wait anymore.

Undress me, and begin digging the pit.

Then, you will put me in.

EPIDEMIC
नरक

Night. Egon Simon is driving his roadcar. Vibrating in his ears are the musical algorithms of the Vortex, one of the busiest diskohaus in Berlin-Brandenburg 7. His overheated liver is filtering alcohol and methamphetamines. The street to Haselhorst sector is becoming narrower. The turn seems unending, Egon's brain turning upside-down together with the roadcar.

He manages to get out of the metal puzzle box. He got lucky: just a broken finger and some scratches. The automatic rescue system turned on right after the crash. They will be here soon. He lies down on the grass, thinks about all those stars looking down at him.

Had they been bottles …

The finger hurts; it is still attached to the hand thanks to a tiny strip of skin. Methamphetamines travel fast in his body, squeezing his brain cells. Dopamine rushes, doing its job.

Fuck, that crystal meth was really strong.

Egon has been more wasted than usual for days. Reality has gotten farther, even without Matko's pills and gin bottles. An ongoing trip.

He touches his dangling index finger, teasing it. Paranoia frees her tigers. The piece of meat seems to him more and more alien. Finally, twisting it sideways, he easily detaches it from his hand. Puts it in his pocket. He knows he must preserve it. They will fix everything up at the hospital. They will stitch the alien back in place.

Help is late. Egon gets up and starts walking in circles, kicking the dirt. Too much silence, few shapes to process, nothing with which to interact. His brain need inputs now; it cannot stay alone with itself too long.

He pulls his severed index finger out of his pocket. Watches it. He tries to bend it, mimicking its movements.

Who the fuck are you, eh?

Blood drips ... red atoms falling in the dark, next to his shoes.

Egon approaches the headlights of the roadcar, lets them illuminate him obliquely. He keeps looking at that piece of himself. Human meat. An imaginary meat skewer.

Then, just like being hit by a stone, the desire to taste oneself.

Egon thinks it is nothing illegal. After all, it is his own stuff; he can eat that, if he likes. Nobody could say anything. He begins biting, tearing away small pieces of meat. His nervous system reacts, activating secondary circuits. Pleasure multiplies.

Better, much better than that fucking crystal meth ... fuck Matko, I can get high for free, here ...

He cannot hold back, keeps nibbling.

Finally, there are just well-cleaned bones.

Shit, they look like an archaeologic find.

Egon is still hungry. He made a mistake trying it. Now the desire gets stronger and stronger. A light wind dries the sweat on his throbbing face. Unstoppable sensations of happiness, of freedom. The stars decide to descend from the sky; they lower, become growing luminous spheres. They surround him, spheres stretching out new limbs, raising an unexpected human head. Egon is no longer alone. Known bodies take shape out of nothingness. Hallucinations.

Cristine, his girlfriend. Her large, swaying breasts, her ass tattooed by cellulite.

Then, more bodies, more human meat spawning.

Gritt, a waitress at the Vortex, whom he once drunk-banged in his roadcar. Her soft skin, too-large firm calves, the magnificent adipose tissues heaped on her hips.

An erection surprises him. He admires the fantasy bodies hovering in the void, hypnotized by the dance of the meat. He masturbates; he cannot avoid it.

He starts nibbling at another finger. After all, that hand is screwed by now.

The dance of the meat goes on, while Death, wearing its old plague mask, directs the concert:

the high-pitched screams of ambulance sirens, the silent and wet slashing of a throat in the Vortex, the splashes into the cold water of Landwehr canal of severed heads and feet, indigested leftovers of a house party, the fast rubbing on the asphalt of a dead man's body, hauled by his ankles with metallex ropes, by a pair of fat sows with flaming paws.

The Apocalypse castanets beat the rhythm of the 21st century's funeral, like Helena's fingernails drumming impatiently on the metaluminum frame of the bed in her hospital room. She is about to give birth, the first contractions bend her back like a pulled slingshot. Restraints hold her wrists, neck, and ankles. She sweats the bluish residues of Cloud 7. Her right leg chewed clean off. Purple flowers of living flesh suck her thick blood. Someone took advantage of her when she fainted in the emergency room.

She has already swallowed her tongue, and cannot wait to get her hands on her juicy, tender baby. She wants to name her Uxor, before turning her eyes upward, like a shark, and sinking her teeth in that first-choice morsel. She wants to taste the caviar of abomination.

ACKNOWLEDGEMENTS

Thank you to my friends, colleagues and readers. Daniele Bonfanti, Sergio Altieri (the first one to believe in 'Naraka', some years ago), Michael Bailey, Edward Lee, Lucy Taylor, Bruce Boston and Marge Simon, Linda Addison, Lisa Morton, Tim Waggoner, Greg F. Gifune, David J. Schow, Jonathan Maberry, Paolo Di Orazio, Stefano Fantelli, Miriam Mastrovito, David Cowen, Robert Payne Cabeen, Ellen Datlow, Gene O'Neill, Ramsey Campbell, Mort Castle, Stephen Jones, Rena Mason, Ann Laymon, Monica O'Rourke, Giampaolo Frizzi, Mark Alan Miller, Lisa Mannetti, Silvia Riccò, Antonia Bonimelli, Charlee Jacob, Stefano Cardoselli, Francesca Noto, Mike Lester, Billy Martin, Lee Murray, Joe Mynhardt and Rocky Wood (I miss you!).

Thank you to beloved authors Henry Miller and William S. Burroughs for being my magic gateways into the world of writing. To my family for everything. Especially to my wife Sanda who saved me from another kind of 'Naraka', here on Earth.

Thank you all for reading my works and for your support.

ABOUT THE AUTHOR

ALESSANDRO MANZETTI IS A BRAM STOKER AWARD-WINNING AUTHOR, EDITOR, AND TRANSLATOR OF HORROR FICTION AND DARK POETRY WHOSE WORK HAS BEEN PUBLISHED EXTENSIVELY IN ITALIAN, INCLUDING NOVELS, SHORT AND LONG FICTION, POETRY, ESSAYS, AND COLLECTIONS.

ENGLISH PUBLICATIONS INCLUDE HIS COLLECTIONS *THE GARDEN OF DELIGHT* (SPLATTERPUNK AWARD 2018 FINALIST), *THE MASSACRE OF THE MERMAIDS*, THE MONSTER, THE BAD AND THE UGLY (WITH PAOLO DI ORAZIO), *DARK GATES* (WITH PAOLO DI ORAZIO), *STOCKHOLM SYNDROME* (WITH STEFANO FANTELLI), AND THE POETRY COLLECTIONS *NO MERCY, EDEN UNDERGROUND* (BRAM STOKER AWARD 2015 WINNER), *SACRIFICIAL NIGHTS* (WITH BRUCE BOSTON), AND *VENUS INTERVENTION* (WITH CORRINE DE WINTER.

HE EDITED THE ANTHOLOGIES THE *BEAUTY OF DEATH* AND *THE BEAUTY OF DEATH VOL. 2 - DEATH BY WATER* (WITH JODI RENEE LESTER)

HIS STORIES AND POEMS HAVE APPEARED IN ITALIAN, USA, AND UK MAGAZINES, SUCH AS DARK MOON DIGEST, THE HORROR ZINE, DISTURBED DIGEST, ILLUMEN, DEVOLUTION Z, RECOMPOSE, POLU TEXNI, NOTHING'S SACRED VOL. 4, AND ANTHOLOGIES, SUCH AS *BONES III*, *RHYSLING ANTHOLOGY* (2015, 2016, 2017, 2018), *HWA POETRY SHOWCASE VOL. 3 AND 4, THE BEAUTY OF DEATH VOL 1 AND 2, BEST HARDCORE HORROR OF THE YEAR VOL. 2, MAR DULCE, I SOGNI DEL DIAVOLO, DANZE ERETICHE VOL. 2, IL BUIO DENTRO,* AND MANY OTHERS.

AWARDS AND NOMINATION:
• BRAM STOKER AWARDS 2015 WINNER
• BRAM STOKER AWARDS 2017 TWO-TIME NOMINEE
• BRAM STOKER AWARDS 2016 TWO-TIME NOMINEE
• BRAM STOKER AWARDS 2014 NOMINEE
• SPLATTERPUNK AWARD 2018 NOMINEE
• RHYSLING AWARD 2015, 2016, 2017, 2018 NOMINEE
• ELGIN AWARD 2015, 2016, 2017, 2018 NOMINEE

WEBSITE: WWW.BATTIAGO.COM

FORTHCOMING BOOKS

KNOWING WHEN TO DIE
by Mort Castle
Collection – **Paperback and eBook Edition**
June 2018

ARTIFACTS
by Bruce Boston
Petry Collection – **Paperback and eBook Edition**
July 2018

MONSTERS OF ANY KIND
Edited by Alessandro Manzetti and Daniele Bonfanti
Stories by: David J. Schow, Ramsey Campbell, Jonathan Maberry, Edward Lee,
Cody Goodfellow, Lucy Taylor, Monica J. O'Rourke and many others
Anthology – **Paperback and eBook Edition**
September 2018

DARK MARY
by Paolo Di Orazio
Novel – **Paperback and eBook Edition**
October 2018

AVAILABLE BOOKS

A WINTER SLEEP
by Greg F. Gifune
Novel – **Paperback and eBook Edition**
April 2018

SPREE AND OTHER STORIES
by Lucy Taylor
Collection – **Paperback and eBook Edition**
February 2018

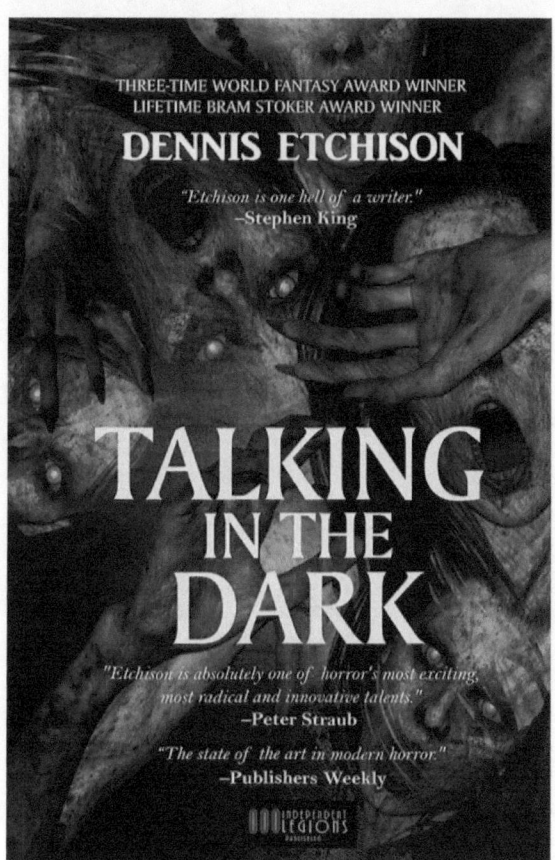

TALKING IN THE DARK
by Dennis Etchison
Collection – **eBook Edition**
December 2017

THE LIVING AND THE DEAD
by Greg F. Gifune
Novel – **Paperback and eBook Edition**
December 2017

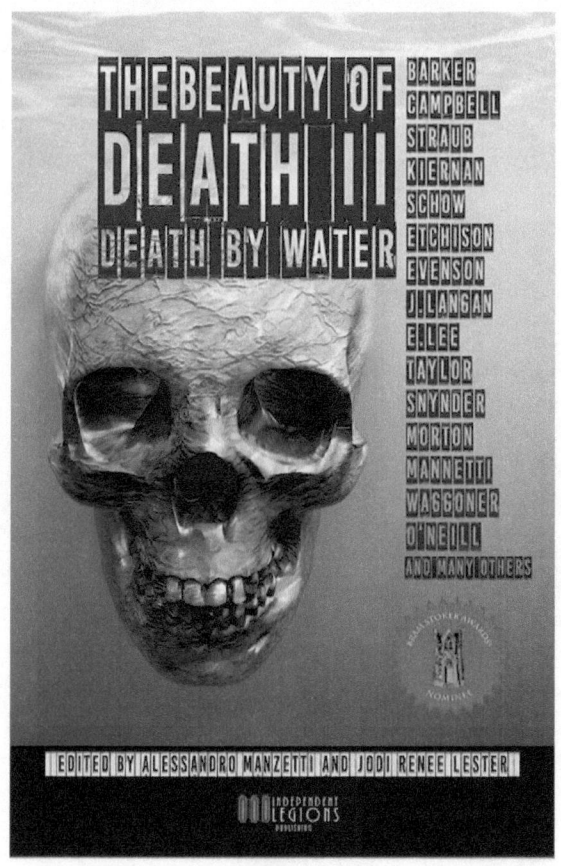

THE BEAUTY OF DEATH VOL. 2 - DEATH BY WATER
Edited by Alessandro Manzetti and Jodi Renée Lester
Anthology – **Paperback and eBook Edition**
November 2017

NICOLE CUSHING

CHILDREN OF NO ONE

The Great Dark Mouth is waiting

INDEPENDENT LEGIONS PUBLISHING

CHILDREN OF NO ONE
by Nicole Cushing
Novella – **Paperback and eBook Edition**
October 2017

DREAMS THE RAGMAN
by Dennis Etchison
Novella – **eBook Edition**
October 2017

THE RAIN DANCERS
by Greg F. Gifune
Novella – **eBook Edition**
September 2017

THE WISH MECHANICS
by Daniel Braum
Collection – **Paperback and eBook Edition**
July 2017

THE ONE THAT COMES BEFORE
by Livia Llewellyn
Novella – **Paperback and eBook Edition**
May 2017

SELECTED STORIES
by Nate Southard
Collection – **Paperback and eBook Edition**
April 2017

THE CARP-FACED BOY AND OTHER TALES
by Thersa Matsuura
Collection – **Paperback and eBook Edition**
February 2017

ALL-AMERICAN HORROR OF THE 21ST CENTURY
Edited by MortCastle
Anthology – **Paperback and eBook Edition**
November 2016

BENEATH THE NIGHT
by Greg F. Gifune
Novel & Novella – **Paperback Edition**
October 2016

THE BEAUTY OF DEATH VOL 1
Edited by Alessandro Manzetti
Anthology – **eBook Edition**
July 2016

DOCTOR BRITE
by Poppy Z. Brite
Collection – **eBook Edition**
January 2017

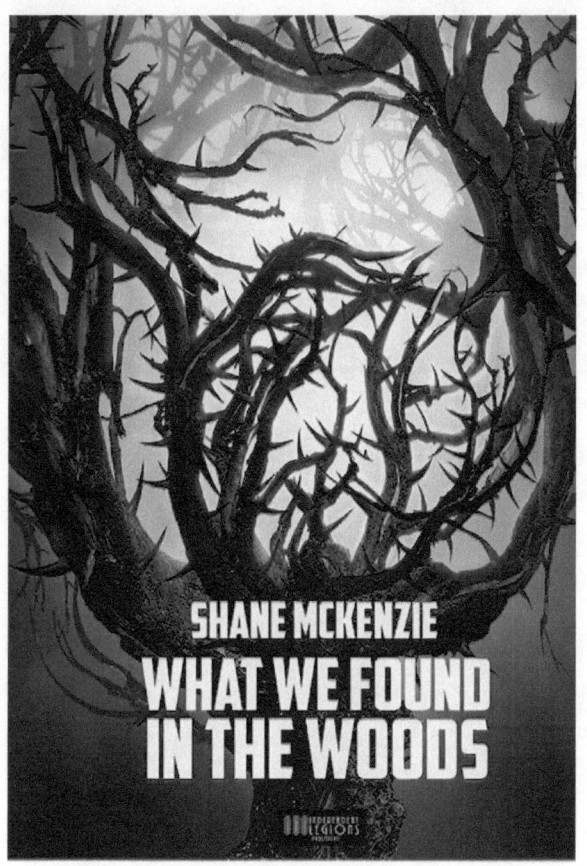

WHAT WE FOUND IN THE WOODS
by Shane McKenzie
Collection – **eBook Edition**
September 2016

USED STORIES
by Poppy Z. Brite
Collection – **eBook Edition**
June 2016

THE HORROR SHOW
by Poppy Z. Brite
Collection – **eBook Edition**
August 2016

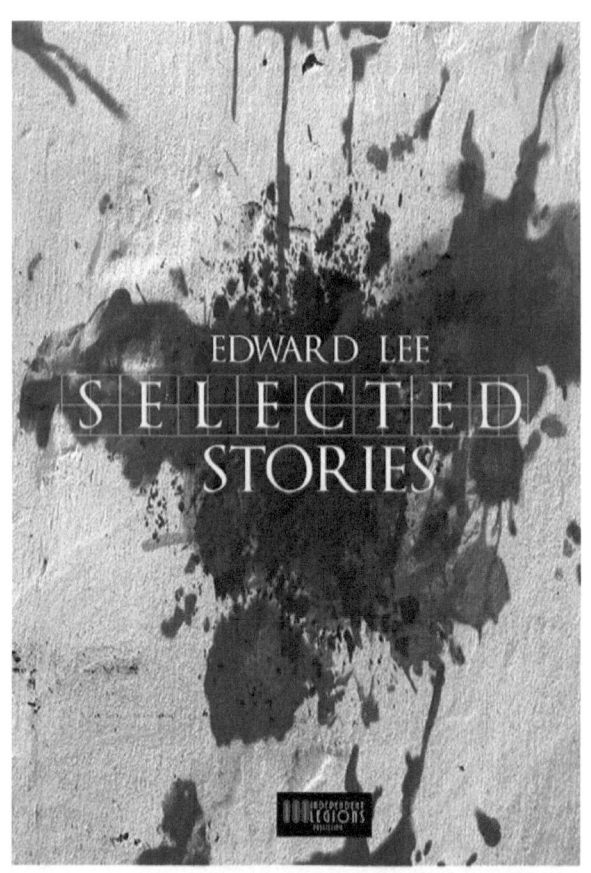

SELECTED STORIES
by Edward Lee
Collection – **eBook Edition**
July 2016

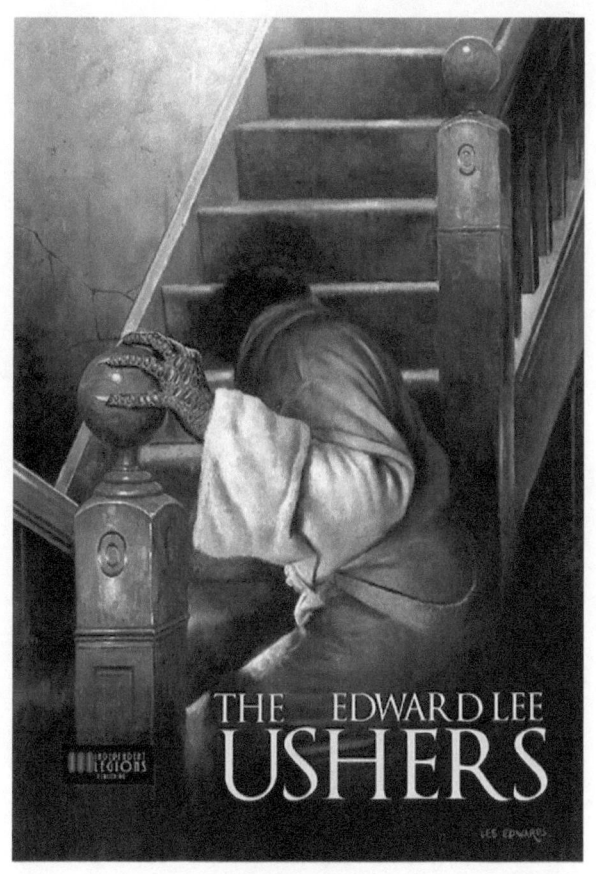

THE USHERS
by Edward Lee
Collection – **eBook Edition**
May 2016

THE CRYSTAL EMPIRE
by Poppy Z. Brite
Novella – **eBook Edition**
May 2016

SELECTED STORIES
by Poppy Z. Brite
Collection – **eBook Edition**
February 2016

THE HITCHHIKING EFFECT
by Gene O'Neill
Collection – **eBook Edition**
February 2016

SONGS FOR THE LOST
by Alexander Zelenyj
Collection – **eBook Edition**
April 2016

INDEPENDENT LEGIONS PUBLISHING

BY ALESSANDRO MANZETTI

VIA VIRGILIO, 10 - 34134 TRIESTE (ITALY)

+39 040 9776602

WWW.INDEPENDENTLEGIONS.COM

WWW.FACEBOOK.COM/INDEPENDENTLEGIONS

INDEPENDENT.LEGIONS@AOL.COM

BOOKS IN ITALIAN:

WWW.INDEPENDENTLEGIONS.COM/PUBBLICAZIONI.HTML

SPECIALTY PRESS AWARD RECIPIENT